Utterly Deadly Southern Pecan Pie

by

Penny Burwell Ewing

The Haunted Salon Series, Book Two

Utterly Deadly Southern Pecan Pie

COPYRIGHT © 2017 by Penny Burwell Ewing

Cover Art by *Angela Anderson*

The Wild Rose Press, Inc.
PO Box 708
Adams Basin, NY 14410-0708
Visit us at www.thewildrosepress.com

Publishing History
First Fantasy Rose Edition, 2017
Print ISBN 978-1-5092-1437-2
Digital ISBN 978-1-5092-1438-9

The Haunted Salon Series, Book Two
Published in the United States of America

Theo's distorted face twisted

as he struggled to breathe. His body jerked, and his clutched hand dug at his swollen throat. He made a harsh sound.

"He's having an allergic reaction," Barbara Herrington screamed, her hands plowing through his coat pocket in a frantic search. "Where's his EpiPen? I can't find his EpiPen!"

I recognized the gurgling sound having heard it in my facial room just before Scarlett choked to death on her own vomit.

With a flash, I remembered that shortly after Scarlett's grisly incident, the entire staff at Dixieland Salon had been trained in CPR and mouth-to-mouth resuscitation. Scrambling to Herrington's side, I fell to my knees, the remembered sound of the instructor's voice guiding me through the steps.

Titling his head back, I placed my ear close to his mouth and then it checked for any obstruction. Taking a deep breath, I pinched his nose closed and sealed my lips around his, blowing deeply until his chest rose with the force of my breath.

I paused, again inhaling deeply.

"What are you doing?" a voice screamed in my ear. "You...get away from my husband!"

Whack! Barbara's shoe connected to my jaw. I gasped, toppling over onto my back, hitting my head on the hard concrete. I must have blacked out for a minute or two because the next thing I remember was intense pain spreading throughout my body. Sagging against the strong hands lifting me from the floor, I inhaled Bradford's familiar woodsy scent, gulping in air and the coppery taste of blood.

Dedication

For my aunt, Mary Sue Altman,
who inspired the character of Deena and
her passionate pursuit of perfection.
Here's to you, Aunt Sue.
The Salter sisters are together again
within the pages of this book.

Cast of Characters

Jolene Claiborne—Word around heaven is this busybody hairstylist is the one to haunt if you have a mystery to solve.

Deena Sinclair—This Tucker sister is looking for love in all the wrong places.

Billie Jo Hazard—Her psychic abilities keep letting her down.

Annie Mae Tucker—This proud southern mama doesn't want to share her secret pecan pie recipe.

Harland Tucker—The Tucker patriarch is back from the dead, but he finds himself buried under suspicion when a long-time rival is murdered.

Detective Samuel Bradford—The Whiskey Creek detective is back in the saddle again after political mayhem almost cost him his job. If he's not careful, he could find himself roped and hog-tied into matrimony with a sassy salon owner.

Theodore Herrington—The bank president ended up in the hottest part of the south.

Barbara Herrington—She married an older man for money. Money can buy many bobbles, but what about love?

Ellie Malone—Her bonnet's set for the banker's son, and she doesn't need permission from his father to rob the cradle.

Victor Redding—Pineridge Plantation is the crowning prize of this southern gentleman's heritage and no damn Yankee will take it from him.

Nancy Chance—The Pecan Festival is her only claim to fame.

Josiah Redding—The red dirt of his plantation hides

blood-soaked Confederate gold, and a secret that has imprisoned him there throughout the 150 years since it claimed his life.

Scarlett Cantrell—This lively spirit refuses to stay within the boundaries of heaven—especially when rumor is her new best gal-pal is headed straight for another war between the states.

Chapter One
The Key

The man leaning against the exquisite mahogany mantelpiece had been dead for one hundred and fifty years and appeared as if he had stepped from the pages of an antebellum romance novel. His hair, dark and flecked with silver, flowed back from a high forehead. Eyes darker than sapphires were set in a face bronzed by the rays of the hot Georgia sun. His lips, firm and sensual, pressed together in a cynical twist, and the gray frockcoat and vest fit snug over a pristine white shirt with a black stock expertly tied at his throat. Black boots shone from beneath gray trousers, and his large, tanned hand held a smoking cigar.

He belonged to another time.

We stared in frozen surprise at one another, as I stood in the open doorway of the library. My hand rested on the brass doorknob while a group of tourists waited at my back until my sister Deena noticed my hesitancy to enter the spacious room.

"What's the holdup?" she asked in a hushed voice. "Did you forget your lines again?"

The acrid aroma of tobacco smoke stung my nostrils. I nodded, my gaze glued to the ghostly specter at the fireplace.

Deena brushed past me in her blue, cotton, hoop skirt and motioned for the group to follow.

"The Rococo Revival furniture was placed in the house by Josiah Redding around the time of 1836 when he built Pineridge Plantation for his bride-to-be, Savannah Childs, and has been lovingly cared for by Redding descendants throughout the years."

She pointed to the dark, heavy pieces before speaking again.

"Josiah's portrait hangs over the chimney, and you can see he was a handsome and wealthy Southern gentleman planter. Painted in 1858 by a local artist three years before the Civil War, Savannah wrote in her journal that her husband would retire to this quiet haven after dinner to smoke his imported cigars."

My gaze lifted to the portrait. The likeness of the man in the painting failed to capture the sense of mystique in the fathomless eyes of the man himself. The illustrated man, and the one standing beneath it were one and the same. *Josiah Redding*, in his astral form. And of course, I was the only one in the room who could see him fade away into nothingness.

Perhaps I should explain.

I see dead people. Celestial citizens of inner space. Transcendent realities. And yes, I suppose in certain circles they are referred to as ghosts. Most are friendly. Some not so much. And then every once in a while I encounter a real pain-in-the-ass spirit.

It all started back about seven months ago, after a client, Scarlett Cantrell, with some help from an outside source, joined the Other Side. It happened in my beauty salon. Scarlett needed help bringing her murderer to justice, and she picked Dixieland Salon as her earthly headquarters. As all of this unfolded, I found myself drafted into helping her. Yep, me, Jolene Claiborne.

Hairstylist extraordinaire, and spirit consultant.

Not everyone in my life is happy about my special gift inherited from my Granny Tucker. Namely, my younger sister, Deena, and my boyfriend, Detective Samuel Bradford, who happens to be her old high school sweetheart. (I picked up the habit of dropping his first name while investigating Scarlett's murder. To me, he's just plain Bradford. Hard nose cop, and my best squeeze.) But that's a long story and Deena's signaling for me to pick up where she left off.

Careful not to brush against the tables and upset the delicate porcelain quail figurines, with my bulky hoop skirt, I glided deeper into the room until I stood beneath the portrait of Josiah Redding.

"The legend of Piper's Gold is well known in these parts," I said with an exaggerated southern drawl. "On July 19, 1864, a small band of Confederate soldiers under the command of Major Travis A. Piper were quietly transporting a cache of gold from a bank in Thomas County to headquarters in Macon, Georgia. As evening approached, they arrived at Pineridge Plantation and were graciously received by Mr. and Mrs. Redding for the night. The officers were given rooms in the main house, and the others pitched tents in a nearby field. As they retired for the night, a message came in warning of an advancing Union troop. Immediately the officers gathered to discuss their orders to hide the gold and retreat south. When the Union troop moved on, they were to retrieve the gold and proceed to Macon taking every precaution to elude capture.

"The orders were carried out. Unfortunately, at dawn on July 20, 1864, the Union troops struck and massacred Major Piper and his small band of soldiers. Heady with victory, the Yankee soldiers stormed the house, and killed Josiah. His youngest son, Asa Douglas Redding mysteriously disappeared from the plantation and history on that same night."

I paused as expressions of horror and gasps of dismay sounded from the group. When they settled down, I continued with my story. "The house and its furnishings were spared as an officer spotted a portrait in the front parlor of Josiah's father wearing his Masonic ring. The officer, a Mason himself, ordered the house placed under guard. But the damage had been done. The eldest son, Randall Josiah Redding, was reportedly killed two days later on July 22, 1864 in the final battle for Atlanta. Savannah Redding and her young daughter Adeline died that winter when they both contracted pneumonia. The remaining son, John Milton Redding, survived the conflict and is the ancestor of the present owner, Victor Redding."

Here I paused again and lowered my voice to achieve dramatic expectation from my listeners. "The gold has never been found. Rumors abound that Major Piper and his soldiers are still guarding their Confederate gold. And watch out for Tempy, the old slave woman. Many visitors claim to see her throughout the main house. Beware. You have been warned."

Muffled cries of anticipation rang throughout the group of tourists. I could see many of them turning their heads to peer into the corners of the richly ornamented room.

"I saw something when I came in here," a man stated.

"As did I," echoed another.

And on it went for several minutes until Deena, with a worried frown directed at me, began ushering the tourists toward the opened library door.

"I wish you wouldn't do that thing with your voice, Jolene," she admonished as I joined her at the rear of the group. "It triggers their imagination."

"In defense of myself, my dear darling sister, it's in the guide brochure, and it's what they expect to hear. People love haunted houses, and I can't help it if Josiah presented himself over by the fireplace when we came in. I get the distinct impression he doesn't like strangers in his house," I teased.

"Please keep it light, not real," she pleaded. "And please don't let anyone see you talking to him. They'll think you're crazy."

"All right, Deena." I closed the library door firmly behind me. "Let's finish this tour so I can get out of this dress and corset."

We were standing outside the library, which occupies the northeast corner of the principle floor, in a large hallway. The walls were painted cream, reminiscent of ancient parchment paper, with electric wall sconces fashioned like candlesticks casting their soft yellow light over worn pine floors.

I took the lead once again. "As you have noticed, the manor house has been modernized by the Redding descendants, but still retains its distinctive historical flavor with nineteen century period furnishings. Before modern lighting however, the plantation mistress oversaw the making of candles for the main house and slave quarters. During the 1850's candle manufacturers made it possible for the richer families to purchase candles instead of making them. Savannah's household ledger, dated in 1860, details purchases of candles from a general store in the nearby town of Albany. Now if you will follow Deena to the front entryway, another guide is waiting to take you on a tour of the sole remaining slave cabin restored to its original condition."

As the group trudged past me I let out a long breath and plucked the damp cotton dress from my sweating torso. Even though it was November in South Georgia, the coolness of fall had failed to arrive and the manor house had air-conditioning only in the upper living quarters. My dark blue gown buttoned up to my throat, and the sleeves were long and tight around my wrists. Not one inch of skin showed and underneath the heavy cloth, all kinds of female paraphernalia had me cinched up tighter than a horse's saddle. All historically correct for the time period, Nancy Chance, the tour coordinator had parroted, but by God, I was hot as Hades and ready to take off these tightly laced ankle boots pinching my toes with every step.

Bringing up the rear, I could hear my sister's voice drone on about the hand-painted wallpaper depicting a classic English garden gracing the entrance hall of the manor house. She spoke of the spacious circular room with a large square rug worn threadbare from years of traffic and the original French crystal and brass chandelier which still hung over the center of the room.

I made my way to the front door with its delicate etchings in the fanlight and sidelights to thank each tourist for their visit as they stepped onto the large front porch. There a man dressed in period clothing waited to take them on a tour of the grounds.

As soon as the door closed behind the last

straggling tourist, I turned to Deena. "Thank God, that's over. My feet are killing me, and I've got to lose the stays. Let's go change and stop by Sonic for a cherry limeade on the way home."

Deena eyed me critically. "You're the one who volunteered us for this gig. Which, I'm glad you did, I should add."

"Of course, you are. You're like a cat lapping up cream in this environment."

She performed a playful pirouette. "An age of enlightenment."

I grimaced as the ankle boots bit into my flesh. "More like the age of confinement."

A small bedroom in the back of the house had been set aside as a changing room for the volunteers, and as Deena and I passed by the library a soft thump sounded from behind its closed doors.

"There shouldn't be anyone in there," I said. We turned back to investigate. When I opened the door and peered into the empty room, I noticed a small book lying on the floor next to one of the cherry bookcases. "A book fell to the floor. You go on ahead. I'll only be a minute."

"Okay, but hurry. We have a tight schedule for the rest of the day. It's eleven-thirty and Billie Jo is going to meet us at your house in thirty minutes to decide on a pecan pie recipe for the contest tomorrow night. And we have to be at the salon by four to do hair and make-up for tonight's beauty pageant."

I groaned. "Don't remind me. It's going be a long week."

Deena left and I returned the book to its place on the shelf. A cold chill swept over my body as the scent of cigar smoke wafted in the stale air. I turned around to meet the appraising gaze of Josiah Redding. The hair on the back of my neck prickled with static electricity.

Once more our eyes locked in frozen tableau. His stare was compelling and magnetic, and I lost all fear. And then suddenly he reached inside his front vest pocket, withdrew a key, and held it out toward me. Without hesitation, I crossed the room until I stood directly in front of him. The shiny key glistened like new. Etched on it was a heart-shaped design with interlinking lines within the heart symbol. He dropped the bronze key onto my outstretched palm, and my fingers closed around the metal.

"What do I do with this?"

Silence met my question.

I opened my hand and stared down at the key, now scratched and dull with age as if the past one hundred and fifty years had accumulated on its surface in a few seconds of time. My head snapped up with the violence of uncertainty, but I stood alone in the cozy room.

I shivered in the warm air.

The murmurings of approaching voices pierced the silence and speared me to action. I dropped the key into the pocket of my dress and bolted to the doorway and paused, gazing around the room one last time before I stepped out into the hallway and eased the door closed. I stood for a moment, my hand on the knob, puzzled and curious about the mystery surrounding the vintage key and its possible meaning. When no answers appeared magically out of thin air, I went across the hall to the bedroom where my sister waited for me.

****

Billie Jo's fork dropped with a clang onto her

dessert plate. "Well, the best Pecan Pie Contest is in the bag for someone else. Worse pie ever."

"Not so," Deena admonished. "We just have to come up with a better recipe."

"That's what you said last week and the week before," she complained. "How many pies do we have to bake before we admit we don't have a shot at winning?"

"We're staying in the contest if we have to bake a hundred pies," I grumbled at my youngest sister. My stomach heaved at the thought of another bite.

Billie Jo frowned. "When this is over, I'll never eat pecan pie again. Not even Mama's."

I nodded my head in agreement. It was two o'clock on Monday afternoon, the first day of Whiskey Creek's annual week-long Pecan Festival, and we were sitting at my kitchen table trying to come up with a viable recipe.

"We can't quit," I said. "Dixieland Salon was nominated as one of the city's ten best businesses, and we're obligated to have an entry in the contest. Besides, I have every intention of winning the all-expense paid weekend trip for the entire staff to Disney World in Florida."

Tempers flared as the afternoon baking progressed with no luck. I was sick to my stomach, had a dozen giggling, teenage girls ready to descend on my beauty shop in a couple of hours, plus two tired sisters, no winning recipe, and a mystery dumped in my lap by a closed-mouth ghost living in an antebellum plantation house.

Crap. Another bad moon rising over the house of Claiborne.

Deena's strident voice crashed my thoughts. I

glanced up to see my sisters frowning at me. Before I could speak, Billie Jo burst out, "Hells bells, Jolene, pay attention. Deena again suggested we get Mama's recipe if we want to win. I told her since you're the one who got us mixed up in this fiasco then you ought to be the one to steal it."

"I'm not stealing Mama's pecan pie recipe. Why don't we ask her again? All she can say is no."

"I tried that this morning," Deena inserted. "She's not interested in sharing her secret recipe with the entire population of Whiskey Creek."

"Oh, for God's sake, it's a pie recipe," I retorted. "What's the big deal?"

"I say we blackmail her."

"And how would you suggest we do that, Billie Jo?"

"She owes us, Jolene. For that whopper of a lie about Daddy. Think of the emotional scars we carry. That's got to be good for one pecan pie recipe."

The lie had been exposed some months back. In the middle of investigating Scarlett's murder, Mama showed up at my front door one night out of the blue. It's time to tell the truth, she'd said. Over coffee she told me the whole sordid tale involving the farm, Daddy, and a loan shark. When Daddy couldn't repay the loan, Mr. Blackstone, the shark, threatened dire consequences. Daddy got desperate and that's when he and Mama came up with 'the plan' to throw the dog off the scent. Well it worked and Mr. Blackstone went easy on Mama—giving her time to repay the loan. *Another long story told elsewhere.*

"Could work," I said. "We could cry foul all over again."

Deena shook her head. "I tried that. She said for me not to go digging up the past. I don't believe there's going to be anymore repentin' from her."

"Do you think she'd give in if we sprinkled holy water on her? I heard that works real well in exorcism. There's a Catholic church in town."

I grimaced in good humor. "She'd just fly away on her enchanted broom, Billie Jo. And speaking of brooms, there's flour everywhere. Deena, you sweep the floor, and I'll wash the dishes. Billie Jo, you clean off the table and then we'll bake another pie."

Billie Jo's face twisted. "Another losing pie."

As a team we cleaned the kitchen and then pulled out the baking tins. Deena had picked out three remaining recipes that sounded promising so we each took one, put it together, and placed them in the oven to bake for forty-five minutes. We were taking them out of the oven to cool when a knock sounded at the kitchen door, and the subjects of our earlier discussion sailed through the door—our parents, Harland and Annie Mae Tucker.

I shot my sisters a Mona Lisa smile then turned to Mama. "We were talking about your secret pecan pie recipe."

Mama threw her purse down on the table. "Sometimes I wonder if the hospital switched you girls at birth. I told Deena this morning that y'all aren't getting that recipe."

"The topic of our conversation didn't include using your recipe, Mama," I said, reaching inside the refrigerator for a pitcher of sweet tea. "We were congratulating ourselves for coming up with a pie that would beat yours hands down. We don't need your secret recipe." I went to the cabinet. "Daddy, would you like a glass of sweet tea? Mama?"

He sat down at the table. "I would, sugar. Fall is awfully warm this year."

Out of the corner of my eye I could see Mama's face as she seated herself beside him. Like an unfinished sculpture, years of hard living had carved out places with an unsteady hand, yet the green fire in her eyes hadn't dimmed with disappointment through the decades. She was pushy, opinionated, and at times, downright unstoppable, but Mama had a good heart, and we loved her dearly.

"Harland, wouldn't you like a slice of that wonderful pecan pie?"

Crap. Up to this point, everything had been progressing smoothly, but Deena's panicked gaze almost derailed my plan to con Mama into handing over her recipe. Whatever happened, I couldn't let them taste those pies. Daddy would lie and make a fuss over our rejects, but Mama would know I was buffaloing her, and we would lose our all-expense paid trip to Disney World.

"It's too hot to cut," Billie Jo blurted out. "We're timing it so we know how long it needs to rest to obtain its optimum flavor."

Mama pushed herself away from the table and took down two dessert plates from the cabinet. She removed two forks from the silverware drawer.

"What are you doing?" I asked.

Mama's mouth twisted. "I'm going to cut two slices from one of those pies behind you on the counter. I assume they're cool since they've been cut into."

Deena stood over by the oven so Mama couldn't

see her mouth open and close like a fish out of water but Daddy did.

He winked at me behind Mama's back. "I don't believe I would like anything right now, Annie Mae. I'm stuffed from that wonderful lunch you prepared."

Mama didn't bat an eye. "Well, I want a piece. We may not have a chance to eat later. You haven't forgotten that we have to man the church booth for the Christmas Bazaar have you? And our granddaughter is in the beauty contest later in the evening. Lynette would be crushed if we missed any part of her special day."

"There's food booths set up out at the fairgrounds, Sugar Plum. We won't starve."

Deena expelled a heavy sigh. "She won't give up, Jolene, until she tastes that pie."

"I know, Deena. But I had hoped to spare her feelings." I shot Mama a sweet smile.

"Humph." Mama scooped up two large pieces of pie onto the dessert plates, returned to the table, and handed one to Daddy. He took a small bite and failed to keep a straight face as he swallowed the pitiful offering.

Mama spit hers back out onto the plate. "Too much salt."

"We know," we said in unison.

"And the others?" she asked.

"We've been baking pies for weeks now, and they're either too salty or sweet or the pie crust is either burnt or mushy," Billie Jo blabbed.

"We can't figure out what we're doing wrong," Deena added. "And we followed the recipe instructions exactly, but not one has turned out right. They all taste bad."

Daddy pointed to the three remaining uncut pies

cooling on the counter. "Maybe one of those turned out."

"Not by the looks of them," Mama spoke up. "The middle sags and the crust is burnt. You're probably using inferior ingredients and your oven temperature was too hot. The best way to judge them is to do a taste test."

"Count me out," Billie Jo grumbled.

"You only have to taste a small piece from each pie," I coaxed.

"Let Mama and Daddy taste 'em," she retorted. "My heart isn't in it any longer."

"We need your stomach, not your heart," Deena huffed.

She shook her head. "My stomach's on fire."

"Your mother and I will do the honors," Daddy volunteered, reaching across the table to pat Billie Jo's hand. "I'm sure one of them will be a winner. Right, Annie Mae?"

"I doubt it," Mama said. "But I'm willing to taste them and give my advice on baking the perfect pecan pie."

Like Billie Jo, my stomach churned like a volcano, and while Deena dished up pie, I downed a couple of Tums with a glass of ginger ale. Billie Jo finished up the pack.

Daddy's face registered surprise after tasting the first sample. "That wasn't bad, girls. At least it wasn't salty."

"Harland, your taste buds are on strike," Mama disagreed. "It smacks of maple syrup. This one is definitely a loser."

Mama rejected the second and third pie as well.

Neither one held up to her high baking standards.

"I'm glad it's over," Billie Jo said when Mama voiced her objection to the last pie. "Now we can stop wasting our time."

"Dixieland Salon will have an entry," I stated, "even if it's in last place."

"Annie Mae, are you gonna sit back and let our girls be humiliated by their lack of baking skills?" Daddy huffed. "You're the best dang baker in Whiskey Creek. They would win hands down with your supervision."

"Oh, no," Deena wailed. "We couldn't ask Mama to share her secret recipe with us. What if we won? Everyone would want her recipe. Why, I heard Diane Downey last Sunday in church bragging that if her son...you know, he owns Don Juan's Plumbing on Pine Needle Drive? Well, she said that if his business wins, she's going to write a cookbook and showcase the winning recipe."

Mama's face went red. "She stole my idea! I told her weeks ago about my dream to write a cookbook. I've even contacted Vanessa van Allen for some advice."

"Not the Vanessa van Allen who writes the bestselling vampire books?" I asked, amazed at Mama's resourcefulness. "She's been on the best-selling lists for weeks."

"Yes, that's her," Mama boasted. When I told her about my idea, she was interested."

"She's local, isn't she?" Deena asked. "I heard she recently bought a big house in Westgate. How do you know her?"

"Her mother, Betty and I went to school together.

Betty told me Vanessa didn't want her living alone after her father died so she bought that big house for the two of them. Well, I had a chance to talk to her one day during a visit with Betty."

"Wow," Daddy said. "Here's your chance, Annie. Think of the publicity and interest you'd generate with the first place winning recipe. Women would be lining up to buy your cookbook. Do you think Vanessa would help you find an agent?"

"She did mention the idea to her agent. He's interested if she co-authors."

"But you don't want to share credit with her, do you?" I asked. "I mean they're your recipes after all, Mama."

"Vanessa said that I could pay her a modest fee to ghostwrite the cookbook."

"If she writes your cookbook like she writes sex scenes, I'd buy it," Billie Jo said with a giggle. "Roddy and I read her books together in bed."

Deena rolled her eyes. "Really, Billie Jo? Sex and cooking? Do you ever think about anything else?"

Billie Jo's smile widened. "Not lately. You?"

"How much is a modest fee for a best-selling author, Annie Mae?" Daddy interrupted. "I'm thinking your idea of dollars and cents differs from hers. She's one of the rich and famous."

"Harland's right. I don't have that kind of money," Mama said. "But I know where to get it."

"Does that mean what I think it means?"

"Yes, Jolene, it does. Dixieland Salon is going to win that contest with a little help from me and my secret recipe. Diane Downey can eat my dust!"

Chapter Two
The Family Law

The noise level in the salon had reached an unbearable level. Someone, probably my niece, Lynette, had switched on the radio. The music blared over the speakers, nearly drowning out the excited squeals of half a dozen giggling teenage beauty contestants and their parents.

"Turn the music down," I shouted at Billie Jo as she passed by my workstation on the way to the shampoo bowl with a blonde haired, blue-eyed hopeful. "I can't work with that racket screaming in my ear."

"I'll turn it down, Aunt Jolene," Lynette hollered, scrambling out of my stylist chair to scamper in the direction of the reception desk where the radio blasted out a rock and roll tune.

As the music lowered to a reasonable level, I could once again hear the chatter of proud parents boasting to one another about the amount of money they had sunk into their daughter's dreams of becoming the next Miss Pecan Festival Queen. I could've bought a whole wardrobe for the price of those custom-made pageant gowns, and briefly wondered how much Billie Jo and Roddy had shelled out for Lynette's pink silk gown.

"Are you sure you don't want your mother to do your hair, Lynette?" I asked her when she plopped back down in my stylist chair. "I know she'd do a great job."

"No way, Aunt Jolene," she said. "I heard you looked like the Statue of Liberty after Mom did your hair."

That had been the day of Scarlett Cantrell's funeral. When Billie Jo had finished anchoring my long, wavy hair into springy curls with bobby pins and a can of hairspray, I didn't have the heart to tell her that on my tall frame the fat curls poked up like the Queen of Liberty's spiked crown.

I leaned down and kissed my niece on the check. "Your mama wouldn't do that to you, honey. She's a fine hairdresser."

"I'm not taking any chances. Let her work her magic on some other unsuspecting contestant. I want to win!"

I fashioned Lynette's light brown hair into a simple French Twist which emphasized the green eyes shining like polished jade in the mirror. She was a striking combination of Roddy's dark, good looks and Billie Jo's delicate beauty. So far, I hadn't seen a more beautiful contestant than my niece.

After a quick dusting of hairspray, she headed off to our nail tech, Ellie Malone for a quick manicure before having her makeup done by Deena. The next contestant took her place in my stylist chair and so the next hour went by.

I had finished with my fifth updo when the door chimes announced the second wave of contestants due to arrive, and my heart sank at the sight of the blonde bombshell entering the salon. Here was Lynette's closest competition.

Her companion, an older gentleman, I recognized from the society pages in the Whiskey Creek Gazette, and a brief introduction to him in the past—Theodore Herrington. The girl must be his seventeen-year old granddaughter, Kandy Herrington.

Several inches taller and about twenty pounds heavier than my niece, she had thick, shoulder-length, honey blonde hair and sky blue eyes. A real looker. When she reached adulthood, which wasn't far off by the curves she displayed, she would resemble a 1940's pinup-girl with voluptuous curves and a come hither smile the opposite sex gravitated to like a bear to honey.

Kandy came from money, and it showed. Even from this distance I could see a confidence and sophistication the other girls lacked, including Lynette, and I hoped my niece didn't walk away with a broken heart tonight instead of the crown and title she coveted.

Several of the other contestants ran up to Kandy and pulled her away from her grandfather. He smiled indulgently at her and seated himself in the reception area. Although I wasn't an acquaintance of the Herrington family, Lynette attended the same high school as Kandy and spoke often of her. I knew her parents were divorced and her father, Ryan Herrington, had recently started dating my nail tech, Ellie Malone. Her mother had remarried and relocated to Atlanta.

To the average observer, one would think, by the innocuous expression on his face that Theodore Herrington was a likeable fellow. But thanks to Ellie and the media my opinion had been colored to the point I continued working without acknowledging his self-important presence.

I knew from Ellie that he had expressed his disapproval of her dating his son, Ryan. His excuse had been her age. She's twelve years older than Ryan and some folks believe that to be too wide a gap to bridge, but age is just a number. One only had to see the couple together to know the attraction was real. The problem is a matter of economics. Ellie hailed from the wrong side of the tracks. She and I share that real estate. We're middle-class, working poor. Not one of the 'beautiful' people.

Oh, and I forgot to mention that Ellie Malone is African American.

Not exactly a candidate for the Daughters of the Confederacy.

As president of the Central National Bank of Georgia, Theodore Herrington and his second wife, Barbara Breckinridge of New York graced the pages of the Whiskey Creek Gazette on a regular basis. Their lavish parties were the talk of the town. A rumor had surfaced that he had flown in rare orchids from Hawaii in the dead of winter just to impress his guest of honor—regardless of the cost. In these times, such flagrant disregard for the value of the dollar came across as obscene. The money could have been donated to one of the local schools for any number of unfunded projects, or a soup kitchen to feed the homeless.

But Theo Herrington was also known for his bad temper and not just his excessive greed. Gossip had it that he had killed his first wife. A disturbing thought as I left my station and approached the reception area. Unfortunately, Ellie crossed his line of sight about the same time I did.

He pointed a finger at her. "Miss Malone," he said in a condescending tone of voice. "I want a word with you."

A warning cloud settled over Ellie's features. Not good. Some people you leave alone. Like Ellie.

"What can I do for you, sir?" Her voice held a challenge.

He reached into his suit pocket and withdrew a pen and checkbook. "It's not what you can do for me. It's what I can do for you. How does fifty thousand sound?"

"Sounds real good in this economy," she said. "But since you're giving away money, make it seventy-five."

He scribbled on the check. "Done. I want you out of my son and granddaughter's life."

My jaw dropped open. "Ellie, what are you doing?"

"Stay out of it, Miz Claiborne," Herrington cautioned. "This matter doesn't concern you." He handed the check over to Ellie.

I ignored him. "Ryan is the best thing to happen to you in a long time, and now you're ready to sell your future with him for seventy-five thousand dollars? Damn, girl."

Herrington pushed himself to his feet and shoved his finger into my face. "I asked you to stay out of this. But now I'm warning you. This is a private matter."

At the commotion several parents turned to gawk in our direction. Billie Jo and Deena both came over to investigate, but I reassured them the situation had been handled and for them to return to what they were doing. I turned back around to deal with my unpleasant guest in a quiet, orderly way, if I could manage to do so without losing my temper. Patience isn't one of my virtues. But to my credit I also have learned how to handle touchy situations. As a salon owner, I have to be—bad hair days and unsatisfied patrons abound in this business.

Ellie touched my arm. "I know you want to help. Trust me. I know what I'm doing."

"I hope so. Don't sell your soul just because you're sleeping with the devil's son. Fire burns, you know."

She tore the check in half. "I never meant to keep it. Just wanted to know how it feels to hold that much money. Ryan is worth more than seventy-five thousand dollars." She handed the torn check to Herrington. "Thanks for the thrill, sweetie."

"You'll regret this, Miss Malone," he sputtered. "You have no idea what I'm capable of, and I promise you that I won't allow you to be a part of my family. If my son persists in this relationship, he leaves me no choice but to resort to drastic measures. When I'm through, Ryan will curse the day he met you."

"I don't cotton up to threats," she snapped back. "I'm not a defenseless little woman who you can bully with big words and threats. Be careful, sir, or you might find yourself on the receiving end of your promise."

At the snarled words, Herrington's face blanched, and his hands clenched and unclenched as if he were trying to restore feeling. For a moment, I thought he would keel over with an apoplexy and that wouldn't be good for business. After Scarlett's unfortunate demise in the facial room, I'd made a promise to myself that there wouldn't be another dead body carted out of Dixieland Salon—ever.

When the overhead bell rang, I glanced over to see my parents enter. Mama saw me standing next to Herrington, and she made a bee line over to us. Ellie excused herself and took the opportunity to escape back to her workstation where the next contestant waited for her.

"This is my lucky day," Mama cooed. "Theodore Herrington, you're just the person I'm looking for. I need to discuss some business with you."

Daddy came up behind her and stuck out his hand. "Theo, I haven't seen you in years... Hey, are you all right?"

Herrington took out a handkerchief and mopped his sweating brow before shaking Daddy's hand. "I'm fine, Harland." He glared over at Ellie. "I'm trying to wrap up some unpleasant business that's proving to be more difficult than I first realized. And speaking of unpleasant business, I was shocked to learn your story. Annie Mae is a convincing liar, but I've known that since high school."

Even though I had been unaware of my parents past relationship with this man, the manner in which he delivered his verdict raised my hackles. There are four people allowed to call my mother a liar. Daddy. Me. Deena. And Billie Jo. I call it the Family Law.

I could tell by the narrowing of Daddy's eyes that he agreed with me. "Now that's uncalled for," he said. "Annie Mae was—"

"He's right, Harland," Mama interrupted. "I'm a talented liar. But that's not important. What's important is a bank loan for publishing my cookbook. That's the business I want to discuss with you, Theo."

"Well, this isn't a good place to discuss private business matters, Mama," I inserted, hoping to calm the growing tensions. "Don't you and Daddy have to be getting out to the fairgrounds? You don't want to be late. Mrs. Downey is a stickler for promptness."

"I have a watch on, Jolene. You go on and leave us

alone," Mama ordered.

Thankfully Deena interrupted us. She greeted Mama and Daddy and then turned to me. "Kandy is draped and waiting. Lynette left her heels at home so Billie Jo is heading out early. She'll meet us out at the fairgrounds later. I called Ted and asked him to come in and help you finish the remaining contestants."

"He didn't mind coming in on his day off?"

"No. He said he was finished shopping at the mall and would run home and change real quick, but I told him to come as is. He should be here any minute."

Reluctantly I returned to my workstation and consulted with Kandy on her choice of hairstyle, but I kept a close eye on the reception area. At first, the conversation seemed to be amicable, but soon after I began fastening sausage curls to the back of Kandy's head, Daddy's roar of outrage sounded the alarm. Both men surged to their feet and stood face to face in a confrontational pose. I dropped my rattail comb onto the counter, and rushed over to plant myself between them.

"What's going on?" I asked in my calmest voice.

"Your father's a hot head," Herrington accused. "I figured all those years in exile would have taught him to control his temper."

"I get steamed up real quick where Annie is concerned," Daddy shouted. "She told me you were awfully attentive after my supposed death. I wasn't even cold in the ground and you were quick to offer her comfort."

"You weren't dead, Daddy," I said.

Theo frowned. "Harland Tucker, you're an old fool. I never laid a finger on your wife."

"What happened to get this started?" I directed the question at Mama.

"Theo said his bank wouldn't lend me the money to get my cookbook published. I'm not asking for much."

"Aren't you jumping the gun a bit?" I asked her. "I told you this wasn't the time or place to discuss this. Make an appointment with a loan officer like everyone else does."

"My bank will not approve a loan for such a losing proposition. That's a bad investment. What if you can't repay the loan?"

"Your bank isn't the only one in town," Daddy told him.

"One word from me and you won't get a loan."

"Why would you do that?" I asked him.

"Because there's bad history between us," Mama replied. "Theo doesn't like to be reminded of certain events that took place amongst friends."

"Friends don't threaten to bury you six feet under the Georgia clay like Harland did me, Annie Mae. I haven't forgotten how you destroyed our friendship. I warned him not to marry you. You almost destroyed him, too."

Daddy launched himself at Herrington. "You son-of-a-bitch! I'm a good mind to tie your asshole in a knot."

Luckily, the father of a contestant arrived in time to prevent Daddy from striking Herrington, which was a good thing because the older man was once again showing signs of intense stress. Hearing the commotion, Deena rushed over and ushered our parents to her office, but I could still hear Daddy's tirade through the barrier of the door. His overreaction to the situation troubled me. Something unspoken had happened between them in their past that prompted the violent anger in my father. And it centered on Mama.

Kandy grabbed my attention as she joined her grandfather in the reception area and requested a glass of cold water for him. When I rejoined them, Herrington hunched over in one of the chairs breathing heavily. His face paled, and his hands trembled as he took the glass from my hand, much like after his confrontation with Ellie.

"Would you like me to call a doctor? Or perhaps I could call your wife?" I asked him.

"No. I'm fine."

"You're not, Grandfather," Kandy interjected. "You've been sick for days, and that argument didn't help. That man threatened to kill you!"

"Go finish your hair, my dear," Herrington said in a strained voice. "I'll be fine by the time you're ready to leave for the pageant."

That prayer I could get behind. The entire salon had witnessed Daddy threaten to snuff out Theodore Herrington. Spooked by the bad vibrations, I crossed my fingers behind my back for good luck and went in search of my next hopeful contestant.

Chapter Three
Blue Suede Shoes

By the time I arrived at the fairgrounds, a foul mood had settled over me. Ted showed up at the salon wearing a plaid mini-skirt so short he must've duct-taped his family jewels (although I use the term lightly) to his inner thigh to prevent them from hanging below the hemline. His entrance set the place on its head, and I didn't blame the parents for grabbing up their daughters and clearing out of the salon. Whiskey Creek lies slap-dab in the middle of the Bible belt and cross-dressing wasn't an accepted Christian practice in this neck of the woods.

My sisters were fussing over Lynette's evening gown hanging from a clothes rack when I found them in the contestant's dressing room area. Several sofas and tables with chairs dotted the large room and I could see by Billie Jo's expression that they were discussing Ted's future employment as she smoothed out wrinkles on the soft pink silk with a hand-held steamer.

"We can't fire him," Deena said. "He didn't break any rules. I am the one who prevented him from going home to change."

"Did he tell you he was dressed like Sweet Sally Mae?" Billie Jo's voice rose with indignation.

I stifled a laugh at Billie Jo's reference to our local streetwalker. Sweet Sally Mae strut her stuff down on the east side in colorful miniskirts hiked high over her curvy thighs. Rumor had it she raked in the big bucks for her naughty display.

"No. I didn't give him a chance to," Deena responded.

"Thank God you're here," Billie Jo said when she saw me. "Deena was telling me about Ted showing up at the salon—"

I dropped the bag of styling tools I had brought from the salon on the table. "I heard y'all. And I agree that we might have a problem, but we can deal with him later. I'm more concerned about Daddy's ugly confrontation with Herrington. There's something bad buried in their past, and I'm worried about it boiling over into the present."

Billie Jo returned the steamer to its holder. "Tonight is important to Lynette. Let's concentrate on her. I don't want anything to upstage her accomplishment."

"She's right," Deena agreed with a bright smile. "Let's enjoy the evening. Bill is joining me after the pageant. Is Sam going to be able to make it?"

"Bradford's working a case but promised to stop in later if he can," I said. "He told me to tell Billie Jo that he's confident Lynette will take the crown."

"I wish I had his confidence," Billie Jo said. "My baby girl is beautiful, but Kandy Herrington is built like a silicone implant display. Good Lord, Lynette is barely out of her training bra. It's a shame she's not stacked like you and Mama."

Stacked wasn't precisely the word I would've used in describing my physique. I much more preferred Bradford's hourglass description of my endowments, but I held my peace.

"These girls aren't being judged for their bust size, Billie Jo." Deena added.

High-pitched giggles could be heard coming our way, and as the girls joined us I turned and greeted my niece and her best-friend, Jennie Wesley.

"Love your dress, Miz Claiborne," Jennie said with youthful enthusiasm. "Cool shoes, too."

I tipped my blue suede heels up for her to get a better look. "Thanks for the compliment. You have great taste."

"Jennie, where are your things?" Billie Jo asked. "It's time to get in your gown."

"Rachel has them," she said. "We ran into Theo Herrington out in the auditorium. That's when he started yelling threats about taking over my father's bank. You know my father's temper."

"Herrington seems to rub people the wrong way," I said when the girls stepped out of hearing range. "That's the third run-in that I know of today. He seems determined to make enemies."

"Not when you consider his reputation, it isn't," Billie Jo said.

"Rumor mill has Roger Wesley's bank is in financial trouble," Deena spoke up. "I have a friend that works as a bank teller there. She told me there's a large amount of money missing and the bank is being investigated for embezzlement."

"Herrington is a bastard. One day someone's gonna put him out of his misery," Billie Jo declared.

"Don't say those things," Deena cautioned. "We're going to enjoy the rest of the evening even if it kills us."

All three of us burst out in laughter, and the depressive spell broke. Rachel Wesley showed up with Jennie's evening gown and accessories and reassured her little sister their father was fine and patiently waiting with the other parents for the contest to begin.

Working together, we dressed the girls in their lovely gowns and stepped back to survey our work. Lynette was a vision in her pink silk evening gown and Jennie just as stunning in teal blue satin.

When the moment presented itself, I pulled Rachel aside. "Jennie told us what happened between your father and Herrington."

"I swear, Jolene, it appeared as if Mr. Herrington purposely provoked my father into that ugly scene," she said. "Which could have possibly given my father a stroke. I'm glad Lynette showed up and distracted Jennie. She doesn't know how bad his health has become."

"Herrington is out of control," I told her. "Earlier at the salon he offered Ellie a fortune to break up with his son."

"Ellie Malone and Ryan Herrington are dating?"

"Yes."

Rachel smiled. "Wow. No wonder Theo Herrington was aching for a fight. He wouldn't want his son in an interracial relationship. Did Ellie take the bribe?"

"No. She told him she might consider it for seventy-five K. He wrote her out a check for that amount."

"And she took it?"

"Yes, but she tore it in half. You should have seen his face. I thought he was going to stroke out for sure."

"No such luck, huh?"

We smothered our giggles when the others turned to glower at us. "After that dreadful scene he got into another confrontation with my parents," I whispered.

"What about?"

"Well, I know it wasn't about the bank loan Mama wanted. I believe it had something to do with an unresolved incident that happened a long time ago."

"That doesn't sound so bad."

"No, the bad part came when Daddy threatened to knock his lights out in front of a salon full of witnesses."

"Wow. If Herrington drops dead, your father is first on the list of suspects."

"That's what I'm afraid of." I crossed my fingers, hoping the man in question lived a long and healthy life.

****

"These three young women are our finalists for this year's title of Miss Pecan Festival Queen, and I would like to congratulate them on their outstanding accomplishments," Nancy Chance announced from center stage. She beamed at Lynette, Jennie, and Kandy and then led another rousing round of applause. Several seconds passed, and an older gentleman came on stage with an envelope in his hand. He gave it to Nancy and then exited to the opposite side of the stage.

Nancy tore open the envelope. "Now, without further ado our second-place runner up is...Jennie Wesley."

A sash was draped over Jennie's head before she accepted a bouquet of peach roses and left the stage amid polite applause. Lynette and Kandy held hands under the spotlight.

Kandy Herrington beamed like a mermaid rising from the waves in a sparkling sea-foam green silk gown that molded to her curvaceous figure like a second skin. I crossed my fingers for good luck and waited with baited breath for the first-place runner up to be announced. Silently, I chanted Kandy's name over and over in hopes that Lynette would be the last woman standing.

"Before I introduce you to the first runner-up, I would like to take this time to emphasize the responsibilities of the first runner-up. If for any reason the winner can't fulfill her obligations, the first runner-up will then be crowned Miss Pecan Festival Queen." Nancy paused for a deep breath. "Drumroll, please," she instructed, and a teenaged boy stepped proudly out onto the stage with a small drum. The drumroll reverberated throughout the room.

Nancy again stepped up to the microphone and said, "The first runner-up is Kandy Herrington."

Applause broke out as Kandy stepped forward with a pasted smile of nonchalance to receive the first runner-up sash over her head and a bouquet of white roses. She exited the stage with her head held high leaving Lynette standing alone at center stage.

"And this year's Miss Pecan Festival Queen is…Lynette Hazard!"

"She won!" Billie Jo screamed in my ear as last year's winner removed her crown from her own dark hair and pinned the rhinestone tiara on Lynette. Whistles and wolf calls echoed throughout the audience as the white sash with Miss Pecan Festival Queen in gold letters dropped over Lynette's head and a bouquet of red roses were placed in her arms.

I could see tears on her smiling face as she strolled across the stage waving to the audience as they gave her a standing ovation. She waved enthusiastically when she spotted us in the crowd.

"I knew she would win," Mama crowed.

"She's a winner, our granddaughter," Daddy agreed. "I've never seen Roddy smile so big."

"He's a proud father," Deena said over the applause. "Billie Jo's crying."

I glanced in surprise over at my youngest sister. Billie Jo hardly ever displayed raw emotion in public. She hated weeping, clingy women. Which told of the importance of Lynette's victory.

Out of the corner of my eye I saw Nancy Chance and another gentleman having a disagreement offstage. From the violent way her arms were waving, something had transpired to upset the pageant coordinator. I watched as she threw up her hands in defeat and came up the stairs to the stage. She approached the center microphone and asked for silence. As the crowd settled down, I noticed Jennie and Kandy reappear on stage and Lynette being asked by the older gentleman to join them.

I didn't need a flash of insight or a clairvoyant vision to tell me the future. Nancy's crestfallen face said it all.

"What's going on?" Mama asked in a strained voice. "Something's wrong."

"I'm not sure," Daddy answered. "Whatever it is, I don't like it."

Billie Jo clenched Roddy's hand. "Don't jump to conclusions, honey," he said. "There's no need to get all bent out of shape until we know what's going on."

"May I have your attention, please," Nancy announced. "There has been a complaint registered anonymously against one of the judges for her previous association with one of the contestants. Because of this charge, her scores are being thrown out and the scores of the two remaining judges are being re-tallied. Until this is resolved, please remain quietly in your seats. I will have the new results shortly." Nancy hurriedly exited the stage with her face adverted from the crowd.

Beside me, Deena gasped as the tiara was lifted from Lynette's head, followed by the Miss Pecan Festival Queen sash. The items were given back over to last year's winner.

Roddy and Billie Jo watched in stunned silence as Lynette stood bravely beside the two other contestants, her face pale, but proud. Jennie's pixie face was anxious. Kandy's hopeful.

A chorus of boos and catcalls from the audience gathered in strength as the minutes passed by, and everyone grew antsy with anticipation, or as in our case, trepidation. Nancy's return to the stage brought immediate silence. She opened another white envelope and withdrew a card.

"The results are in and the second runner-up is…"

The audience held its breath. We held hands and climbed to our feet.

"Lynette Hazard."

Sporadic applause sounded around the audience. Like a balloon with a sudden tear, we collectively sat down and watched Lynette receive the second runner-up sash and the bouquet of flowers with her head held high. Nancy waited until she had gracefully exited the stage before continuing in a flat, monotone voice.

"The first runner-up is Jennie Wesley."

Jennie receive her recognition as Kandy Herrington beamed from center stage. I hate to admit it, but I wanted to wipe the smile from her chubby face. I couldn't, but I wanted to.

Nancy didn't wait for a drumroll introduction this time. "And Kandy Herrington is this year's Miss Pecan Festival Queen," she said and strode off the stage leaving a stunned audience.

I didn't wait for Kandy's crowning, but bolted out of my seat and rushed to find Nancy. I caught up with her backstage amid the hum of conversation of bewildered contestants.

"Explain to me how my niece was dethroned in front of her family and friends," I said in a low, composed voice not wanting her to feel the brunt of my anger. Nancy had been a patron of my beauty shop for years and I knew her reasonably well. She wasn't responsible for what had just taken place.

"This is the first time in the history of this contest this has happened. A judge's scores have never been rescinded."

"The judge?"

"Miranda Moore," she said.

"She's Lynette's former ballet teacher. But she's taught dance to half the girls in this town. I know for a fact that she wouldn't throw the contest Lynette's way. Miranda Moore despises Billie Jo. They butted heads so often, Roddy insisted Lynette be pulled out of her class."

"You and I know that, but the committee listened to the anonymous complainant."

"Who?"

"You know I can't divulge that information, however I can tell you this person carries a lot of weight in this city."

His name popped up like a brain freeze. "Theodore Herrington."

She shook her head negatively. "No, not him. He is pushing to have me thrown off the festival committee. But you're close. Think family member."

"Had to be his wife. Barbara was with him at the pageant and I noticed her slip out of her seat after Kandy was named first runner-up," I parried. "She's the dog, right?"

She nodded in affirmation. "As I previously stated, I can't divulge the information."

"Thank you, Nancy. I should have figured he was behind it. From my limited association with Barbara Herrington, she comes across as a woman who would bend under pressure, especially from her controlling husband. Can we appeal the decision?"

She frowned at the suggestion. "Of course you can, but that's a waste of time. The festival will be over before the committee can reach a decision. Theodore Herrington—"

She broke off as several contestants ran past us like the building was on fire. "What on the earth is going on out there?"

The sound of thumping crashes and raised voices came from the stage area. I didn't wait to see if Nancy followed, but dashed in the same direction the girls had taken. When I emerged onstage, I could see Daddy tussling with Theo Herrington on the floor in front of the stage.

I heard a whack—a fist connecting with flesh. I winced when I heard another whack.

"Hellfire!" Daddy raged from the floor. His punch connected with Theo's jaw.

Several stunned bystanders watched at a distance, but no one interceded to break up the fight.

Mama screamed and struggled against Billie Jo and Deena who flanked her from both sides, their arms interlinked with hers. "Stop it, Harland," she screamed. "You and Theo are going to kill one another."

Adrenaline kicked in and I rushed for the stairs. From my perch on the stage I could see Daddy penned underneath Theo's punishing blows. For one moment Theo loosened his hold and Daddy rolled onto his side and made it to his feet, blood dripping from his nose.

I made it to the bottom stair as Daddy charged like a bull. The sickening thud of bodies connecting brought cries of fear from the female observers. Both men fell to the floor with Theo, the heavier of the two, on top of Daddy. Fists continued to fly as I launched myself at Theo's back and hung on like a champion bronc rider.

"Get off me, bitch," he roared, bucking and twisting, trying to dislodge me.

To this day, I can't explain why I sank my teeth into his shoulder. I suspect it was an automatic reaction to being called a bitch by this nasty old man or my overprotective nature of Daddy. Anyway, Theo bellowed in pain, reached up, grabbed my dress and yanked.

I kissed the floor and rearranged my nose. Spots danced in front of my eyes as excruciating pain blazed a trail from my face to my brain. I gasped for breath and tasted blood.

At this point, Roddy and several men entered the fray to pull the two men apart. Deena's boyfriend, William Maloney lifted me to my feet and handed me a handkerchief. It took several seconds for the dizziness to subside before I stood on my own and pressed the handkerchief to my nose—groaning with aggravation at my bloodstained dress and shoes.

Both men were breathing heavily, and Daddy also sported a bloody nose. Theo had a split and bleeding lip. Barbara Herrington wept on the sidelines, and as soon as the two men stopped struggling, she rushed to her husband's side.

"Someone, call the cops," she screamed, and then pointed at me and Daddy. "I want both of them arrested for assaulting my husband."

"Your husband is at fault here," I cried. "He's the one going to jail. He broke my nose!"

"What the hell is going on in here?"

I turned with relief at the sound of the husky, authoritative voice of my boyfriend, Detective Samuel Bradford. Crap. From the deep frown marring his face I concluded that he wasn't happy to see me. His words confirmed my suspicions. "Why am I not surprised to find you in the middle of this, Jolene? You realize what this means don't you?"

****

Bradford arrested all three of us. No amount of protesting changed his decision, and we found ourselves being transported to the hospital to be checked out by a doctor before heading off to jail. I wasn't scared or nervous about being incarcerated since I'd done this before. Actually, being Bradford's girlfriend (at the moment), and a repeat offender, had earned me special handling.

My face upset me the most. I had a broken nose and a skinned up chin, and the doctor predicted I would have twin black eyes. Ordinarily, I'm photogenic, I told the police photographer, and I don't have to buy any of the prints if I didn't like them. I laughed, but he frowned at my witty conversation and told me to turn to the side for a profile shot.

Bradford maintained his professional distance during my booking. He hadn't come near me after our initial encounter at the fairgrounds auditorium. I wasn't holding out much hope that he and District Attorney Randy Fallon could find a way to get me and Daddy sprung from lockup before the media plastered our pictures on the eleven o'clock news. Bradford had to maintain his professional distance until the proper procedure was followed. Besides, he was pissed.

Officer Diamond Presley awaited to escort me to my temporary holding cell, and I was glad to see my old friend. Bradford had introduced us when he placed me in protective custody from the mob. (It's a long story and best told elsewhere.)

"Your fingerprints are on file, so you don't have to submit to that procedure tonight," she said. "We can proceed directly to your overnight accommodations."

"I think my luck is turning, Diamond. It's my good fortune you were on duty when I was brought in."

"Well, I'm surprised to see you, too. I heard you bit the shit out of that old codger." She chuckled.

"I swear I don't know what came over me."

Her lovely brown face broke into a wide smile. "Girlfriend, he asked for it. I would've taken the starch out of his shirt too if he beat up on my pappy."

We reached my overnight accommodations. Diamond opened the door, and I held out my hands for her to remove my plastic bracelet.

"Diamond, do you have any information on Daddy?" I took a seat on the small bed and awaited her answer.

"He's fine, honey. Sam's taken extra good care of him. Don't you worry none. You and your pappy will be out of here in no time."

Diamond stayed with me for a few minutes more and then left. Another hour passed before she returned and unlocked the door. "I told you it wouldn't be long before you'd be going home. All the charges have been dropped." She held up my purse. "I'll give this to you out in the waiting room. Have to follow the rules, you know, especially with Mini Pearl."

Mini Pearl was my .32 caliber snub-nosed revolver and my constant companion. I carry her safely cradled in a pink holster tucked into my purse or in certain cases, strapped to my thigh or ankle for easy access. My Georgia Weapons Carry License makes it legal for me to carry a concealed weapon so I'm never without a means to defend myself.

I stared at her in amazement. "How did that happen? So fast, I mean. I thought I'd be here overnight."

"Sam arranged it," she said. "Herrington and your pappy talked it out. A misunderstanding about the beauty contest. Your pappy said he overheard one of the parents saying old man Herrington boasted about stealing the crown away from Lynette to give to his granddaughter. Well, Sam convinced both men to let it drop and all interested parties get to go home. You don't have a problem with that, do you?"

"No, Diamond, I don't." I followed her back down the same corridor we'd taken earlier. "I'm ready to go home and take a long hot bath."

She shook her head. "You look like you've had a hard day. Now, mind you, I don't mean that in a bad way… It's just that, well, you're banged up real good and your clothes are ruined."

"My blue suede heels are definitely ruined," I agreed. "Would you believe today is the first time I've worn them? And I laid out two hundred bucks for them."

"You could try an old country remedy my granny told me about. She said it would take blood stains out of anything. I bet it would work on suede."

"I'll try anything."

"Warm cow pee."

I stopped in my tracks. "Geez, Diamond, that sound's funky."

"My granny is as southern as cheese straws, but she swears by it."

"Where do you buy cow pee?"

"How the hell would I know? I'm a city gal. Buy a new pair. That's the American way to stimulate the economy, you know."

We were still laughing when I spied Mama and my sisters pacing in the front waiting room. Daddy was nowhere in sight when I joined them. Deena rushed up when she spied me and Officer Presley standing in the doorway.

"Jolene, thank God. Are you okay?" she gushed. "We were so worried."

"I'm fine," I replied. "Just ready to go home."

Diamond handed me my purse and excused herself when Mama and Billie Jo joined us. "I'll go see what's keeping your pappy."

"Thank you, Diamond," I said as she turned to leave. "Let's have lunch soon. My treat."

She gave me a quick nod and disappeared down the hall. Mama, Deena, Billie Jo, and I settled ourselves on one of the many white plastic chairs to wait. I opened my purse, relieved to see Mini Pearl resting comfortably in her pink leather holster.

"It's like a miracle," Mama said. "I can't believe what Sam did for us, Jolene. He kept you and your father out of a lot of trouble. We have to find a way of repaying him."

I was half-listening and glanced up to see her lift an eyebrow suggestively. "Of course, you're not at your best tonight so you might want to wait." Her soft voice sounded eminently reasonable. "You're gonna need a plastic surgeon. Whatever possessed you to jump onto Theo's back? I swear I could see your panties. I bet everyone else did, too."

Oh, hell. Why couldn't she cut those damn apron strings?

"Thanks for the advice, Mama," I responded sarcastically. "I'll find a plastic surgeon in the yellow pages tomorrow morning. And as far as everyone seeing my panties, well, you'd better be glad I decided to put some on at the last minute or they would have seen my *twinkie pie*."

Her nostrils flared. "You've always been my problem child. I think you say things like that on purpose to rile me up. And lower your voice, people are staring."

She was right. People were staring, but I didn't care. More devastating things had transpired tonight than my exposed panties.

Like Lynette having to give back the tiara and title of Miss Pecan Festival Queen.

I glanced over at Billie Jo sitting several chairs down from us, and went to sit beside her.

"How's Lynette?" I asked. "I know how teenagers feel about being embarrassed in front of their friends. I'm so sorry for my foolish behavior."

Billie Jo's brow puckered. "Don't apologize. If anyone is to blame for this mess, it's Herrington. I blame him for stealing Lynette's title and for starting the fight with Daddy. And one of her friends caught the whole fight on video and uploaded it to You Tube. The video has gone viral. The house is packed with teenagers. Roddy had pizza delivered to feed them all."

"I'm on YouTube? Crap. Bradford's pissed and now this. What am I going do?"

She didn't have a chance to respond because Bradford escorted Daddy into the room. "Here he is, ladies," he said, his gaze on Mama. "You can take him home and put him to bed. I'm sure he's going to be sore in the morning."

"We owe you a debt of gratitude, Sam. If it hadn't been for your interceding, Harland and Jolene would still be in a lot of trouble. Thank you." She hugged his neck.

"A simple misunderstanding, Mrs. Tucker. Herrington is as anxious as you to put this behind him."

Deena and Billie Jo expressed their thanks also and followed Mama and Daddy out of the station leaving me alone with Bradford. Finally, he turned to stare at me, his brows drawn together in an agonized expression. "We need to talk." He took me by the arm and propelled me out the door.

"Where are we going?"

"To my office where it's private."

Well, it didn't take a rocket scientist to know that my sweet, handsome cop had every intention of dumping me. Damn. Just when I was getting use to a steady diet of sex after a long haul of celibacy. The thought of another extended dry run turned my smile upside down, and I was surprised when I heard Bradford say in a stiff voice, "Stop scowling at me. I just wanted to inform you that I had to agree that you would enroll in anger management classes to appease Herrington for biting him."

I gawked across the desk at him. "Anger management classes. That's what you wanted to talk to me about?"

"It was that or a psychiatric evaluation. I figured you would prefer the anger management. Was I wrong?"

"No, of course not," I conceded. "I thought you brought me back here to your office to dump me."

He raked his fingers through his hair, leaned back in his chair, and for a moment, his sapphire gaze studied me. "I thought strongly of it," he admitted. "I've never dated a woman who keeps me guessing the way you do. God, Jolene, you're like a wild horse that refuses to be tamed. I'm not sure that's a good thing."

I lifted my chin higher. "I'm not the type to beg. And I'm fairly certain I'm not going to change at this late stage of my life. I'm quirky at times, but I'm comfortable in my skin just the way it is. I'm not going to reinvent myself for a man…even if that man is you."

Hurt by his, what I saw as rejection, I didn't give him a chance to respond. Instead, I gathered myself together and marched out of his office and out into the November evening where my family awaited me.

Chapter Four
Mint Julip Tea and Murder

Tuesday morning dawned bright and warm. I had slept well after a disastrous Monday, and when I studied my image in the mirror after my morning shower, a banged-up face smiled back. However, my nose had swollen to the size of a small dill pickle, and after I removed the clear hospital tape, it appeared slightly crooked and sore to the touch. Makeup would disguise the worst of it, as well as my yellowing eyes and scratched chin. All in all, I was optimistic that, with time, I would heal up nicely and no one would be the wiser of my latest mishap.

To booster my confidence and draw the eye away from my face, I dressed in a form-fitting, knee-length faded blue denim dress and matching heels. Since Deena and I were conducting tours at Pineridge Plantation later in the morning, I styled my hair into a becoming chignon.

Dressed and ready to leave, I fed Tango, my orange tabby, poured coffee into a disposable cup and headed out the door, my period antebellum gown slung over one arm. The sight of the dress brought the vintage key to remembrance, and I was anxious to return to the mansion and begin my search for the mysterious lock the key fitted.

Traffic was light as I sped down Main Street

toward the salon. I flashed by the courthouse square, made a right on Love Avenue and pulled into Parkers Place—a small cluster of boutiques and a quaint café. As I came around the corner, to the back of the salon, I spied Deena's green Buick. She was in the kitchen when I came through the back door.

"Is that you, Jolene?"

I stepped into the small kitchen. "Yep, in the flesh."

She spooned coffee into the paper filter. "You sound chipper. I thought you'd be more subdued after your run-in last night with Theo Herrington and another trip to jail." She giggled. "I wish I had thought to take a picture of you when you jumped on his back. We could've had two prints made. One for my scrapbook and have the other framed and hung in the reception area for our clientele to enjoy."

"Don't mention his name to me." I sat down at the small dinette table. "Because of him I have to take anger management classes."

She turned around. "Oh, Jolene, your face! Does it hurt? What did Sam say after we left? I'm sure he was upset to see your beautiful face messed up."

"You wouldn't believe what he said," I murmured.

"Oh, yes I would. His face said it all. I know Sam. Pissed off for sure."

I started to share the details of his anger when the sound of a female voice drifted from the front of the salon. There would be plenty of time to pass along my single status to her on the long drive out to Pineridge Plantation.

"Nancy's here," I said, glancing at my watch. 7:00 a.m. "I've got one perm and a head of foils scheduled before we leave at ten so I'd better get to work."

"We're not finished with this conversation," Deena said. "I can tell that something's bothering you."

"My nose is bothering me," I said as I exited the kitchen. Nancy and another woman were waiting in the reception area.

She greeted me with a, "Oh, my dear, you look dreadful. I regret telling you about Herrington being responsible for Lynette losing her crown. How is Billie Jo taking it?"

"I haven't talked to her this morning." I led the way to my stylist chair. "But I'm sure she's fine. One of Lynette's friends filmed the whole damn scene and uploaded it to YouTube. Her friends thought it was the coolest thing. You know how teenagers are."

Holly, our receptionist and shampoo girl, hadn't arrived for work yet, so I draped Nancy and led her back to the shampoo bowl.

"I'm sorry you were arrested. Detective Bradford wouldn't listen to me when I tried to explain the situation."

I wet her hair and squirted a generous dollop of shampoo into my hand. "Yeah, I know. I appreciate what you tried to do for us. Thankfully the charges were dropped and we were released."

"Too bad Detective Bradford couldn't have left Theo behind bars," she said. "He's making my life miserable. Thanks to him this may be my last year as director of the Pecan Festival. I've been doing this for fifteen years, you know."

"I'm sorry to hear he's giving you a hard time. The committee would be lost without your expert direction. They should rethink their position."

We finished at the shampoo bowl and returned to my chair. As I wrapped her hair in perm rods we chatted about tonight's pecan pie bakeoff. Nancy tried to steer the conversation back to last night's fight, but I remained resolute. Theo Herrington was one subject I wanted to put to rest.

By the time I finished wrapping her hair, the staff arrived, and the salon began filling with clients and their excited chatter. I had a hard time keeping my temper reined in. I wasn't in the mood to talk about my arrest or my face being plastered all over YouTube.

With twenty minutes to burn before I had to rinse the permanent wave solution from Nancy's hair, I headed back to the kitchen to find Billie Jo seated at the table nursing a cup of coffee.

"Morning." She yawned sleepily into her mug. "We had a late night with a house full of teenagers." She glanced up. "You might need to call a plastic surgeon like Mama suggested."

"Morning to you too, sis. And thanks for the compliment." I laughed. "Deena said the same thing. How's Lynette after last night's fiasco?"

"Better than expected. You'd think she'd invented Facebook the way those friends of hers are carrying on. They've started a petition online to have the Miss Pecan Festival Queen title rescinded. At last count I believe they had collected over two hundred signatures."

I poured a glass of water and joined her at the table. "The salon is buzzing with it this morning and it's all over the morning news. Kandy's picture is plastered across the front page of the Whiskey Creek Gazette. She seemed delighted with the reversal last night."

"Herrington is an asshole," Billie Jo spat. "I wouldn't be surprised if he didn't bribe Miranda Moore to confess to padding Lynette's scores. She'd do it just to spite me."

"Actually, Barbara Herrington officially lodged the complaint. Not Theo."

"Did Nancy tell you that?"

"Yes and no. She didn't say Barbara's name but it doesn't take a master's degree to know she's the guilty party. It had to be her acting on his behalf."

"So besides that, what else is bugging you?"

"Bradford dumped me last night."

"Why?"

"My screwed up personality, what else?"

"I don't see it."

"You wouldn't, Billie Jo. You're a lot like me."

"So what did you say back to him?"

"I told him that I liked myself just the way I am."

"Good for you." She squeezed my hand.

"And I wasn't going to change. Even for him."

"Good for you. Do you think he's been thinking about this for a while? Or was it your arrest that sealed the deal?"

I shrugged. "He's had a hard time accepting certain things about me since we started dating."

"Like seeing dead people?"

"That's one of them. Bradford doesn't believe in ghosts."

"I used to believe the same. Remember when you told me about Scarlett hanging around after she was murdered? Well, I came around didn't I? Hey, speaking of coming around, did you encounter any ghosts while you were out at Pineridge?"

"Billie Jo, you're incorrigible."

"No, seriously, Jolene, answer the question."

"Why are you interested?"

"Because I ordered one of those Paranormal Investigative Kits online," she said. "Next time I'm out at Pineridge, I'm gonna see if I can communicate with one of 'em."

I grinned at her. "You ordered a ghost-hunting kit?"

"Nooo. I didn't order a ghost-hunting kit. It's a Paranormal Investigative Kit. You know, for us amateurs. Not everyone can communicate with dead folks, and I don't have your special talent."

"You should be thankful," I said with a sigh. "My life would be easier if I was normal like you." The timer on the table buzzed, and I pushed back from the table. "I've got to rinse Nancy's hair."

"Hey." Billie Jo grabbed my arm. "Have you told Deena about your breakup with Sam?"

"I haven't said anything to her or Mama. Would you mind if we kept this between us for now? There's been so much for the family to deal with lately, and I don't want them worrying about mine and Bradford's relationship."

She nodded. "I will if you answer my question."

"Yes, Billie Jo. I saw the ghost of Josiah Redding. Happy?"

"Extremely."

Nancy was on her cell phone when I approached my workstation. "But Mr. Lampton, you've only heard his side of the story." She sputtered. "I can explain myself if you would give me a chance...yes sir, I understand. I'll be there as soon as I'm finished here."

She threw her phone inside her purse. "Another anonymous complaint filed against me. I have to appear before the festival board to answer the charge."

I led her to the shampoo bowl. "I'm sure you'll be able to answer the allegations to their satisfaction." I turned on the warm water, removed the plastic cap, and leaned her head back into the tepid spray.

"Jolene, if I lose my position as director of the Pecan Festival because of this ridiculous trumped up charge, I promise you I'll be gunning for Theodore Herrington."

Silently, I wagged my head in response to her passionate declaration. In my opinion, it might be a good idea to cancel the festivities before someone else got hurt. Theodore Pain-In-The-Ass Herrington seemed determined to collect enemies, and this situation stunk worse than a politician's opinion.

****

"The manor house at Pineridge Plantation is a two-and-a-half-story red brick mansion standing amid a tranquil garden of pines, live oak, magnolias, and azaleas. The century old Shortleaf pines towering over the house brings cooling shade from the scorching sun and gives the plantation its name."

"I'm glad you're rehearsing your lines," Deena said as we were changing into our period costumes in the back bedroom of the mansion. "Your southern drawl needs work, Jolene. Not enough twang."

I plopped down onto one of the brightly colored upholstered chairs and tried to take a deep breath. "I don't think I can lace up these boots. My nose throbs every time I bend over, and I feel like I'm going to faint in these tight stays. Can you help me?"

Deena sank to her knees and grabbed my foot. "So are you going to tell me what's bothering you?"

I pointed at my face. "Isn't this enough?"

She finished lacing up one foot then grabbed the other. "No, it isn't. I know you're neurotic about your appearance, but something's up. I only want to help, you know."

The old idiom *Take the bull by the horns* came to mind as I listened to her prattle. Deena's like a bull with a cow in heat. Once she smells a problem, she'll bang the hell out of it until it's either dead or pregnant with the solution.

Her cell phone rang as she finished lacing up my boot. "You'd better answer your phone," I said, relieved for a short reprieve. "It could be important."

She picked up her purse from the bed, and dug out her phone. "It's Summer."

I tried not to eavesdrop as I stood before the full-length mirror fastening a snood over my hair. The conversation was brief. Deena snapped shut the phone, threw it in her purse, and began fumbling at the buttons on her gown.

"Summer found a lump in her breast. She's at the hospital for a biopsy. I've got to go. I'm sorry but you'll have to handle the tours on your own."

Butterflies assaulted my stomach. Cancer popped into my thoughts and fear like the quick, hot touch of the devil's pitchfork shot through me. I swallowed with difficulty and found my voice. "Don't worry about the tours. I can handle them. Your daughter needs you."

"I'm scared." She spoke in a suffocated whisper. "What if it's cancer?"

"Don't say it, Deena. Never say *that* word."

Together we stripped off her gown and somehow managed to get her redressed into street clothes. She grabbed a hanger and reached for her gown, but I stopped her.

"Leave it. I'll take care of your things. Get out of here. And call me with any news."

Deena started toward the door, but stopped and turned back. "I rode with you. How am I going to get back to town?"

"Take my car." I dug through my purse for the keys to my new red Mustang. "I'll hitch a ride with one of the other volunteers." I tossed them to her.

"Call Sam," she suggested before she disappeared into the hallway.

"I'm the last person he wants to hear from right now," I said to the empty doorway. "Of course, you don't know yet."

A quick memory of our last date shot through me and the urge to call him had me reaching for my phone, but Rebel pride overrode the impulse, and I dropped it back into my shoulder bag. Called me a wild horse, did he? Well, here's one wild horse that wasn't gonna slip on a bridle!

Chapter Five
My Old Nemesis

The tour group, made up of senior citizens from a
nearby retirement village, were waiting for me when I
stepped onto the front veranda. A chorus of oohs and
aahs sprang forth from wrinkled lips as they gathered
around to inspect my antebellum day gown.

After I restored order to the lively group, I
conducted them on a tour of the house, pausing
frequently to answer questions posed about the duties of
the plantation mistress and the treatment of slaves. A
few of the men in the group were knowledgeable of the
times and challenged me for a better explanation on
every answer.

We'd stepped into the main floor dining room
when the familiar sensation of shifting cosmic space
pinged me. Out of the corner of my eye I could see the
misty shape of an old black woman garbed in a long,
striped cotton dress similar to the one I wore. On her
head was a red bandana tied in the traditional African
head-wrap slave women favored.

"*I be Tempy.*"

The words planted themselves in my mind. With a
group of tourists surrounding me, I gave her the briefest
nod of acknowledgement, then pointed to the dark
antique table dominating the room. "The Sheraton-style
table is original to the house and you will notice the

convex mirror over the fireplace mantel dates to the Regency period. The watercolor of the house on the right of the chimney was completed in 1860 by the same local artist who painted Josiah Redding's portrait in the library."

The air danced with movement as Tempy drifted a few feet over to stand beside an elegantly dressed woman in the group. Fascinated, I watched as ghostly fingers touched the woman's chocolaty cheek.

"She be of my clan."

Looking about her with unease, the woman reached up to caress her cheek in the same manner as Tempy had and smiled. Apparently she sensed a presence and reacted without knowing it was her ancestress' touch. Seemingly satisfied, Tempy disappeared.

The rest of the tour passed uneventfully, and it wasn't until I had ushered them back out to the veranda where another volunteer waited that anticipation took root. Finally, I could search for the mysterious lock. I reached inside the front pocket of my dress and clasped the key tightly in my hand. Immediately it grew warm, sending a slight tingling up my arm. On quiet feet I made my way to the library, paused outside the closed door, and glanced back over my shoulder. Alone. Good. Explaining my furtive actions to any observers would take precious time I didn't have.

Stepping inside I closed and locked the door. A swift survey of my surroundings exposed no supernatural guests in the empty chamber. My gaze traveled to the cherry bookcases where a small box stashed among the books would be hardly noticed.

Fifteen minutes of frantic searching produced no results so I abandoned the bookcases for the small desk on the opposite wall. Perhaps I would have better luck over there but again after several minutes of ransacking the drawers, I had no luck. With care I replaced the articles in the drawers as I had found them and paused in my search. My gaze probing into the corners of the room for any indication of an undiscovered hiding place.

Nothing. I had searched every likely nook and cranny and came up empty-handed. Another brick wall. No answers in here.

So where to continue my search?

Mentally I recalled each room on the ground floor. The small drawing room next door, with its beautiful marquetry desk and antique tables, offered a wealth of hiding places. With that destination in mind, I started for the door when I felt the air crackle and the faint distinct sound of feminine laughter behind me. The hairs on my nape rose as I glanced over my shoulder and saw the familiar ghostly figure materialized on the chintz covered sofa.

My old nemesis, Scarlett Cantrell, lounged over its shiny surface like a South Georgia coon dog on a short leash.

"So you're back." I let out a sigh of aggravation.

Her expression held wicked amusement. "With a vengeance," she purred. "Fancy meeting you here."

"What are you doing? Why aren't you…" I pointed heavenward. "You know, up there?"

She stretched lazily, her blue-green eyes never leaving mine. "I might ask you the same thing. I'm here for an interview. And you?"

"Playing Scarlett O'Hara," I twanged in my best southern accent.

"That's debatable. You're dressed like an indentured servant."

"I will have you know my gown is the historically correct clothing of plantation mistresses. They were hard-working farm hands who worked from sunup to sundown just like any field hand. Few ever wore Hollywood's glamourous portrayal of silk gowns and frivolous bonnets."

"Still pushy and opinionated, I see."

"And you're still vain and self-centered. How is it they haven't kicked you out of Heaven?"

Scarlett gave a humorous laugh. "They keep threatening to, but my probation isn't up so I have a tad more time. That's why I'm here. To help, that is."

"Oh, God, please tell me you're not here to help me."

"No, I'm here to help him." Scarlett waved a transparent hand at the fireplace.

Josiah Redding stood just as I had first seen him yesterday morning with the tour group. His piercing gaze passed over me and settled on Scarlett. With the ease of a leaf blowing in a gentle summer breeze, she drifted over to him.

Observing their animated conversation was like watching a silent movie without the by-line scrolling across the screen to tell you what the actors were saying. Therefore, I could only guess as to what was going down a few feet from me.

Finally, after what seemed like forever, Scarlett left Josiah by the fireplace and resumed her position on the sofa. "Aren't you going to congratulate me? I got the job."

"And what job would that be?"

"Josiah is in need of an interpreter."

"I'm afraid to ask why, but I'm sure you're dying to enlighten me."

"So he can communicate with you," she said. "He can't cross over until the mystery of the massacre is solved."

"No mystery there. It's a documented fact that Union troops murdered his family."

"Not according to him."

"Why can't he communicate with me himself? You haven't stopped talking since the day you died."

"He bears a terrible secret. So terrible he can't speak of it."

"He spoke to you," I pointed out.

"We're on the same plane of existence. But he won't even tell me his secret."

I opened my hand. "Here's the mystery. A big help would be for him to point me in the right direction. How am I supposed to find a lock to fit this key in this oversized house?"

At my last word, a brown leather bound book flew out from one of the bookcases landing with a loud thump on the hardwood floors.

"He said you would find answers in there," Scarlett said.

I picked up the book and discovered it was an old ledger dating back to the 1840s. "He expects me to read this?" I held up the key again. "I want to know about this."

"Too late, he's gone back into hiding. He doesn't like strangers trampling his property. Although he did mention something about mint julep tea and murder."

"Well, that's just great," I pronounced with a sigh.

"How am I supposed to solve this mystery if I can't get any help from the man with the problem? I take it you're sticking around to assist me with this?"

"Sorry, I'll be going, too. I'm wrapping up a case and my client is waiting for a report on her lost pussy. A calico named Pumpkin."

I rolled my eyes. "Is that why you're dressed like Sherlock Holmes? If you're going to hang around here, you need to blend in. Borrow something from Vivian Leigh's closet like you used to do when we worked together on your case, okay?"

The library door rattled. Shoot, someone wanted in. Unbuttoning several buttons, I shoved the ledger inside, re-buttoned the bodice, and pocketed the key. Looking down in dismay at the awkward outline of my breasts, I tried unsuccessfully to reposition the ledger. The knocking grew more pronounced with every second. Hastily, I shifted the ledger one more time, sent a prayer heavenward, and opened the door to see Victor Redding standing there with a perplexed expression on his ruddy face.

This modern-day plantation owner didn't resemble his ancestor at all with so many generations of mixed blood between them. Josiah, tall, dark-haired with refined features, Victor, of small statue with silver-streaked red hair, brown eyes, and plain features.

"Why is the door locked?" he asked in a business-like tone. "And who's in there with you?"

"No one, Mr. Redding." I stepped back to allow him entrance. "We were told to straighten the rooms after the tour. The door must have jammed."

He rubbed his chin. "I could have sworn I heard voices in here."

"No, I talk to myself. I'm sorry if I startled you."

He stared at me as he stood on the threshold, as if he expected something to happen. He didn't have long to wait. Scarlett, annoyed by the interruption, got up from the sofa in a huff, headed for the door, and whooshed straight through him.

I darted out the door behind her and into the small drawing room next to the library. Breathlessly, I leaned against the door listening for any tell-tell sign that I had been followed. I was sure he hadn't because he'd been too dumbfounded when Scarlett had passed through him.

For one frightening moment back there, when he stared so hard at me, I'd thought he detected the ledger clearly outlined against the material of my dress. Now, I removed it and set it on a nearby table and then did a quick search for any hidden locks.

After several unsuccessful minutes of rummaging, I concluded that the room held no clues, and I needed to get moving in case Redding decided to spy on me. I lifted my dress, inserted the ledger beneath the petticoat at the waistline, and smoothed the dress over it. Cautiously, I opened the door and peered into the empty hallway.

Across the hall in the bedroom, I changed into my street clothes and stuffed the ledger into the garment bag. I gathered mine and Deena's things and headed to the front of the house. I needed a ride back to town. The place seemed deserted, and no way would I beg a ride from Redding after our earlier meeting, so I stepped out onto the front veranda to see if anyone else lingered behind.

"Jolene?"

Bradford's deep voice caught me by surprise. I turned and watched him rise from one of the veranda rocking chairs.

"What are you doing here?" My voice came out sharper than intended, but his sudden appearance made me feel a mite guilty. Was it possible Redding had reported the missing ledger hidden in my garment bag? Technically, I guess I was committing a crime; a misdemeanor, of course. Nothing serious, but still unexplainable to certain individuals within the law enforcement community.

He took a step in my direction. "Deena said you needed a ride back to town."

"Oh, sorry, she doesn't know about the breakup," I stammered.

"I thought as much from the phone call."

He twisted his cowboy hat in his hands. A habit. My heart jolted at his vulnerability, but my feet remained glued to the porch.

"She asked me if I knew what's bothering you," he said. "I didn't give her an answer, because, actually, I'm glad you didn't tell her. You stormed out before I could explain myself."

"I understood perfectly."

He took a step closer. "No, you didn't. Can we talk?"

"Yes, on the way back to town." I wiped my sweating palms down the side of my dress.

"Here, let me help you with those."

He took the garment bags and I followed him around to the back of the house to his unmarked police car. He opened the passenger side door, and I climbed in as he loaded my things into the back seat and then slid into the driver's side.

"Deena said she had an emergency," he said as he turned the car around and started down the long tree-lined dirt driveway. "Is everything okay with your folks?"

"As far as I know. Summer called. She's the emergency."

He glanced over at me. "You're tight-lipped this morning."

I laughed to cover my nervousness. "Hard to believe I'm tongue-tied, isn't it? But I don't know what to say to you at the present moment."

"Then let me do the talking."

I turned my attention away from the passing landscape. "I'm listening."

"Jolene, I meant everything I said to you last night. You're impetuous, exasperating, and headstrong. You make snap decisions without regard to the safety of others. You have a bad temper. You're kooky—"

"Now wait just a damn minute—"

"Shut up and let me finish," he commanded in a strong voice. "What you didn't give me a chance to say is that you're the most exciting woman I've ever known. You trample across the universe like it's your playground, and you gobble up each day like it's your last. Your greatest strength is your sense of humor, and I was instantly attracted to your ability to laugh at yourself. Even now with two black eyes, a skinned chin, and a busted nose, you're unaware of your attractiveness. You're pushy and cushy in all the right places, and you're not ashamed of your body. You love for me to watch you naked. That's sexy as hell, woman."

"I don't understand," I stammered. "Last night you weren't sure dating me was a good thing."

"And I still feel the same way this morning. You radiate life. The good, the bad, and the ugly of it. The problem is when I'm around you I can't seem to think straight."

"So what are you saying?"

"Honestly, I don't know," he answered. "But wherever we're headed, I wanted you to know how I feel about you. All of it and not just certain parts spoken in the heat of the moment. Perhaps if we dialed it back a notch we'd better understand how to proceed."

"Dialing it back a notch? I believe that means no sex," I informed him.

Bradford glanced over at me. His brow arched. "I didn't mean that far back."

"Good," I said. "No sex, no Jolene."

This amused him and his serious expression melted into a smile. "I'm glad that's settled. Now maybe we should stop overthinking this relationship and just enjoy the benefits."

For a split second I allowed myself to lapse into reality. Bradford had said all the right things I'd longed to hear, but the real problem between us hadn't even been voiced. We were skirting around the issue of my paranormal abilities, and it needed to be addressed if we wanted to have a chance at happiness together. Even though we had a temporary understanding between us, the day of reckoning couldn't be postponed forever. One of Daddy's wise quips.

Not wanting to break the easy camaraderie that had sprung up between us, I left my doubts unspoken. The rest of the trip went fast and several minutes later

Bradford pulled into the salon front parking lot. Loaded down with my things, he followed me into Deena's office and deposited the garment bags on the sofa. Then he pulled me into his arms and brushed a gentle kiss across my lips.

"I'll see you out at the fairgrounds for the pie bake-off tonight," he promised and then headed for the door.

Billie Jo had just finished a haircut when I stepped out of Deena's office and went back to her station to speak with her. "It looks like you've had a busy morning. The reception area is packed. Do you think the staff is going to be able to handle the overflow with us out this afternoon?"

She removed the cape from her customer's neck. "I think so. They won't be able to take walk-ins, though. I instructed Holly to recommend other salons if they can't wait for an appointment."

Her customer eyeballed me. "Honey, I gotta couple of friends that would be happy to take care of the jerk that punched you. I could give 'em a call if you'd like."

"Don't go troubling yourself, Roy," Billie Jo said. "We can't afford any more incidents."

He gave a gap-toothed smile. "Just being neighborly. No harm meant."

She brushed his neck with talcum powder. "None taken."

He handed her a twenty. "Keep the change." He slapped his cap on, and then tipped it in my direction. "Take care, ma'am."

"He's a character," I said after he left. "I believe he would've done it."

She put her combs into a jar of blue germicide. "He would. Never encourage him to take an interest in your problems or you'll have problems."

"I'll keep my distance."

"Sam dropped you off?"

"Yeah, Deena called him and told him I needed a ride back into town."

"So, did you two talk? Are y'all a couple again?"

"For now, but I don't know how long it'll last" I said. "We have issues to work out."

Billie Jo stood with hands on hips. "Jolene, men are like baseball bats. You have to try them out until you find the one that feels right in your hands. Some fit and some crack under the pressure. Enjoy it while it lasts is my advice because you never know when you're gonna strike out."

"Where you do come up with this stuff?"

"I hear things. Here and there. Mostly here."

"That explains it." I glanced at my watch. "I'll help you clean your station before we leave. We're running out of time." I picked up a couple of dirty towels lying on her workstation counter.

Billie Jo placed her barber clippers in the drawer. "Deena called. They're waiting for Summer's biopsy report to come in. She said she would meet us at your house as soon as she could. Mama will be there at one."

We cleaned her station and gave final instructions to the staff before we loaded my stuff in Billie Jo's Charger and set off for my house on Pinecone Lane. Five minutes later I unlocked the door and we stepped inside to see Tango sitting on my clean kitchen counter.

"Damn cat refuses to sit on the floor," I said as I shooed him off the counter and headed down the hall. I turned off the security alarm and took the two garment bags to my room leaving Billie Jo in the kitchen.

My curiosity would have to wait until later tonight to read the contents of Josiah's ledger. I tucked it under a couple of magazines in my nightstand and went back into the kitchen to find Billie Jo feeding the cat.

"I figured you wouldn't mind," she said. "He wouldn't stop yacking and I had to shut him up—"

Deena burst through the kitchen door. She threw her purse on the table. "They found a cyst! A cyst! I'm so relieved. When was the last time you examined your breasts? It's been ages for me so we're going to do one right now on each other."

Not me," Billie Jo declared. "Roddy is the only one who's allowed to do any breast examinations on me."

"Deena, that's real good news," I said. "And we're thrilled at the false alarm, but don't you believe you're overreacting? Besides, Mama should be here any minute."

Deena proceeded to unbutton her blouse. "Mama can do one, too. Come on, please do this for me. "

"Are you crazy? What if someone comes to the door?" Billie Jo's voice came out in a choked squeak.

Deena's bra hung over the back of a chair, and she had one hand lifted high in the air and the other roaming over her breast, pressing and pushing. I flushed when she caught me staring.

"Don't be embarrassed," she said. "Y'all are my sisters."

"Sisters or not, I'm not baring the girls," Billie Jo said.

"I'm with Billie Jo on this one." I held up my hand as if making a pledge. "I'll wait and do mine in the shower tonight and report the results to you tomorrow."

"Me, too," Billie Jo echoed.

In retrospect I should have expected Mama to march through the kitchen door without knocking.

"Yoo-hoo, it's me… Harland, stop! Don't come any closer. One of your daughters is in a state of undress."

"In the kitchen?" came Daddy's voice from the carport steps.

The door banged shut. "Deena, what in God's name, are you doing? Have you taken leave of your senses? This isn't like you." Mama slanted me a black look. "What did you do to her, Jolene?"

"Nothing to explain her behavior," I said. "Probably a meltdown of some kind."

Deena retrieved her bra and slipped it on. "Summer found a lump on her breast this morning, and I've been at the doctor's office with her." She picked up her blouse. "That's why I'm doing a self-examination. I've had a terrible scare. What if she had breast cancer? And there's something else—"

Mama opened her arms wide and enfolded her in a tight embrace. "Oh my God, why didn't you call me? I'm sorry I yelled at you, honey. Is everything okay with Summer?"

"They found a cyst. She's fine." The words were muffled by Mama's shoulder.

"I'm going to bake a chocolate cake for her."

Deena sniffled, pulling back. "She'll love that."

Mama handed her a tissue from her pocket. "Dry your eyes, baby."

Another knock sounded. "Is everything okay in there?"

I opened the door. "All's clear, Daddy."

He came in and handed me a five pound sack.

"Here's the peanut flour I promised to pick up for you from Golden King Peanut, honey." He slid a cautious glance over the kitchen. "Billie Jo, I have your case of peanut oil. Would you like me to put it your car?"

"Thanks, Daddy," I said, placing the sack of flour on a shelf in the walk-in pantry. Billie Jo and Daddy were outside when I stepped back into the kitchen. Deena had pulled herself together and was rechecking her digital camera. Mama was stacking dishes in the sink.

"Can you think of anything else we need for the bake-off?" I asked her. "We're out of luck if we forget something at home. We can't borrow ingredients from another team, and we can't leave the baking area once we start."

"No. I have everything we need in the car," she replied. "Let's get going. I still have to make my homemade crusts."

"You should have grabbed a couple of frozen ones from the grocery store in case yours doesn't turn out," Deena said. "Things don't always turn out as planned."

Mama frowned. "Bite your tongue, child. I've been baking most of my life, and I don't plan to screw up now."

"There's a first time for everything," I muttered to myself as I locked the kitchen door behind me on our way out. "Especially the way our luck is running."

Chapter Six
Utterly Deadly Southern Pecan Pie

The fairgrounds large kitchen had been partitioned into ten portable areas complete with a stove, a small refrigerator, and counter-space for preparing food. Our assigned space was at the end of the line and closest to the public restrooms. A low murmur of voices scattered with occasional bursts of laughter and clanking pans filled the large room where the contestants were beginning to filter in. Deena snapped a few pictures of milling people for our festival scrapbook as we made our way down the line and to our portable kitchen.

"Set that box down there on the counter, Harland," Mama instructed. "And then get yourself one of those chairs over yonder. You're gonna need it before the judging later tonight."

Daddy ambled off in the direction Mama had indicated. A man in faded jeans and an equally faded cowboy shirt stopped by with a list of contest instructions pertaining to set-up, ingredients, breaks, and time limits.

"Please take notice to the warning under the ingredients list, ladies," he said. "Don't use any of the products listed in that section. Understood? Did you remember to submit your recipe with the contest officials?"

"No, I forgot when we registered," Mama said.

"You'll have to wait until after the photo op now," he said. "I see the judges finishing with Rosie's Flower Mart. You're next. Any questions before I leave?"

"No," we said in unison.

"Good luck, then," he said and left.

"We don't need luck—we've got the winning recipe," Mama said to no one in particular, and started unpacking the box and setting up her kitchen.

"What can I do, Mama?" I asked her.

"You can put those eggs and butter in the ice box. Billie Jo, you can go see what's keeping your father. I want him in the pictures. Hurry, I can see those judges headed our way."

Deena snapped a picture. "Ignore the camera. And please try to act natural."

Mama set out her canister of flour, pie pans, light corn syrup, salt, and vanilla extract on the counter. "Get plenty of pictures for my cookbook." She turned and presented her profile. "Pay special attention to this side of my face. It's my best side."

Daddy sported a huge grin when he and Billie Jo returned several minutes later. He placed the chair down outside the cubicle and out of the way of foot traffic and sat down.

"Where've you been, Harland?" Mama wanted to know.

He raised an eyebrow at her. "I ran into a friend. I'm here now so stop carrying on. I swear woman you can't stand for me to be out of your sight for more than five minutes."

She frowned. "There you go wishing again."

The approaching judges halted any further bantering between the two. Daddy stood up and pushed his hands deep into his pockets. Mama went to stand beside him. My sisters and I flanked them.

We all wore plastic smiles.

The three men and two women, and a photographer, stopped at our cubicle.

I winked at Bradford. He winked back.

Nancy Chance regarded us and then down at her clipboard. "Entry #10: Dixieland Salon. Check. Before we start, let me introduce the four judges: Theodore and Mrs. Herrington, Victor Redding, and of course, Detective Samuel Bradford of the Whiskey Creek Police Department."

Hands were shaken, and pleasantries exchanged, however restrained, and each person lined up as Nancy directed. Wisely, she sandwiched us between Victor Redding and Bradford with Herrington and his wife at the end.

The photographer took several shots. Nancy, satisfied with the photos, wrote on her clipboard, and motioned for the judges to please follow her. Bradford gave me a quick peck on the cheek before being whisked away with the others.

Mama grabbed her purse off the counter. "Harland, you keep an eye on our kitchen while the girls and I submit our recipe to the contest officials. Don't leave and if anyone comes looking for something to borrow, you be sure and tell them no, you hear? I only brought enough for three pies. Oh, and stay out of the whiskey."

Daddy relaxed back down in his chair. "Yeah, I hear you, but no promises on the whiskey."

We left Daddy and headed for the registration desk, but hadn't moved ten feet before Mama caught sight of Diane Downey barreling toward us.

"Oh, mercy," she moaned, picking up her pace. "I do believe my bad luck is back. We don't have time to stop and chat. Quit dawdling, Deena. I didn't mean for you to take a picture every minute."

I turned around to see the grand dame of Whiskey Creek waving her arms in the air as if she were flagging down a speeding car. The oversized purple dress, a fashion faux pas on an inordinate scale, hung shapeless and clashed horribly with her bright orange-red hair; bottled, of course. And I know because I'm her hairdresser. Yippee.

"Yoo-hoo. Annie Mae! Wait up! It's me, Diane."

"I think she saw me looking back at her," I confessed. "She's waving at you."

Billie Jo pulled Mama to a stop. "Give it up. She's not going to."

Diane breathed an audible sigh when she caught us. "If I didn't know better, I would suspect you're trying to avoid me, Annie Mae." She again took several deep breaths.

"No, never, my dear," Mama grated. "You know I'm beholden to you for your invaluable help stemming church gossip after Harland's unexpected return. I didn't see you. We were rushing to submit our recipe, right girls?"

Deena snapped a couple pictures of Diane. "That's a lovely dress. I hope you don't mind if I photograph you for our festival scrapbook?"

Behind Deena's head, Billie Jo rolled her eyes heavenward and mouthed, "Liar."

I smiled, stifling the urge to give her the thumbs-up gesture in agreement.

"Why no, honey, I don't mind," Diane puffed. "I

think that's a great idea. You don't mind if I copy it do you? I love scrapbooking."

The line of Mama's mouth tightened a fraction more, and her brows pulled into an affronted frown.

"Like my cookbook idea." I heard her mutter.

"What did you say, Annie Mae?"

"Mama said you were welcome to copy the idea," I replied for her.

"We're in a hurry, Diane. Something in particular you wanted?" Mama's tone tightened.

The woman's lips cracked a small smile. "I wanted to wish you good luck in the contest. May the best man or woman win."

"She will," Mama boasted. "I'm confident of that."

Diane opened her mouth to answer, but Mama kept talking. "We do have to get on over there and submit our recipe. Good luck to you and yours."

With that, Mama stalked off and left Diane staring after her, uncertain if Mama had offended her or not. Deena turned around and snapped a last shot of the woman standing there with hands on hips and mouth hanging open. "I thought she would make a good target for darts," she said when we followed after Mama's retreating figure.

"Hey, better not let Bill hear you speak that way," I said lightly. "He wouldn't approve."

"Yeah, preacher boy would lecture you on proper Christian etiquette," Billie Jo teased.

"Bill's a stuffed shirt."

Billie Jo and I exchanged knowing glances. For Deena to criticize Assistant Pastor William Mahoney could only mean trouble in paradise.

Hallelujah! A revolution I could encourage. Bill

was a sanctimonious moral meter and from my dealings with the human race no one is without fault. The skeleton hidden in his closet probably had clothes on so as not to be caught with his pants down.

The registration desk wasn't busy, but the young woman in charge left us in doubt that our recipe would be safe in her keeping. After several minutes of listening to her bumbling conversation with a late entrant, Mama decided we would wait for her replacement, which was due to arrive shortly according to the woman herself.

Well, it took ten more minutes of waiting until the replacement arrived. Mama grilled him until she was satisfied of his ability to file the recipe in the appropriate place.

She also decided to take the long way around the building to avoid Diane. Twenty minutes later we arrived back at our original destination to find Daddy's empty chair.

****

"I swear, Annie, I wasn't gone more than ten minutes," Daddy drawled when he returned several minutes later. "The restrooms are right over there, and I couldn't hold it any longer."

Mama glared at him. "I told you not to leave. What if someone came in here and snatched those pecans I brought from home? We'd be out of the contest before it began."

"Did they?"

"Did they what?"

"Snatch your pecans?"

"No, they're still in the canister."

"Then stop complaining, woman, and put all that

zest into those pies you need to start making."

Deena raised the camera again. "Smile and say cheese, you two."

I smiled at them posing arm in arm for the camera. "That looks like flirting to me."

"It is," Billie Jo said while Deena panned the camera around to take a couple of shots of us and then stepped into the cubicle for a snapshot of the set-up for the cookbook layout.

Mama disentangled herself from Daddy. "Time to bake pies, girls. Billie Jo, you shell those fresh pecans, and Jolene will measure out the flour for the pie crusts."

Daddy plopped back down in his chair and turned to watch the buzz of the contenders. I moved into the kitchen, grabbed a bowl and measuring cups, and placed them on the counter. Seeing a pile of loose flour around the canisters, I wet a paper towel with water from a spray bottle and wiped the counter clean before reading the recipe Mama had given me beforehand. I measured out the flour and dumped it into the bowl.

"So what did y'all name your entry?" Daddy asked, turning around to watch us scurrying around the small enclosure. "Nancy Chance stopped by. She said you failed to write down the name of Dixieland's entry on your registration form. I thought y'all knew this. She said she was going to find you."

"Well, she didn't," Mama said. "Are you sure you heard her correctly? This is the first I've heard about naming our entry."

Billie Jo stopped shelling pecans. "What do you call it at home?"

"Have you ever heard me refer to it as anything other than pecan pie?" Mama answered.

"Just asking."

"Just answering."

Daddy rolled his eyes. "I should've stayed home where there's peace and quiet."

"Shut-up, Harland," Mama said.

"Hand me those contest instructions that man dropped off earlier and I'll see if it mentions anything about it," Deena suggested. Mama handed it to her. "Hmmm. Yep, here it is. Each entry is to be named. They even give an example to help you come up with one of your own: Henry's Heavenly Pecan Pie."

"How about Dixieland Delight Pecan Pie?"

"That's a good name, Daddy."

"Well, I don't like it, Jolene. What about Annie Mae Tucker's Southern Pecan Pie?"

"Because I don't like that name, Mama. I like Perfectly Georgia Pecan Pie," Billie Jo stated.

"God knows, Annie's recipe is one of the richest, most deadly desserts of my knowledge," Daddy said. "And it's utterly deadly on my waistline."

"How about Utterly Deadly Southern Pecan Pie?" Deena suggested.

"That's brilliant," Billie Jo said. "I love it. What about y'all?"

"With a name like that how can we lose?" Mama agreed.

"I second the motion," Daddy cheered.

"Y'all, I think we need to choose another name," I argued. "That sounds dreadful."

"Jolene, don't pee on the fire," Billie Jo said. "Majority rules."

"Now we have to cross our fingers that no one else has come up with the same name," Mama said.

Overruled, I gave in gracefully and Deena left to register Dixieland Salon's official entry with the name 'Utterly Deadly Southern Pecan Pie'.

The rest of us got back to work and soon the smell of baking pies permeated the air. Deena returned with the welcome news of our chosen name being accepted by the contest officials and held up a copy of the laminated sign that would grace our coveted spot at the judging.

It read: Entry #10: Dixieland Salon—Utterly Deadly Southern Pecan Pie.

Hmm. As I continued to stare at the sign, the hairs on my scalp prickled as a creepy feeling crawled down my spine leaving me more than a tad worried that we had acted in haste in choosing such a dreadful name. I shrugged it off, blaming the heartburn on the corndog I had eaten for lunch. Besides, what could happen with a pie?

****

An attractive young woman made her way up to the podium in the front of the room. She smiled at the crowd and spoke into the microphone.

"Good evening, ladies and gentlemen. My name is Tammy Hodges from WXYB Channel Ten News, and I would like to welcome you to the Fifteenth Annual Pecan Pie Bake-Off. For those of you who are attending for the first time, tonight's competitors include the top ten businesses nominated for their outstanding services by you, the tri-county citizens."

The applause from the large crowd of spectators rang across the room. Deena snapped shots from our assigned seats facing the judges table which had been set-up with the ten entries.

"Our pie looks the best," Mama boasted. "See how plump and golden brown the pecans are compared to the others? The crust is perfect."

"They all look the same to me," Daddy said.

"That's because you left your glasses at home, Harland."

I shifted in my chair aware of the glaring looks directed our way by several of the other contestants, but kept my mouth shut because the more I interfered in my parent's bantering, the more they would continue.

"This year we are going all out on our first-place prize," Tammy continued. "The winner of the Best Pecan Pie Bake-Off will receive an all-expense paid trip for their entire staff to Disney World in Orlando, Florida."

A rousing applause and cat calls rang out at her announcement.

"Now, before we get started with the first phase of the bake-off, I would like to introduce the judges. Please help me welcome Theodore Herrington, President of Central National Bank, and his wife, Barbara. Next are Victor Redding of Pineridge Plantation, and lastly, Whiskey Creek Police Department Detective Samuel Bradford."

A light applause broke out as each person stepped up to the podium.

Billie Jo leaned in closer. "Herrington and his wife don't seem like they belong together, do they?"

"Stiff as a corpse on a cold day," I whispered back. "I wonder why such an attractive woman would marry a man so much older than her."

"She married him because he's rich, and he married her because she's young and pretty," Billie Jo offered.

Mama pinched me hard on my upper arm; a childhood tactic utilized to gain our attention. I shot her daggers. She didn't get my message, just smiled sweetly and pointed to the judges making their way to the long table.

"And now for the first phase of the contest," Tammy said. "The judging criteria will be: Overall appearance; Texture and consistency of crust, and of course, Taste. Then each entry will be given a score for Overall Impression. The scores will be tallied and set aside for the second judging. The first contender is Don's Delectable Delight by Don Juan's Plumbing."

We watched while the judges each took a small bite of the pie and swirled it around in their mouths, enjoyment written on their faces. After a slight nodding to one another, the scores were entered on the sheets they carried. As they went down the line Tammy gave a running account of each entry's name and the business it represented.

Mama let out a long, audible breath, resting her hand over her chest. "We're next."

"The suspense is killing me," I said.

"And the last contender in the first judging is Utterly Deadly Southern Pecan Pie by Dixieland Salon," Tammy announced.

With fingers crossed, I fastened my gaze on Bradford's face as he picked up a clean fork, broke off a piece of pie and slipped it into his mouth. Immediately, his expression twisted.

I leaned closer to Mama. "There's something wrong with your pie. Bradford's scowling and the others are, too."

"Looks like our pie stinks," Billie Jo said. I frowned at her.

"Give them a second," Mama cut in. "The flavor is fixing to burst on their tongues."

"Something's bursting on their tongues," I heard Daddy comment.

Light chatter broke out around us. The judges wrote on their score cards and handed them over to Nancy Chance. With a quick wave to the crowd, she stepped behind the podium.

Tammy stepped back up to the microphone. "The score cards in the first round of competition have been turned in, and the second round will begin shortly after a brief ten-minute intercession. Remember, interaction between the judges and contestants are strictly forbidden."

People stood up from their seats, began milling around, and exiting the room. Mama and Daddy had their heads together talking in low voices so I left them to themselves, searching the crowd for any sign of Bradford, but he and the rest of the judges were nowhere in sight.

Deena turned to me and Billie Jo. "Did you notice anything wrong when the judges were sampling our entry?"

"You'd have to be blind not to," I said. "Bradford's face was twisted up like a barbed wire fence."

"Theo Herrington looked kinda green to me," Billie Jo added. "What do you suppose happened? Do you reckon the entries could've been switched?"

"I can't see how," I said.

"I guess we screwed up again," Deena said. "That or we're cursed."

"I don't believe that," I murmured.

"That's the only possible explanation," she said. "We're terrible bakers. What does Mama think?"

I glanced over at Daddy planting love pats to her back. I couldn't hear what he was saying, but their body language spoke volumes. "I think this contest means more to her than we realized."

"And look who's heading this way with a smile as wide as the Great Divide," Billie Jo said. "That woman has the gait of a construction worker."

"Diane's come to gloat," Deena accused. "Better warn Mama."

I stepped over and tapped Mama on the shoulder. "Heads up, we've got company." Her eyes held a fragile spark. Underneath Mama's gruff exterior beats a tender heart.

She and Daddy climbed to their feet as Diane plowed to a stop in front of us. "Diane, I'm so glad you stopped by," Mama said. "I was telling Harland about your wonderful dress, and suddenly, poof, there you are—a great, big, purple vision of loveliness. Right, Harland?"

"Um-um-um, you're right, Annie Mae…loveliness."

"Thank you for your kindness, Harland. I came by to—"

"Wish us luck in the second round," I supplied. "Same to you, Mrs. Downey."

Her smile wilted a bit. "Hmm. Yes, that's what I wanted to say. Good luck in the second round. I'd better get back to my seat. I see the judges are returning."

The judges were lined up behind the long table, ready for the second round. Daddy winked at me as he seated himself beside Mama.

"Do you think our second pie turned out like the first?" Billie Jo wanted to know.

"We'll know soon enough," I said.

Tammy Hodges stepped back up to the microphone. "Welcome back to the Fifteenth Annual Pecan Pie Bake-Off, phase two. This is the last chance the contenders have of impressing the judges with their entries. At the end, the scores will be added to the first round and the contestant with the highest score will be this year's Best Pecan Pie winner."

Applause rang out at her announcement.

The second round turned out to be a repeat of the first, if not worse. When the judges came to Dixieland Salon's entry, they hesitated, which sent the crowd buzzing. The judges jotted down their scores and handed them to Nancy before stepping away from the table. Bradford averted his eyes from mine so I knew it was bad.

"Well, now we know," Billie Jo said.

Amazingly, Mama kept her head held high during the entire second round. Pride to her was like a giant ocean wave. When you're in deep water, it picks you up and tosses you up onto the beach. Your mouth may be full of gritty sand but your butt is on dry ground, thanks to that mighty wave carrying you through the turbulent waters. Mama's wise like that.

I reached over and squeezed her hand. "Thanks, Mama."

"For what?"

"I know you did this for the salon and not for yourself."

She patted my hand. "I'd do anything for you,

honey, but I did this for my cookbook."

Before I could respond, Tammy tapped on the microphone and the crowd settled down. Mama kept my hand in hers as we returned our attention to the woman at the podium.

"Ladies and Gentlemen, the scores from both rounds have been tallied and the moment we have all been waiting for is finally here. The winner of this year's competition is..." She took the envelope from Nancy Chance and opened it. "Don's Delectable Delight by Don Juan's Plumbing."

The crowd erupted in cheers and sporadic boo's.

"Would the winners please come up to the front and receive your prize?" came over the microphone.

Oh, well, so Dixieland Salon didn't win. But we could still make a trip to Disney World happen. The idea had been mulling around in my mind since forever. I turned to Billie Jo and Deena and said, "Listen, I been thinking. Why shouldn't Dixieland Salon take the staff to Disney World anyway and pick up the tab?"

"We can have staff meetings and write it off as a business trip," Deena added. "What do you think, Billie Jo?"

"I'm good with it. Roddy's been looking forward to a vacation."

"Let's take Mama and Daddy with us, too," I suggested. "The trip will help her forget this fiasco."

Without warning, a loud coughing, choking sound echoed above the din. Then, a scream rent the air.

"Someone call 911—"

Startled, I swung my head in the direction of its source and saw Barbara Herrington kneeling over someone collapsed on the floor. I couldn't be sure of the identity of the victim with so many people scrambling about. For one shattering moment I thought about Bradford, but then, the sea of people parted, and I recognized Theo Herrington's crumpled form thrashing about like a fish on dry land.

Well, at least it was over. That bad moon I'd been expecting for days had finally crested on the horizon in the form of a pie. Unfortunately, from the reactions of the judges, I suspected it'd been our Utterly Deadly Southern Pecan Pie that'd delivered the dirty deed.

Chapter Seven
The Finest Kentucky Bourbon

"If there is a doctor in the building, could you please come to the front? We have an emergency!" Tammy yelled over the microphone.

I pushed through the crowd of onlookers. Like a slow motion movie, the scenes unfolded in agonizingly clear detail. Theo's distorted face twisted as he struggled to breathe. His body jerked, and his clutched hand dug at his swollen throat. He made a harsh sound.

"He's having an allergic reaction," Barbara Herrington screamed, her hands plowing through his coat pocket in a frantic search. "Where's his EpiPen? I can't find his EpiPen!"

I recognized the gurgling sound having heard it in my facial room just before Scarlett choked to death on her own vomit.

With a flash, I remembered that shortly after Scarlett's grisly incident, the entire staff at Dixieland Salon had been trained in CPR and mouth-to-mouth resuscitation. Scrambling to Herrington's side, I fell to my knees, the remembered sound of the instructor's voice guiding me through the steps.

Titling his head back, I placed my ear close to his mouth and then it checked for any obstruction. Taking a deep breath, I pinched his nose closed and sealed my lips around his, blowing deeply until his chest rose with the force of my breath.

I paused, again inhaling deeply.

"What are you doing?" a voice screamed in my ear. "You…get away from my husband!"

Whack! Barbara's shoe connected to my jaw. I gasped, toppling over onto my back, hitting my head on the hard concrete. I must have blacked out for a minute or two because the next thing I remember was intense pain spreading throughout my body. Sagging against the strong hands lifting me from the floor, I inhaled Bradford's familiar woodsy scent, gulping in air and the coppery taste of blood.

"Bloody hell, she busted my lip," I managed to croak.

"Don't try to talk," he said, smiling down on me. "You're bleeding all over my new white shirt. Here, hold my handkerchief over the cut. You might need stitches to close the wound."

Wincing as I held the coarse cotton against my painful lip, I asked, "Theo?"

Slipping his arms under my knees and around my back, he lifted my one-hundred and sixty pounds with effort. "The paramedics are with him now. Several doctors also responded to our call. He's in good hands. Let's get you back over to your family while we wait for the paramedics to check out your injuries. Harland is bellowing like a bull."

"Put me down. I can walk. If Mama sees you carrying me, she'll start fussing like a mother hen. Besides, it's only a split lip."

"And possibly a concussion. You smacked your head on the floor. You were coming to when I reached you. It won't kill you to be pampered."

"You don't understand, Bradford. Mama hasn't cut the umbilical cord, yet."

Boy, I called that one right. The second Bradford and I broke through the wall of people she flew to my side.

"Are you all right? Oh, your lip." She clucked in alarm. "Sam, set her down on this here chair. Billie Jo, see if you can find some ice. Harland, you go pack the car so we can get her to the hospital. Deena, put that camera down and fetch that bottle of bourbon from the kitchen and a glass, too. For the pain."

Bradford sat me down on the chair, waiting until Mama stopped to take a breath. "Calm down, Mrs. Tucker. One of the paramedics will be right over as soon as Herrington is stabilized."

"I'm fine, Mama." I batted her hands away. "But I would like a shot of that whiskey."

"Sam, what happened?" Daddy asked. "Did he have a heart attack? It sure looked like one from here."

"I'm not sure, but with Jolene in good hands, I need to get back over there. Would you excuse me?" He turned to Mama. "Mrs. Tucker?"

"Of course, you go on. We'll keep an eye on Jolene."

After a hardy handshake with Daddy, Bradford drooped a kiss on my forehead and barreled his way through the crowd gathered around Herrington. I leaned back against the chair and closed my eyes against the harsh, white overhead lights. The events of the past few days seemed to rush through my mind. The war of words between Ellie and Herrington, my parents and Herrington, the botched beauty pageant, the fight, and now this—Herrington collapsing after eating Dixieland

Salon's entry.

I groaned at the last thought.

"Here, Jolene, drink this."

My eyes opened to Daddy holding out the shot glass filled with his best bourbon whiskey. I gulped it down, sputtering as the amber liquid burned a path down to my gut, spreading immediate warmth and comfort to my frazzled nerves. Daddy gave me a second glass which followed the first.

"Slow down, girl. That's my finest Kentucky Bourbon you're guzzling. You have to sip it to appreciate its unique flavor, right, Roddy?"

"That's a fact, Mr. Tucker," Billie Jo's husband said, I think, from somewhere behind me.

I held out the glass. "Another, please."

Daddy poured another shot, and I downed it like the previous two. I held out the glass toward Daddy. "One more for the road."

"She's had enough," Mama said, handing me the handkerchief instead. "Put this on your lip."

The ice-filled handkerchief eased the throbbing and with the whiskey-induced euphoria spreading through my veins I began to feel better.

An EMT broke through the crowd and approached us. He dropped his emergency bag on the floor. "Let's see what's going on, ma'am." He knelt beside me. I grimaced when he examined my lip. He held a stethoscope to my chest. "Breathe deeply a couple of times for me. Okay. Have you been drinking?"

I hiccupped. "Yep, three shots of fine Kentucky bourbon."

"For medicinal purposes only, young man," Mama added. "Look at her."

"Yes, ma'am, I am," he said. "She's banged up, but her vitals are normal. I don't believe she needs stitches for the cut on her lip. However, Detective Bradford said that she hit her head on the floor and blacked out. She could have a concussion. As a precaution, I would recommend she be transported to the ER."

"I'm not going to the hospital for a split lip and a bump on the head," I protested.

"Listen to the nice young man, honey," Daddy said, trying to soothe me but I wanted no part of it.

"Jolene, you're being stubborn."

"No hospital, Billie Jo."

"Okay, since she refuses to be transported to the hospital on my recommendation, she'll have to be monitored throughout the night," the paramedic said. "If there is any problem waking her, or if she shows any sign of grogginess, call 911 immediately."

"Thank you," Mama said. "We appreciate it. Before you leave, could you give us any news on Theodore Herrington's condition? He's a family friend."

"I'm sorry, ma'am, but I'm not allowed to give out any information on another patient, you understand. You can ask Detective Bradford. He's headed this way."

The EMT left us and I could see that he had stopped for a word with Bradford—probably about my refusal to cooperate with his suggestion for an ambulance ride to the hospital, but I'd had enough. My mood didn't dictate another lecture from an emergency room doctor. Not my fault this time. I was trying to save a man's life when I'd received my injuries.

Bradford joined us, his expression somber. "I've

got some bad news for y'all," he said with a shake of his head.

"Today's the day for it, Sam," Daddy replied. "Give it to us straight."

"Theodore Herrington didn't make it."

"He's dead?"

"Yes, Mrs. Tucker. They were unable to revive him."

"Goodness gracious, how could this happen?" Mama asked, as though she could hardly believe it herself. "How's Mrs. Herrington holding up?"

"I haven't told her, yet," he said. "Victor Redding convinced her to step out of the building for a breath of fresh air. She hampered the resuscitation effort."

"A heart attack?" Daddy wanted to know.

Bradford shook his head. "It appears to be an allergic reaction from something he ingested. Mrs. Herrington couldn't find his EpiPen in his suit pockets. She said he carries one with him at all times."

"That's strange he didn't have it, today," Deena observed. "And convenient if you know what I mean."

"Could've been something in the pies?" Billie Jo asked.

"An autopsy will answer that question," he said.

"Herrington could've ingested something out on the fairway," I said. "I saw him out there this afternoon when I was at the corndog stand."

"That's possible," he said. "For now, I need y'all to hang tight. An officer will be by to take a statement from each of you."

"Not another official investigation?" Deena grumbled. "I'm not over the last one."

"You don't have anything to worry about. This

looks like an unfortunate accident," he said. "Until the cause of death is called, all pies and ingredients from the contest will be confiscated and tested for the allergen."

Daddy hugged the bottle to his chest. "Not my aged Kentucky bourbon."

"Did you include bourbon in your entries?"

"Two tablespoons in each pie," Mama said.

"The bottle will be returned to you when we're finished," Bradford tried to assure Daddy.

"Sam, if you don't mind me asking, what is the allergen you're looking for?" Roddy asked.

"According to Mrs. Herrington, her husband had a severe allergy to peanuts."

"That being the case, you won't be needin' my bottle of bourbon," Daddy told him. "No peanuts in there."

Bradford took out a small notepad. "I'm sorry, but we've got to cover all the bases. The ingredients you used for your entries are still in your assigned space in the kitchen?"

"They're in a box on the counter," I said. "Except Daddy's bourbon."

"Good, return to your assigned space and wait for an officer to collect your statements and the box of ingredients." His powerful gaze swept over me. "I need to get back over there. Are you gonna be okay?"

Holding the soggy handkerchief to my lip, I sighed. "Yeah, but I look like hell."

He chuckled. "Yeah, you do at that. You need some rest." He brushed his lips softly across mine and left me staring after him.

Rest, huh? What about another shot of that fine

bourbon whiskey to speed it along?

****

As luck would have it, we didn't make it out of the room before Bradford informed Barbara Herrington of her husband's death. With a screech as high and loud as an agitated barn owl, she flew past him, wrapped herself around the body, wailing. Oh my. A bad scene for all.

Unfortunately, her caterwauling only served to make the situation worse. Instead of exiting the building as being directed by the authorities, the crowd surged forward to catch a glimpse of the weeping widow and her dead husband. Chaos broke out.

Bradford's call for crowd control blasted over the noise. Pushing through the bodies, we finally made it through to the kitchen, but lost Deena in the crowd.

"Billie Jo, go find your sister," Mama promptly told her.

"No way in hell I'm going back in there," Billie Jo said.

"I'll go." Daddy clutched the bourbon bottle to his chest.

"No, let me," Roddy responded then sailed back through the kitchen door.

The four of us made our way back down the row of cubicles until we reached the last one. I excused myself and hurried to the ladies restroom. My luck held. The line was short, and I didn't have to explain my beat-up appearance more than a half a dozen times. I was surprised to see Ellie entering as I exited.

"Did you just get here?" I asked her.

She gave me a quick hug. "No, Ryan and I have been here for a while. We were sitting in the far back so his father wouldn't see us together and start another public fight. We don't have to worry about that now, do we? Ryan's gone to find Kandy. He doesn't want her to hear about her grandfather's death from a stranger or the media wanting to interview her. What happened to your lip?"

"Barbara Herrington decked me when I was trying to give her husband mouth-to-mouth. I guess she panicked." I touched my bruised lip. "She sure packs a wallop for a small woman."

"I missed that. We could hear the shouts, but couldn't see over the people rushing up front."

"She kept screaming for his EpiPen. He's allergic to peanuts."

"I heard he was poisoned," she said.

Taking her by the shoulders, I drew her out of the restroom entrance and away from listening ears. "Why that's nonsense, Ellie. Where'd you hear that?"

"I overheard a big woman in purple."

"Did she have orange-red hair?"

"Yeah, come to think of it, she did. She looked familiar. I know I've seen her in the salon, but I can't recall her name."

"Her name is Diane Downey and she looks familiar because she's my client."

"You might want to know that I heard her say it was your momma's awful pie that killed him!"

"You must be mistaken. Diane is Mama's friend from church."

"She's no friend. Just one of them 'good Christian bitches' my momma warned me about." Ellie's mouth twisted in a bit of a sneer. "They go around testifying about Jesus when they haven't met 'em for themselves.

No mistake. That woman said some nasty things about your pie. Great name, by the way."

I let her words sink in. "Don't say anything to Mama about what you overhead, or anyone else for that matter, okay? The sooner this day is behind us the better, and I don't want anyone reminding her of it. I know how to shift the gossip back on Diane without anyone being the wiser."

"How's that?"

I smiled. "I'm her hairdresser. Accidents happen, you know."

She chuckled. "Remind me not to piss you off. You're my hairdresser, too."

Glancing over at our cubicle, Mama motioned for me to return. "I need to get back. Tell Ryan I'm sorry about his dad and if there's anything we can do, just holler."

"Well, there is one thing," she said. "Ryan feels it would be best if Kandy is with her mother in Atlanta until the funeral. We're driving up and I'm not sure what time I'll be back, so I need to reschedule my morning appointments. Is that okay with you or would you like me to clear it with Deena?"

"You take tomorrow off. Holly can reschedule your appointments. Kandy's not going to leave without a fight, you know. She'll want to stay here."

"I tried to tell Ryan that but he won't listen. See you later," she said and headed toward the exit.

A young policewoman was taking Mama's statement when I returned to the cubicle. Deena and Roddy hadn't returned, and Daddy and Billie Jo were watching Mama with wary eyes. I could see why. From her defensive stance and the expression on her face I discerned that she wasn't happy with the young policewoman's presence or attitude or whatever Mama perceived as an offense.

"What's going on with her?" I asked Billie Jo.

"The nice policewoman wants her to clarify the ingredients in the box."

"I don't understand—"

"Neither does Mama," Billie Jo said.

"I'll have you know, Miss—"

Mama's voice held an edge that I recognized from my childhood. Scared and desperately trying to hide the fact, her brave front threatened to crumble soon. I'd heard and seen much through the hard years when Daddy wasn't around and the farm struggled to stay afloat. Tears would follow if we didn't wrap this up and get her out of here.

"Where's Deena and Roddy?"

"I don't know," Billie Jo said. "I hope Roddy is able to find her soon."

"That's Officer Groves, ma'am," the exasperated policewoman said over our chatter. "I'm not questioning your statement, Mrs. Tucker. But I have a few questions about the ingredients in that box."

"Annie Mae, let the officer do her job," Daddy said. "Go back over that list of ingredients so the rest of us can give our statement. I'm tired and ready to go home."

Mama huffed. "This, Officer Groves, is flour, butter, sugar, corn syrup, and salt. Am I going to fast?" She pointed to each ingredient. "This is vanilla and left over eggs I didn't use. Oh, and pecans. I'm forgetting something." She tapped her finger on the side of her head, smiling. "Oh, yeah, Harland's best Kentucky bourbon. Hand it over to the nice policewoman, Harland."

Officer Groves scribbled in her notepad. "I'd like to take your statement next, sir," she said to Daddy.

Roddy and Deena walked up as Daddy was finishing up his statement. Officer Groves stopped scribbling on her notepad. She pointed at me and Billie Jo. "I'll get you two next and then the other two."

I grabbed Deena's arm and took a couple of steps away from the officer so she couldn't overhear our conversation. "Where've you been?"

"I was looking for Bill," she retorted, slipping her camera into her should bag. "He said he'd be here, but I couldn't find him. And then I had a clear shot of Theo's body so I took a couple of pictures before the cops ran me off."

"That's good thinking, Deena."

She shrugged. "I remembered those pictures I took of the facial room when Scarlett died, and how helpful they turned out to be so I started snapping away. Hey, how's your lip?"

"Sore and my head hurts, but I'll live."

"You were amazing by the way. I'm glad we took those CPR classes. You might've saved Mr. Herrington's life if his wife hadn't decked you."

I touched my sore lip. "True. Listen, I ran into Ellie outside the restroom a few minutes ago. She and Ryan are driving Kandy to her mother's house in Atlanta tonight. Ryan wants to get his daughter out of town for the next couple of days. I told her it was okay."

"Did she say how Ryan was taking his father's death?"

"No, but he must feel horrible. But Ellie isn't

grieving his passing."

"That's understandable. The man treated her like a pariah."

"She told me another piece of interesting news. Get this. Diane believes Herrington was poisoned by Dixieland's entry."

"That's crazy talk. Why would she say such a horrible thing? Does Billie Jo know? Mama?"

"I haven't had a chance to tell her, and I don't want Mama to know her friend is spreading rumors. She's been through enough today. We all have."

"Agreed. Let's give our statements to the police so we can leave."

Together, we stepped back over to Officer Groves. When it was my turn I gave my account as I recalled it. Officer Groves, satisfied with our statements allowed us to leave. The ride home was a long silent one. My thoughts traveled back to Rachel Wesley's remark last night. *If Mr. Herrington drops dead your father is first on the list of suspects.*

Disaster had once again parked on our doorstep. Herrington *had* dropped dead. Deena had been right when she said that things don't always turn out like they're planned. Never had there been a truer statement spoken under the hot Georgia sun.

Chapter Eight
The Ledger

When I arrived home I fed the cat and downed a couple of pain relievers for my headache, took a long hot shower, and slipped into warm, comfortable pajamas. After brewing a cup of hot herbal tea, I climbed into bed with the ledger I'd smuggled out of Pineridge Plantation. Tango curled up at the foot of the bed and began cleaning himself.

For several seconds I stared down at the hardbound ledger encased in soft brown calf covers. The book, in pristine condition for its age, probably hadn't been moved from the library shelf but for the occasional dusting for the past century. Awed by the history, I opened the front cover and fingered the yellowed parchment. The handwriting was hardly legible, the period ink faded, but the name Josiah Redding and the dates, 1840 to 1843 were recognizable midway down the page.

Leafing through the fragile pages, I examined the intricate details of the entries. The result was a beautiful example of nineteenth century plantation record keeping.

Sure that I'd be blind by the time I read through the entire ledger, I got up, went into my office, dug out a magnifying glass to read the spidery script, found pen and paper to jot down notes, and returned to my bedroom. Skimming down the columns for any information that stood out from the ordinary, I paid close attention to purchases of lockboxes with keys.

My cell phone jiggled from the nightstand. I answered with a cheery, "Hello."

"Hey, I'm at the kitchen door." Bradford's husky southern voice sounded over the line.

"Okay, I'll be right there." I snapped shut my phone, stashed the ledger in the nightstand drawer, and padded down the hallway to the kitchen. Tango shadowed me with yowls of anticipation of another meal.

"Come here, you," Bradford said, sweeping me into his arms when I opened the door. "Um, fresh from the shower," he whispered, his breath hot against my ear. Butterfly kisses trailed across my check until his lips clamped over mine. Strong fingers brushed against my breasts, and then traveled down to hook a thumb inside the elastic waistline of my p-jays.

Pleasure bubbled up in the form of a groan which he mistook as pain. He broke off the kiss. "Sorry, sweetie. I forgot about your lip."

I removed his cowboy hat, threading my fingers through his silver-streaked dark hair. "It's much better, but I'm going to have a bruised mouth to match my black eyes. How's Mrs. Herrington?"

He set me away from him, sat down at the kitchen table, and reached down to pet Tango, meowing at his feet. "How about a cup of coffee and I'll fill you in."

"Okay," I said, moving over to the counter. "I'm listening."

"She didn't take her husband's death well."

"That's an understatement," I said from the sink as

I filled the carafe with water. "I've never heard a woman scream so loud."

"That was just the beginning. The M.E. arrived and wanted to examine the body. She got all riled up when I raised the sheet and started screaming for Victor Redding."

Taking the creamer from the refrigerator, I put it on the table with the sugar and cups. "I didn't know they were friends."

"They're not according to Redding—only acquaintances. Anyway, he hadn't left yet so he sat with her while Crosby examined the body. She cried the whole time on his shoulder. I felt kind of sorry for him."

I sat across from him. "What did the M.E. think about the death?"

"On cursory inspection of the site, he said it looks to be accidental. Naturally, it'll be thoroughly investigated by his office and mine."

"What about Ryan Herrington? He was there with Ellie Malone. I ran into her and she told me they were driving to Atlanta tonight. He wants Kandy out of town until things settle down." I placed a plate of cookies I'd picked up from the bakery on the table.

"Yeah, I talked with him. Wanted to know how long it would take before the body would be released for burial. I told him it depended on the autopsy and the investigation. He promised to get back with me in a day or so. I can understand him wanting to protect his daughter from the media. He said only a couple of words to his stepmother before leaving. There's definitely a strain between those two."

"She's young enough to be his wife, not his

stepmother," I huffed. "And she's attractive, too. I wonder if she ever put the moves on him. That goes on a lot when an older man marries a younger woman. Or perhaps Ryan objected to his father marrying her. That would create tension within the family."

"Jolene, is the coffee ready?"

I got up and poured him a cup. "I could be right, you know."

"And you could be wrong." He poured cream and spooned sugar into his cup. "Anyway, she doesn't have any family here in Whiskey Creek so Redding suggested she stay out at Pineridge Plantation until her family could make arrangements to fly in from New York. His housekeeper will watch over her for the night. The paramedics sedated her so she shouldn't be much trouble."

I took the chair opposite him. "Everyone seems to be certain it was accidental?"

"We won't know for certain until the M.E. has completed the autopsy and a preliminary investigation is conducted. Now I'd like to change the subject and ask if you would accompany me to dinner and the gospel sing out at the fairgrounds tomorrow night."

"I would love to have dinner with you, but I'm not taking another step out there. One of us is jinxed. I'm leaning toward it being the fairgrounds."

He chuckled. "Jolene, it's you. You can't help yourself. You're a trouble magnet. Remember Mayor Payne's fundraiser? Upside down and inside out. You and your meddling."

"I caught Scarlett's killer."

"As luck would have it, I arrived in time to rescue you from a desperate killer."

This time I chuckled. "I remember it differently, gallant knight. The gun was in my hand and my finger on the trigger."

"My point exactly," he parleyed, "a trouble magnet."

"I don't do it on purpose, you know," I protested. "A girl has to defend herself."

He drummed his fingers on the table, glancing down at his watch. "Are you sure you're going to be okay here by yourself tonight? I know you said earlier that you didn't want company, but I could stay although I have to be up at the crack of dawn. I have a witness to interview in Macon in the morning."

I shook my head. "No, I'll be fine. There's a book I've been dying to read and your snoring is distracting. Is the witness for the Herrington case?"

"No. A homicide down on the East side." He rose from his chair. "I'll be back around noon. Call my cell phone if you need me. Is six o'clock okay to pick you up for dinner tomorrow evening?"

"Six is fine."

At the door he settled his cowboy hat on his head and smacked me on the butt with the palm of his hand. I locked the door behind him, reset the alarm, and padded back to the bedroom and the awaiting ledger. Tango settled at the foot of the bed when I finally climbed in and dug the ledger out of the nightstand drawer.

It cracked open in my hands.

I opened to the bookmark and resumed reading. Accounts of crop harvesting, cotton shipments. Purchases of clothing for the field workers and their children filled the next couple of pages. I turned the next page, pausing over a detailed account of a large sale of lumber to a Mr. John Winston for a small sum of money. Noted underneath the column were the words in parentheses, (house fire—has pregnant wife and five kids. The man won't accept lumber as charitable donation—sale will be at a loss for PP).

"Tango, our friend, Josiah Redding was a kind and conscientious man. He sold his lumber at a loss to help out a neighbor who'd lost his home in a fire. John Winston had a burned-out house, five kids and a wife to support and still refused to accept charity from his neighbor. Men back then had a lot of pride. I'm glad Josiah found a way to help without stripping the man's self-esteem."

Tango lifted his head. His bushy tail began to whip back and forth in an agitated manner before he sprang off the bed with a loud hissing noise and bolted out of the room. A tiny pinprick of light at the foot of my bed began to undulate and take the shape of a woman.

Of course, I knew my late night cosmic visitor could only be Scarlett Cantrell.

"You need to get a dog," she said. "Your pussy is finicky. You'd think he'd never seen a ghost."

I bookmarked the ledger, and returned it to the nightstand. "Never mind the cat, Scarlett. What drags you out so late? I thought you were working on a case in the hereafter."

"Oh, I was in the neighborhood and thought I'd stop in and see what's new with you besides your busted lip."

"You noticed?

"Hard not to," she said. "What happened?"

"Theodore Herrington died tonight. His wife slugged me as I tried to help."

She arched a brow. "How ungrateful of her."

"You didn't know? I thought you might've seen him up there."

"Oh, I knew he'd kicked the bucket. He's the reason why I'm out and about in the neighborhood. Want to know why?"

"I don't think I'm going to like your answer."

"He's my new client."

I groaned. "Scarlett, I'm not getting involved in Herrington's death. I swore off investigating. And how can you do two jobs at one time? What's Josiah think about you moonlighting with another client?"

Scarlett cocked a haughty pose. "There's no time on the Other Side, smarty-pants. And I'm not asking for help. I'm capable of multi-tasking on my own. Theo is being held in Purgatory until his trial. Rumor has it he's headed south. I'm looking into a personal matter for him."

"Well, you're dressed for it."

Scarlett unbuttoned her tan coat and slipped it off to reveal a stunning butter-soft sweater dress with shimmering golden threads. The brown slouch Fedora hat joined the coat on the bed. She cocked her head sideways to show off exquisite waves curled close to her face in a style reminisce of the 1930s.

I whistled appreciatively. "Nice. Is that the newest fashion for a dead PI?"

"It is for this one," she said. "I'm headed for Pineridge Plantation."

"Whatever for?"

"To inspect Herrington's wife."

"You're wasting your time, Scarlett. We don't know if Herrington was murdered. Although, I'm sure he had plenty of enemies who wished him dead. Kinda like you, Scarlett. When you were alive," I added when she gave me the evil eye.

"I never mentioned murder."

"Then what's the deal with looking over his wife?"

"I'm not at liberty to say."

"So you won't tell me why you're spying on Barbara Herrington?"

Ignoring my question, she put on her coat and hat. "I saw what you and your sisters did at Peaceful Valley the other day."

"It was your birthday."

"Yellow roses are my favorite."

"Yes, I know, Scarlett. And you're welcome."

She faded from sight and I went back to my perusal of the ledger. There was a purpose for Josiah Redding wanting me to read the plantation account book, and I had to find it. Two pieces of the puzzle were in my possession—the key and the ledger, but instinctively I knew more of the mystery awaited me out at Pineridge Plantation.

Chapter Nine
The Journal

Wednesday morning, anxious to get started, I awakened earlier than usual and set out for Pineridge Plantation. When I pulled around back I spotted Victor Redding's BMW. As planned, I'd arrived before the other volunteers.

With fewer people present in the mansion, I could search out the upper vacant bedrooms without detection. Excited at the prospect of finding answers, I retrieved the garment bag that held my period costume and boots and approached the back entrance. Twisting the knob and finding it locked, I used my key and slipped into the mud room. Snatches of conversation from the kitchen filtered through as I relocked the door behind me. The rich aroma of fresh brewed coffee and sizzling bacon brought a rumble from my stomach reminding me I'd skipped breakfast—too late to think about that now.

"Stop dawdling over your breakfast, Jack," the housekeeper said. "I expect Mr. Redding and his guest any minute, and I want you gone before they make an appearance."

"Ah, Maude, I'm not through with the morning paper. There's a good piece on the front page about Mr. Herrington. Better hide it from his widow or she'll start crying again. Never heard a woman carry on so."

"Hush now and get going."

A chair scraped across the hardwood floor alerting me that Mr. Turnipseed would catch sight of me in about fifteen seconds if I didn't slip into the hallway and make a dash for it. Clutching the garment bag to my chest, I streaked across the mudroom, into the hallway, and down to the small bedroom assigned for volunteers, and deposited the bag on the bed. I then slipped back out into the hallway. As I approached the front stairs, I paused, listening for any sign of life coming from the upstairs. Hearing nothing but the clanging of pans from the kitchen, I crept up the stairs and into the first bedroom, then eased the door closed, careful not to make a sound.

I made a quick survey of the chamber. Faded blue wallpaper coated the walls like a crisp cloudless day. The rosewood bed, crafted entirely by hand, had an intricately carved headboard and footboard decorated with acanthus leaves. Spiraled bedposts wound into the ivory lace canopy at the top and disappeared into the colorful patchwork quilt at the bottom. A parade of boyhood toys marched and sailed across wooden shelves lining the fabric-covered walls. In the corner, with a realistic mane and red leather saddle, a rocking horse had been rescued from the attic still bearing signs of loving abuse by generations of Redding children.

With no luck in finding the lock I needed, I crept into the sitting room next door and did a thorough search, finding nothing. The next door down the long hallway was shut, and when I pressed my ear to the panel I could hear shuffling within so I backed away and dashed into the closest open door.

I found myself in the green room. A charming

bedchamber with pastel green painted paneled walls and alabaster silk drapes pooling on the polished hardwood floors. My gaze gravitated to the Charleston "rice" bed dominating the room. Josiah's wife, Savannah, had given birth to their four children in the massive bed. Her portrait hung on the wall over the bed, and the serene eyes that stared out across the room gave one the feeling of peace and tranquility.

"You were the picture of long ago Southern aristocracy, Savannah," I whispered. "Your lifestyle is forever dead in the ashes of the Civil War."

"Very poetic, Jolene," a silky voice said behind me. "But she can't hear you. She's moved on."

"I'm well aware of that, Scarlett." I turned around to see her lounging over one of the plush upholstered chairs flanking the chimney. The Fedora still perched on her head, and a cocky half-smile highlighted her face.

"May I inquire into your future course of action? It doesn't appear you're making much headway in your investigation. Would you like some tips I've picked up in my recent endeavors?"

"No tips this morning." The antique jewelry box on the dresser caught my eye. "Keep a lookout and let me know if anyone is heading this way."

"What are you looking for?"

I held up the key. "The answer to this riddle."

"Try it."

Slipping the key into the lock, I jiggled it several times. "Nope, this isn't it."

"Someone's coming," Scarlett warned.

The key wouldn't budge when I tried to remove it. "It's stuck—now what?"

Scarlett's head disappeared through the door then reappeared. "Victor Redding is heading this way. Boy, is he unhappy."

"Oh, great," I moaned, jiggling the key several more times. Scarlett floated over to me. "The doorknob is turning. You'd better come up with something quick."

Dashing over to the bed, I rumpled the covers and dumped the handmade quilt on the floor. The door opened and Victor stepped into the room. Surprised, he stopped midstride and scowled at me.

"Miz Claiborne, what are you doing here? I thought I heard voices."

"I'm sorry I disturbed you." I smoothed the covers on the bed. "I noticed several tourists bolt back downstairs yesterday after the tour. I was afraid they might have been exploring without a guide so I came in early to check the rooms and I'm so glad I did. What a mess. The talking you heard was me—bad habit of mine. I hope I didn't inconvenience you by coming in early? Nancy made us promise to recheck the rooms before leaving and yesterday I just plain forgot."

He quirked an eyebrow as my nervous rambling stuttered to a stop, but I hoped to keep his gaze from straying to the key sticking out of the jewelry box. My luck held. Out of my peripheral vision I caught a glimpse of Scarlett on the move. First, she circled Victor several times before planting herself face to face with him.

"Ask him about Barbara Herrington," she said.

Reaching down, I picked up the quilt from the hardwood floor. "How is Mrs. Herrington this morning? I heard she spent the night with you."

"How did you know she was here?" Exasperation tinged his voice.

Now what? Confess that my boyfriend, Detective Samuel Bradford spilled the beans last night in my kitchen or do I go with the curious ghost of Scarlett Cantrell? I fidgeted with the blanket as I placed it on the quilt tree at the foot of the bed, stalling for time for an answer that wouldn't come back and bite me.

"Um, honestly, I'd rather not give out the identity of the person involved. I'm sure she didn't mean any harm—"

His fist smacked against his palm. "Say no more. I'm sure I can guess who's responsible for loose gossip. But don't believe everything you hear, young lady. Barbara Herrington is a fine upstanding citizen of impeccable manners. And furthermore, I am a respectable bachelor with the utmost concern and respect for a widow. I would never presume to approach a lady so soon after her husband's unfortunate accident. Diane Downey should be ashamed of herself. I shall call and speak with her husband about this most unpleasant business!"

I arched a brow, surprised at Victor's passionate defense of himself and Theo's widow. Which left no doubt of his honor in question, but for my sake, I'd better get him off the trail of the grand dame. The aging socialite could be a formidable opponent, and I didn't want my name associated with any conversation he might have with her husband.

"Mr. Redding, I didn't mean to imply that Mrs. Downey was the person responsible for my knowing Mrs. Herrington is here," I backtracked. "Think no more about it, please. I haven't drawn any conclusions other than your kindness to a suffering soul in need. Perhaps we should drop it. The least said the better, don't you agree?"

He nodded. "Yes, I agree. Wise course of action."

"May I ask you a question?"

"Regarding what?"

I offered him an easy smile. "I want to know about the slave woman, Tempy."

A black scowl crossed his face. "That black witch? Because of her many of my people perished. But if you want to know, she's the one who alerted the Yankees about the gold shipment and the Yankees slaughtered innocent civilians to obtain it. Thank God, Josiah had already hidden the gold and their attempts were thwarted."

His answer raised more questions in my mind. "But how could a slave, and a woman at that, have the resources to pull it off? Her every move was monitored."

"Not in this case. Tempy was a trusted member of the family according to several family diaries, and word passed down through other local plantation families," he said. "She had freedoms few slaves enjoyed. She wasn't held by the plantation's boundaries."

"Then why didn't she flee to the North when she had a chance? Instead, she stayed. Her grave is in the slave section of the family cemetery. What's the evidence of her guilt?"

He paused for a moment. "What's your interest in this?" he countered. "These events were documented by the locals. Are you questioning their authenticity? Follow the history in the brochure. The gold has long since been recovered and turned over to the authorities."

Hmm. So the gold had been recovered? Then why allow the rumor of its existence to continue? Did it not foster trespassers on the property? This merited further investigation, but the approaching click-clack of heels sounded out in the hallway.

Victor Redding must've heard them, also. "That must be Mrs. Herrington now. If you'll excuse me, I'll see she has a good breakfast before returning home. Her sister from New York will be arriving to help with the funeral arrangements later this afternoon." He waved a hand at the bed. "And thank you for respecting my home. I appreciate your devotion."

Guilt hammered me at his kind words. Oh yeah, going through his possessions without his knowledge was certainly respectful. To help his ancestor, of course, but it didn't assuage the undesirable feeling making its presence known in the pit of my stomach.

Scarlett shadowed Victor's retreating figure. "I'll join them for breakfast and meet back up with you later," she said. "I don't trust that woman. She's up to something."

Returning to the jewelry box, I jiggled the key until it came loose in my hand. An eerie feeling of being watched came over me. A reassuring glance backward turned up no other wandering soul of the dead so I shrugged it off as nerves.

With time running out, I made a quick sweep of the bedroom next door, but came up empty-handed. Disappointed, but not stymied, I made my way downstairs to change into my period costume and meet Billie Jo. The next tour started in ten minutes. Hopefully, I'd have better luck next time in my quest to find the treasures hidden in this house so haunted by its bloodied past.

****

Billie Jo, the blonde beauty of the family, fidgeted at the foot of the staircase in a pale yellow cotton day dress with white collar, cuffs, and frilled white apron.

"Are we having a problem this morning?" I inquired.

She gasped for breath. "How do you stand this contraption?"

"Oh, you get used to it. Take shallow breaths and you'll be fine."

"I'm thinking not. After today, I'm wearing my bra and that's that. No corset for me. How can I hunt ghosts if I can't breathe?"

"You're not here to hunt ghosts," I said. "You're here to help me conduct tours of the plantation manor house."

"I'm well aware of that."

"Are you packing?"

"Of course, not," she huffed. "My gun's locked up in the glove compartment of my car."

I pointed at a bulge in her dress. "Then what's in your apron pocket?"

She withdrew a small black gadget similar to a television remote. "It's an EMF meter. Did you know that electromagnetic energy has long been associated with ghosts and hauntings?"

"No, I can't say that I have. And whatever you do, don't turn it on." As the words left my mouth, a high-pitched beeping echoed throughout the front foyer.

She swung the instrument in an arc around her head. "I knew this place was a gold mine for ghosts," she gushed. "Tell me what you see."

"I see a nut-bag, Billie Jo. Now turn it off. There are tourists waiting for us."

The sound died as did Billie Jo's enthusiasm. I felt a momentary pang of regret for my harsh words, but I had no choice. I couldn't tell my baby sister the truth—that the front foyer was now filled with curious spirits from beyond.

That would be like turning a hound dog loose on the scent of an injured coon.

"Jolene, can I have a word with you about your sister?" Scarlett asked me from her perch above on the chandelier. "The others are demanding she refrain from disturbing their sleep. All the racket she's making effectively halted my morning conference with my client who's anxious for an update on his case."

I considered answering her with a bloodcurdling scream when Mr. Peabody opened the front door and ushered in a group of chatting tourists made up of mothers and young children with sticky hands.

"I'm getting a headache," I mumbled.

"I'll take the lead," Billie Jo said, stepping past me to address the group before I could stop her. "Ladies, if I can have your attention I would like to welcome you to Pineridge Plantation, the most haunted house in Georgia. The land runs red with the blood of massacred Confederate soldiers."

Several young children started crying, and a twitter of excited voices rose like a roar in my ears. If brains were leather, Billie Jo wouldn't have enough to saddle a ladybug!

"*What* Mrs. Hazard meant to say is that Pineridge Plantation is haunted by a violent past as is most of the

South, ripped and torn by the bloody battles of the Civil War," I twittered, making my way to my sister's side, patting her hand and giving her a huge smile. "It was a tragic time in United States history, and only by the grace of the Almighty was this grand ole estate snatched from the hands of fate to rise above its tragedies and emerge victorious in a new age of enlightenment and freedom for all."

The group burst out in applause, and I smiled in appreciation of their robust enthusiasm. But somehow I had to quell Billie Jo's desire to communicate with the dead. At least while we were conducting tours. Perhaps Scarlett would help?

"Good save, Claiborne."

Speak of the devil's mistress.

"Momma, the chandelier is moving," a boy said from the group.

"Hush, Tommy," his mother admonished. "It's only a breeze."

I glanced up and sure enough, Scarlett was still perched on the light fixture.

"Head them into the front parlor, Billie Jo and relate the story of Savannah Redding's needlework sampler on the wall," I directed in a low voice. "I'm going to kill two birds with one stone."

Billie Jo's brittle smile softened, slightly. "How come you're the only one who gets to talk about ghosts? You tell the story of Tempy's lost spirit in the old kitchen."

"But not with young children in the group," I stated. "And I keep it on the low when they are."

"You're right. I wasn't thinking. No ghost stories for this group."

I waited until she had led the group into the front parlor and closed the door before addressing Scarlett. "So what did you learn over breakfast?"

"Unfortunately, not a lot," she said beside me. "The widow seems sincere in her grief. I suppose that should make Theo happy to know his wife didn't marry him for his millions."

"I'm having the same bad luck." I held up the key.

"Josiah has faith in you," she encouraged. "Keep looking and you'll find it when you least expect to."

"Good advice." I paused for a second before continuing, "I have a favor to ask you, Scarlett. It involves Billie Jo."

"I figured as much. Don't make it too complicated, I'm overworked now."

"Could you manage to make yourself known to her?" I released a tired sigh. "She's wearing me out with this ghost-hunting business and if she catches a glimpse of you, maybe she'll be satisfied and calm down."

"Y'all are an uptight bunch," she mused. "Okay, I'll do it for the sake of Sisterhood. A state I never enjoyed being an only child. But mind you, this isn't going to be easy. You see, your sister isn't tuned into the metaphysical world. Deena, on the other hand—"

"Leave Deena out of it," I cautioned. "Concentrate on Billie Jo. Keep it simple and wait until I'm with her, okay?"

"I'll do my best, but no promises. I'm not a magician."

The sound of approaching footsteps stilled our conversation. Scarlett vanished through the wall, and I turned around to watch Victor and the attractive widow step down the sweeping staircase.

Primarily because I wanted to observe their interaction, I remained quiet, not alerting them to my presence in the far corner of the foyer. From this distance I could see Barbara had been crying. The skin around her eyes appeared swollen and red-rimmed, and the expertly applied make-up had failed to disguise the shadows brought on by lack of sleep. Her pale hair was slightly mussed, as if tucked in by trembling fingers, and her attire hastily donned.

Victor sat her overnight case on the floor. "Would you like to wait here while I bring the car around?"

Barbara spied me. "Ah, Jolene, I would like a word with you, please."

Her companion's face gave nothing away as he turned and nodded in my direction. "Miz Claiborne, this is unexpected finding you here—again. I do believe the tour has already begun?"

Think fast, ole girl. Ah, just the thing. Taking out a bubble gum wrapper I had placed in my pocket earlier, I held it up for his inspection.

"Kids, again," I said, smiling. "This group is full of them and I saw this lying on the floor when my sister led the group into the front parlor." I turned to Barbara. "My family is so sorry for your loss."

She lifted a tissue from her purse and dabbed her eyes. "I want to apologize for my behavior last night when you were assisting my Theo, but I thought you were trying to finish the job you and your father started the other night at the pageant."

Good Lord, the woman couldn't possibly believe Daddy and I would conspire to kill her husband! We were a tight-knit family for sure, but the *Sopranos* we're not. Words failed me and I stood there staring at her with what I'm sure was a stupid grimace on my face.

Redding picked up the overnight bag. "If you will excuse us, my guest has a plane to meet and you have a tour to join, right?"

Relieved, I bobbed my head like an idiot and stepped away toward the front parlor. Billie Jo was finishing her story as I joined them.

"Now, if you will follow me we'll proceed to the upstairs bedrooms," she said with a gracious smile.

Following in the wake of the group, my mind pondered all that I had and hadn't learned this morning. I allowed Billie Jo to take the lead and brought up the rear—encouraging stragglers to keep up with the group and only adding information when needed.

No further incidents occurred until we reached the library. When I threw open the double doors, Josiah stood at the fireplace with cigar in hand. Scarlett lounged across the long sofa leafing through a magazine, which fell instantly to the floor upon our entrance.

"I smell cigar smoke, Momma."

"Hush, Tommy."

"There's a pretty woman on the sofa."

"Tommy, what did the doctor tell you about your overactive imagination? Be quiet and listen to the nice ladies tell us about the family that lived here long, long ago."

"But Momma, she's there...and a man, too."

Several of the mothers in the group nodded their heads in sympathy and gathered their children closer to them as if the affliction were contagious. Tommy's mother blanched at their insensitivity.

"Now there's someone I can work with." Scarlett materialized at my side. "Josiah said he has something for you. Watch for it."

"Not now," I whispered. "That kid is watching us."

Billie Jo recited the history of the room, and told the tragic story of Piper's Gold, conveniently leaving out the sightings of ghostly Confederate soldiers guarding their treasure.

"And now we will proceed to the old kitchen where slaves prepared meals for the Master and his family," she concluded.

Pleased with the outcome, I ushered the group toward the library doors when a book fell from the bookshelf to land with a thump on the floor.

"Momma, did you see that book fly off the shelf?"

"Come along, Tommy. It's time to go home and call the doctor."

I winked at the kid as his mother steered him out of the room. Not waiting, I dashed back inside, scooped up the small leather volume, and cracked it open to see Josiah's spidery script splashed across the page. Tucking his personal journal in the large pocket of my dress, I went to join the tour group in the old kitchen.

Chapter Ten
Rednecks and Mosquitoes

"Looks like we're in for another nasty scandal," Mrs. Eisenberg told me later that afternoon when I returned to work. "Mister wants to move to Florida. I pitched a fit and told him we were too old. That old man has flipped his lid if he thinks I'm leaving my home."

Smiling at her reflection in the mirror, I grabbed a roller from the trolley. "What scandal is on your radar? There's at least a dozen according to the gossipmongers. And let me say I'm glad you're staying. You're one of my favorite customers."

"Jolene, honey, you're a kind soul," she said. "Now you tell me if it isn't any of my business what I'm going to ask you and I'll shut up real fast, okay?" She waited until I nodded before continuing. "What happened to your pretty face? It looks like you've been wrestling the devil."

I chuckled. "It is bad, isn't it?"

"The worst I've seen in a long time, my dear, and I was an ER nurse for twenty-five years. Were you involved in another automobile accident?"

That incident took place a couple of months back when a mysterious man in a dark blue sedan peppered my car with bullets. Sigh. Another long story told elsewhere.

"No, Theodore Herrington is responsible for the broken nose, skinned chin, and two black eyes. His wife gets credit for my spilt lip." I retold the details of the fight and the ensuing incident at the pie bake-off.

"That woman has a good face and a bad heart. Such a shame about her loss, although, I must say she shouldn't have hit you when you were trying to save her husband."

I secured the last roller in her silvery hair and made no comment on her last statement. Death being the last subject I wanted to discuss as I was sick and tired of talking to or about dead people. Escorting her to the dryers lined up along the back wall of the salon, I handed her a magazine, and headed for the kitchen to grab a bite to eat while her hair dried.

At the reception desk, Holly, on the phone, motioned to me so I slipped behind the desk to check my schedule for the rest of the day until she finished her conversation.

"Barbara Herrington called," she said as she replaced the receiver. "Her usual hairstylist is sick, and she needed an emergency appointment. You had a cancellation at three so I booked the appointment."

I let out a sigh of aggravation. "Holly, can't Ted take her? Or one of the other stylists? I planned to leave early."

Holly shook her head. "You're the only one with enough time to fit her in. Should I call her and cancel?"

"No, of course not. What's she wanting done?"

"Highlights."

I groaned at the extra work. "If any of the other stylists have a cancellation, see if it would be okay to move her to their book."

"Oh, and I booked her sister with Billie Jo for a haircut," Holly added. "Her name is Anita North."

"Fine, I'm going to grab a bite to eat while Mrs. Eisenberg is under the dryer. Put her in my stylist chair when she's dry."

"I'll see to it," she said and turned to answer the phone.

Deena joined me from her office as I headed for the kitchen.

"How'd it go with Billie Jo this morning?" she asked. "She was so excited last night when I talked to her. I've never heard her so animated about giving tours at Pineridge before."

I pulled my homemade chicken salad out of the refrigerator. "Well, she started off on the wrong foot mentioning blood and ghosts in the same breath in a room full of kids."

Deena grabbed a loaf of bread from the cabinet. "I bet that went over well with the parents."

"Yeah, well, I redirected the history lesson onto safer ground. After that, she was great," I said, making myself a sandwich.

The kitchen door sprang open and Billie Jo marched in. "Damn stomach's been eatin' at my backbone. Is there enough left for me?" She reached for the bread and chicken salad.

Deena grabbed the chips from the cabinet and then three soft drinks out of the refrigerator and sat down at the table. "I hear you did exceptionally well with your first tour at the mansion."

Billie Jo took a bite out of her sandwich. "Interesting place," she mumbled.

I downed a swig of soda. "Barbara Herrington and

her sister are coming in this afternoon for the works. Her hairdresser is out sick."

"Kind of surprising after she decked you last night," Deena said. "Seems like she would avoid us at all costs."

"She apologized to me this morning. Said she wasn't thinking clearly and believed me and Daddy were out to finish the job we started at the pageant. Crazy broad."

"That's an understatement," Billie Jo mumbled with her mouth half-full.

"I think she's sincere," I added. "Theo's death has been a shock to her, but that doesn't mean I'm happy about doing her hair. I wish she'd go elsewhere."

"Tell Holly to cancel if you're uncomfortable with her," Deena advised.

"Holly offered to, but the tongues are wagging enough already," I said. "It's only this one time so I'll stick it out."

"Have you talked to Mama and Daddy this morning, Deena?" Billie Jo asked. "I'm worried about them. They took Theo's death hard last night. He was a high school friend after all."

"They're both fine," she replied. "Daddy was on the phone when I got up. I'm not certain, but I believe he was looking for an apartment to rent."

"He's been living with you for seven months now," I piped up. "He's bound to want his own place."

Deena set her drink down. "I know, but if he leaves then I'll be alone again and I have so much space. Why should he waste his money on rent when he can live with me?"

"Maybe he might want to have sex and he can't if

he's living with you," Billie Jo commented.

"Our parents are divorced," Deena replied.

Billie Jo shrugged. "And that's supposed to mean they can't have sex? You're divorced. I suppose you're not having sex?"

Deena blushed. "None of your business. William and I aren't ready to take the next step."

"That's a shame," Billie Jo said. "Sex is as vital to life as breathing. It keeps you young and vibrant. I wouldn't go one day without it."

Holly was a welcome sight when she sailed into the kitchen, interrupting Billie Jo. Mrs. Eisenberg was out from under the dryer and waiting in my stylist chair. Deena shooed me out of the kitchen, promising to clean up so I returned to work in a good frame of mind.

Promptly at three, Barbara and another woman, who could only be her sister—so close was the resemblance—breezed through the front door. Ryan followed in their wake. After leaving them in the reception area, he made a beeline to Ellie's station.

God, how I dreaded this appointment but I pasted on a welcoming smile and marched up to her. "Mrs. Herrington, how nice to see you again." I turned to the woman seated beside her on the sofa. "And you must be her sister from New York." I extended my hand. "It's nice to meet you, I'm Jolene Claiborne."

"Anita North."

Her handshake was like holding hands with a sweaty ice cube. I wiped my hand down the front of my apron. "I hope you find our fair city to your liking while you're here."

"I doubt that," she snorted. "As soon as Barbara has buried her husband, I hope to convince her to return home with me. Why Theodore chose to live down here is beyond my understanding. There's nothing here but rednecks and mosquitos."

In a different setting I might've been tempted to acquaint Miss High-and-Mighty with my redneck origins, but the only feature left undamaged on my face were my perfectly straight white teeth, and I wasn't about to sacrifice them to the cause.

With my fighting instincts tampered down for the moment, I turned to Barbara. "Billie Jo will take good care of your sister so you and I can get started on your highlights."

She followed me back to my station and after a quick consultation I made my way to the dispensary to mix a batch of powdered bleach and developer. Voices coming from the kitchen interrupted my prep work.

"I warned you this would happen, Ryan," complained Ellie's testy voice. "Why did you have to aggravate him so much? His reaction was only natural."

"What are you implying? That I hurt him on purpose? Things snowballed out of control."

"But to do that to him—"

"He didn't suffer. Think about him in a better place."

"I can't bear to think about him at all. I wanted us all to be a family."

"Every time he saw us together…he took out his anger on you."

"Ryan, he didn't mean it. He was old."

"Well, he's gone, and now we can move in together."

"Yes, it's what I've wanted for a long time."

Their voices dissolved into sounds of intimacy. I

backed away from the door in confusion. A cold knot formed in the pit of my stomach when I thought about Herrington's untimely death. Could Ryan and Ellie have conspired to murder the old man for interfering in their relationship? No, I shook my head. Preposterous. I stared down at the bowl of highlighter in my hands. Bleach fumes. Yep, I'd been sniffing bleach and perm solution too much, an occupational hazard that leaves your brains scrambled and your imagination dreaming up murder.

Chapter Eleven
Where's Your Southern Hospitality?

When five o' clock rolled around and my last client waltzed out the door, I sang a short halleluiah chorus and danced a jig to my station to clean up. After overhearing that disturbing conversation between Ellie and Ryan, my day had gone downhill from there. Barbara had proven to be a difficult client and in the end, to get rid of her and her overbearing sister who could be heard complaining from the reception area, I had given her a substantial discount on the price of her highlights.

The usual salon noises—chatting stylists with their customers, phone ringing, running water in the shampoo basin, background music—had finally stilled for the day, and my sisters and I were relaxing in Deena's office. Bradford would be picking me up around six, so I only had a few minutes to chat before I headed for home to shower and change.

"Well, that was a day from hell," Billie Jo said, leaning back in the chair. "I'm thinking about learning a new profession. That North woman made me want to get out of the business. She didn't shut up the whole time she was in my chair."

"How'd you keep your cool?" I asked.

She laughed. "Easy. When she finally slowed down, I politely explained that we rednecks here in the

South owned cell phones and even had access to the internet. Then I told her we had running water and inside toilets that actually flushed just like her fancy throne in the Big Apple. She clammed up after that but I was finished so it worked out real good."

"What did she say about the haircut you gave her?" I asked.

"She tipped me twenty dollars so I guess I did all right. I'm not sure how long she's gonna be in town, but I told Holly not to put her on my book if she calls."

Deena continued to fidget with a supply catalog on her desk and cast longing glances at her cell phone. She had been preoccupied ever since Billie Jo and I had entered into her office. Something had a hold of her panties for sure.

"Is there a problem you need to discuss with us?" I asked her. "I mean about the salon. Or anything else for that matter, right, Billie Jo?"

"Sure, I've got a couple of minutes. Fire away."

Deena's eyes held a trace of sadness. "Would it surprise you to learn that I've always wanted to be more like the two of you?"

Billie Jo's face registered the same surprise as mine. If the truth be told, I secretly harbored the desire to be more thoughtful and serene like Deena. My habit of diving into chaos without question landed me in an unenviable state. All one had to do was to see my face to see the results of my actions.

"Sis, the world couldn't stand another me," I said with a grin. "Ask Bradford. Remember, my dazzling personality landed me in anger management classes. And I'll probably have to have surgery to fix my nose. And don't forget my repeated trips to jail. You don't want to be anything like me. And Billie Jo's a hothead. Just ask Roddy."

"What brought this on?" Billie Jo asked.

"A man brought this on," I answered for Deena. "William Mahoney, Assistant Pastor of First Baptist Church, namely. I'm right aren't I?"

"He's been acting strange ever since the other night," she replied. "We had a situation come up between us and he hasn't been the same. I'm losing him, and I don't have the courage to address the subject with him."

"What happened?"

"Sex happened, Billie Jo." Deena slapped her hand over her mouth. "I mean almost happened," she recanted with a sigh. "Bill freaked out and is now avoiding me."

"I wouldn't worry over-much about it," I advised. "These things usually work themselves out between couples. I know y'all have deeply held beliefs concerning these matters, but I wouldn't spend a lot of time feeling guilty."

"This explains why you were so touchy about the subject earlier," Billie Jo mused. "I'm sorry if I embarrassed you, Deena. The problem will resolve itself, you'll see."

"I'm not as confident as you, Billie Jo, just hopeful that William and I will work it out in time."

I redirected the conversation to a more pleasant subject. "Has Daddy said anything to you about him and Mama getting back together?"

"He refuses to discuss it with me. More than one time, he's told me to mind my own business. However, Theo's death has him thinking about how short life is."

"Death tends to do that to you," I said. "Barbara said pretty much the same earlier. She's on the board of directors at Theo's bank and wants to stay and work in Whiskey Creek."

"Her sister's not gonna be happy," Billie Jo inserted. "I almost feel sorry for Barbara having to tell her she's decided to stay here with us rednecks and mosquitos."

"Well, I'm thankful we're not having to go through another murder investigation," Deena added. "I know it sounds horrible, but I'm glad Theo's death turned out to be an accident and we're not involved. Right, Jolene?"

So much for subtlety. I had to smile at Deena's way of telling me that I wasn't dragging them into another funky set of circumstances like I did when I investigated Scarlett's death.

"Rest assured, I have no such intentions. Although I overheard a most particular conversation between Ellie and Ryan today. I swear if I didn't know better I'd believe that they…oh, never mind. It's not important, and I need to get out of here. Bradford is picking me up for dinner at six."

"How's thing's going between you two?" Deena asked.

I stood up. "Like a roller coaster, so you see, you're not the only one with relationship problems. See y'all in the morning."

"I think I'll be heading out, too," Billie Jo said. "Roddy's in the mood for fried chicken tonight, and I'm gonna stop by the Colonel's for a bucket and all the trimmings. Deena would you like to join us?"

"Yes, Billie Jo, I believe I would. With Bill acting the way he is, we both could use a night off. Thanks for the invite. I'm definitely not in the mood to be alone."

Together we locked up the salon and headed for our cars in the rear parking lot.

****

My cell phone jangled as I pulled into my driveway.

"Hello."

"Hey," Bradford said. "I'm stuck on the east side of town on a homicide case. Can you meet me at Fancy's on Broad around seven?"

I agreed and hung up. Since I had extra time, I poured myself a glass of wine and took a long bubble bath. When I emerged, I reapplied my make-up and slid into a dark blue pantsuit and heels. Tango protested loudly when I gathered up my purse and keys from the counter and dashed back out the kitchen door.

****

Fancy's was lit up like a holiday display when I pulled into the back parking lot. White lights, resembling snowflakes, twinkled from towering pines up to the veranda winding around the house. Personally, I believed the restaurant owners would attract more business if they'd left off the distracting lights and restored the old home back to its former glory of the roaring 20s. The modern day additions detracted from the beauty of the century old architecture.

I spotted Bradford seated at one of the tables on the large veranda when I walked up the front stone steps. He rose in one fluid motion to pull out a chair beside him. His blue jeans and black button-up cowboy shirt emphasized his tall male physique and I couldn't help but notice several women send covert glances his way. Not that I blamed them, he looked positively yummy.

I crossed the veranda and slid into the chair. "Thank you," I murmured, "It's a lovely night for dinner under the stars. The night is so warm for November."

"Yes, my thoughts exactly. I took the liberty of ordering iced tea with lemon. You look great. I can't even tell you've been in two fights," he said with a smile.

I peered up at his ruggedly handsome face so familiar, his dark brown hair edged with silver and cleanly cut and eyes unchanged by time. And for the first time since we had started dating, I wanted to lose my heart to this man. I smiled at the thought. "Thank you, Bradford," I replied. "You look nice, also."

He chuckled at my compliment and picked up the menu in front of him. "Now that that's settled, let's see what we like. I've never been here before, but I've heard some of the guys down at the station raving about the prime rib. What about you?"

"I've been here a couple of times with the gang." I read through the menu. "I've ordered the fried catfish, but tonight I think I'll try the grilled quail with steamed vegetables."

Bradford slapped down his menu. "I'll have the same." He waved his hand at the waiter standing nearby and ordered our meals. After the waiter left, we both relaxed and sat in compatible silence for several minutes. Soon, our salads arrived with a basket of Fancy's signature freshly baked bread and butter churned daily by hand on the premises.

Bradford buttered a slice liberally and shoved it into his mouth. "My cholesterol is going to shoot through the roof after tonight," he said between bites.

I nibbled on my salad. "Dr. Gaines warned me last week about mine. I swear the way he went on you'd think I had Crisco running through my veins."

"Well, in that case, I'll eat the rest of this so you're not tempted to," he said, buttering another slice of bread.

"One can't come to Fancy's and not sample the wares, my dear," I teased, reaching across the table to retrieve a slice of warm, crusty bread.

The waiter brought our entrees, and we fell silent as we consumed the grilled quail. After we had finished eating, coffee and a small slice of chocolate cake for each of us was served for dessert. I waited until the server left and we were alone before broaching the subject upmost on my mind.

"Barbara Herrington and her sister from New York paid us a visit this afternoon," I said lightly. "Anita is determined that her sister return to civilization as soon as the funeral is over, but Barbara wants to stay here. She's on the board of directors at Herrington's bank."

Bradford laid down his fork. "I know what you're doing, Jolene, so stop the chit chat. You're fishing for information on Herrington's autopsy."

"Okay, guilty as charged. I do want to know what the M.E. found, so tell me."

"Ordinarily, I wouldn't be discussing this with you. But since the M.E. has ruled this as an accidental death, and the report will be made public, I can tell you he found peanuts in Herrington's system. He died of cardiac arrest brought on by anaphylactic shock."

"Peanuts killed him? Wow, how strange, but it's what you expected."

"I've seen stranger. His wife told me he failed to

134

carry his EpiPen on his person. I checked her story and there were several incidents of him being treated at the emergency room for accidental ingestion of peanut products. The M.E. said his heart disease had progressed to the point that it couldn't deal with the stress of a severe allergic reaction and gave out. I'm waiting for the analysis report on the ingredients of each pie before officially closing the case."

"So there's no question here of murder?"

He leaned back in his chair and crossed his arms over his chest. "Where'd that come from? Murder was never mentioned. Do you have something you'd like to share with me?"

In my mind, I ran over the conversation I'd overheard earlier between Ellie and Ryan. According to them, with Ryan's father dead, they were free to pursue a life together. Keep your mouth shut, Claiborne, until Bradford has his report back or more damning evidence comes to light.

Now was a good time to redirect the conversation, a helpful habit I'd learned being a hairdresser. "Bradford, can you tell me why you and the other judges rejected Dixieland's entry in the contest, and don't lie, I saw your face when you tasted it."

"You're evading my question, Jolene," he said. "Why did you say murder and Theodore Herrington in the same breath? What are you up to?"

"Are you interrogating me, Detective Bradford?"

He reached out and caught my hand in his. "You started it, Miz Claiborne. Now answer my question."

The caress of his lips on my hand seared a fiery path to my brain. "This feels a little like coercion, I must warn you."

"There isn't a man on the planet with balls big enough to coerce you."

"Not true, Bradford. Let's go home and play bad cop," I said in a breathy Marilyn Monroe voice. "I promise to spill my guts after you supply sufficient coercion."

A deep chuckle greeted my words. "Evasion is in your blood, my dear."

I started to protest, but his cell phone shrilled. He answered it, and by the conversation I knew we wouldn't be indulging in any bedroom games tonight. He signaled for the check.

"Sorry to cut out on you, but duty calls." He pushed back from the table. "Raincheck on the rest of our date?"

Hand in hand we strolled around to the back parking lot. At my car, Bradford brushed a gentle kiss across my lips. "There's a costume ball at Pineridge Plantation on Saturday night."

"Yes, I'm looking forward to it. You?"

"Only if you're my date."

"I wouldn't dream of denying you anything," I responded in my Marilyn Monroe voice. Call me later? We can pick up where we left off. And bring your handcuffs," I suggested.

"Don't tempt me. I'm libel to chain you to the bed until the Herrington case is closed." He dropped another kiss on my forehead and waited until I had unlocked my car and slid in. "This could be an all-nighter so I'll call you sometime tomorrow."

He followed my car out of the parking lot and waved as I turned toward home. I had just turned onto Dalton Road when a ghostly form materialized on the passenger seat, startling me. "I wish you wouldn't do that, Scarlett," I screamed. "Can't you give me some warning before popping in? I almost ran off the road."

She made an impatient motion with her hand. "Jolene, you're such a drama-queen."

"What do you want?" I asked as the oxygen returned to my lungs.

"Nothing. I was in the neighborhood and thought I'd pop in and say hello."

"Hello. Okay, so we said hello. Don't let me keep you. I'm sure you've got places to go and ghosts to see."

"Where's your southern hospitality?"

"Gone with the wind, Scarlett."

"That's not funny."

"Sorry. Payback is hell."

"No, hell is payback," she snickered with abundant meaning.

"I guess this means you're coming to my house?"

"No, I've got places to go and ghosts to see."

And with those parting words she vanished.

My hands gripped the steering wheel. "Geez, I've got to get one of those ghost-buster meters Billie Jo had this morning."

Chapter Twelve
How to Host the Perfect Southern Funeral

The shrilling phone greeted me when I unlocked the door and stepped into my kitchen. I shooed Tango off the counter and reached for the receiver.

"Hello."

"Jolene, where've you been? I've been calling for hours."

"Hang on, Mama. I've got to turn off the alarm."

When I returned I pulled out a chair, sat down, and kicked off my heels. "Hours, Mama? Really? Why didn't you call my cell phone if it's that important? Bradford and I were having dinner at Fancy's."

Tango wound around my feet meowing with purpose so I got up and filled his bowl with Friskies while listening to Mama complain about a phone call she'd received from one of her church friends. Finally, she paused long enough for me to say, "What did Mrs. Bowen say?"

"That my pie killed Theo! Can you imagine such nonsense? And who would start such a rumor. Terrible thing. I swear, I don't know what I'm gonna do. Why even Diane avoided me at church tonight."

Well the rooster had finally come home to roost, and the henhouse was all astir. God I hated church gossip. Whatever happened to love thy neighbor? The Good Samaritan hadn't put in an appearance in many a month of Sundays at our church, and it seemed to me all that pew sitting only served to make our butts wider and our hearts colder. Should I tell Mama the truth and thereby hurt her feelings or lie to spare them? The latter appealed to me most.

I made the sign of the cross over my chest and crossed my fingers for protection against cosmic backlash. "Mama, I wouldn't put a lot of stock into what Mrs. Bowen repeats. She's a hundred years old, and her hearing isn't reliable. Most likely, she misunderstood."

"She is getting up in years," Mama conceded. "And Diane probably has a lot on her mind. Which would explain her behavior. Why yes, Jolene, you're right. You said you had dinner with Sam?"

"Yes, at Fancy's on Broad Avenue. The food is excellent. You and Daddy should try it."

"That's nice, dear. Did Sam mention Theo?"

"No, but I did in a roundabout way. Turns out Herrington died of a heart attack brought on by anaphylactic shock. Herrington had a severe allergy to peanuts."

"I've known that for years, dear. He collapsed one day back in high school after eating peanut butter pie in the school cafeteria. He was known back then to be reckless. He's always been especially jealous of Harland."

"Well, thank goodness there weren't any peanuts in your recipe. But it's strange he collapsed right after eating those pies."

"Theo wasn't allergic to nuts, Jolene. Pecans are nuts and peanuts are legumes."

"I know that Mama. I grew up on a peanut farm."

"Then what are you getting at? Are you suggesting someone put peanuts in the pies to murder Theo?"

"That's silly, Mama. I'm not suggesting anything of the sort. I'm merely thinking out loud."

"Well I don't like the direction your thoughts are taking, young lady. Don't be a harbinger of evil tidings."

Since I'd boxed myself into a corner, the wisest course of action was to come clean with her and confess my overactive imagination had flared up again. That explanation would get me off the hook and I wouldn't be guilty of spreading conspiracy theories involving the dead man's son and his girlfriend.

"Mama, I believe the repeated blows to my face and head has knocked a couple of screws loose. Why I even had a conversation with Scarlett in the front seat of my car tonight. She needed my advice on how to host the perfect Southern funeral."

As expected, the phone line went dead. Relieved, I took a quick shower, changed into my night clothes, and dug out Josiah's journal from the nightstand. Tango ambled in and settled at the foot of the bed.

A trickle of worry wormed its way into my thoughts. I put down the diary, replaying my earlier conversations with Bradford and Mama. What if peanuts were found in one of the entries? Especially Dixieland's? If my suspicions turned out to be true, and Ellie and Ryan were involved in Herrington's death, I might be guilty of withholding evidence. Bradford had to be told. He could determine whether to investigate the pair or not. My identity would be withheld, and I would be safe from any retribution from the either of them.

I tried to shake off the feeling of impending doom, but it clung to me like static on a dryer sheet. I grabbed up the phone and punched in Bradford's number. It rang several times before he picked up.

"Detective Bradford."

"I need to talk to you right away."

"I'm at a crime scene. I can't talk now."

"But it's important."

"It'll have to keep until tomorrow."

"Call me first thing."

Disappointed, I hung up, and reached inside the nightstand for a pen and notebook to organize my thoughts for clarity. Bradford would want the details written out so he could go over them as many times as needed.

First, I recorded Tuesday's date and the time of Theo's death. Then I wrote down everything I could remember about that night. Next, I drew a diagram of the fairgrounds kitchen and where each business had been partitioned into ten portable areas. I wrote the name of the business in each space.

A time-line from the moment we arrived until Herrington collapsed was recorded along with what I could remember of our activities. Mentally, I tried to reconstruct our every move but that was proving to be difficult. In my mind's eye, I could see when we left to register our recipe, and had left Daddy behind to watch over our ingredients. He said he left to use the men's room. Which meant our ingredients could've been sabotaged during his absence. I recorded Diane Downey's accusation Ellie overheard after Theo's death.

Next I wrote down Ellie and Ryan's conversation

I'd overheard while mixing bleach in the dispensary. Then there was Nancy's off-handed remarks about gunning for Herrington if she was booted off the festival committee, and also the judge tampering at the beauty contest. The seventy-five thousand dollars bribe Theo offered Ellie to stay away from his son and granddaughter. If I suspected it, I wrote it down. Lastly, I jotted down my observations of Barbara Herrington and her sister, Anita North.

At ten, I put away my notebook and went into the kitchen to make a cup of hot herbal tea to help me sleep, and padded back to my room. The tea didn't help much so I switched on the late news for any further updates on Herrington's death.

Tammy Hodges from WXYB Channel Ten News reported that the Herrington family wanted to express their thanks and appreciation for the calls and flowers pouring in from all around the state. In lieu of flowers, please make a donation in Theodore Herrington's name to Hospice or Whiskey Creek Animal Shelter, his favorite charities.

The news anchor went on to report an ongoing investigation continued into his death and if the public had any information to contact the police department at the number on the screen.

The weather report came on next so I turned off the television and took my tea cup back to the kitchen. As I crawled back into bed my knee hit something hard. I turned over the covers and spotted Josiah Redding's forgotten diary.

Still keyed up, I picked it up, cracked it open and began to read.

Chapter Thirteen
Destiny's Heavy Hand

April 2, 1842

Purchased buckskin stallion and three mares from William Greene for the purpose of getting some colts. Planted corn in the west field. Went hunting. Killed two deer.

Nothing of importance happened on this day other than the usual men stuff like hunting and killing, and digging in the dirt.

April 3, 1842

Sunday. Intended to go to church. Dressed, examined critically my tout ensemble, was about to depart, when lo, Savannah became sick. Unfortunate circumstance! Spent the morning reading the Bible to her. Our closest neighbors, Mr. and Mrs. Major arrived for luncheon. Savannah stayed in her room.

Josiah Redding suffered with a touch of vanity, but most of us do in one way or another. I, personally, take great pride in my matching my handbags and shoes.

April 5, 1842

Savannah sick. Dr. Thomas sent for. Tempy says the baby is coming early. Young Ben sold to Frank Hilton for the sum of three hundred dollars. Agricultural meeting in nearby town of Albany.

Go figure, things haven't changed all that much in a century and a half. Women still get sick during their pregnancies and the men find a way to get out of the house. Thankfully, the atrocious buying and selling of human flesh had been eradicated from the South. Freedom bought with the blood of our young men. The repercussions still ring across the land today.

April 8, 1842

Friday. Commenced planting cotton with seven hands. Weather extremely dry. Praying for rain. I am worried about Savannah. Rode new stallion over to Rolling Oaks this evening. Mrs. Major promised to visit Savannah soon.

*A*tta boy, Josiah, go horseback riding when your pregnant wife stays at home confined to her bed. Thank God, for Tempy's faithful companionship.

April 10, 1842

Sunday. Intended to go to church. Randall is sick with the croup. Savannah in labor. Sent for Dr. Thomas. Household in uproar. The newest addition, a small baby boy born late in evening. Dr. Thomas fearful for his survival. Savannah is bleeding heavily and is unconscious. Lord, save my wife and son. This is a bad day for Pineridge Plantation.

Okay, so maybe I was a mite harsh in my judgment. At least he expressed his pain and suffering on the fragile yellowed pages. How frightened he must have been to witness his wife struggling to bear their second child and not knowing if he would be burying one or both of them. I thought back to the recent birth of my granddaughter, Hannah. Born seven months ago at one of the top-rated hospitals in the state, she and my daughter, Becky, had received the best medical care available. Savannah's fate hung in the balance.

April 11, 1842

Monday. The boy grows weaker as Savannah hasn't regained consciousness and unable to nurse the child. A wet nurse is brought in from the slave quarters. Rose is a new mother with plenty of milk for both children. Dr. Thomas is adamant that Randall be kept away from his mother while she and the new baby are so weak. Mrs. Major stopped by for a short visit with Savannah. Continued cotton planting.

I turned the page, unable to tear my eyes from the ancient writing.

April 12, 1842

A fine name has been chosen for the boy. He shall be named John Milton Redding in honor of Savannah's father, John Milton Childs. Savannah opened her eyes today. Although weak, Dr. Thomas is encouraged that she and the child will recover. Randall is asking to see his mother. Dr. Thomas promised the boy he could go outside for a short time instead. Three hands down sick with a severe bowel complaint.

Life continued to throw problems at the plantation owner. Now he had three more lives to worry about. Reading this made me appreciate Pepto-Bismol and Imodium.

April 13, 1842

Wednesday. Still no rain. Breeding buckskin stallion to Lady's Chance. Hoping to locate additional breeding stock. Nance supervising soap-making. Sending George into Whiskey Creek for supplies. Sick field hands better today. Back out in west field finishing up corn planting. Israel working in kitchen garden. Savannah still weak but insisting on seeing John. Became distraught. Dr. Thomas sent for. Savannah given sedative. Randall recovered.

Poor Dr. Thomas. The life of a country doctor must've been brutal back in the horse and buggy days. And today doctors complain about being underpaid and overworked!

April 14, 1842

Barn fire at John Winston's farm. Lost dairy cow in fire. Mrs. Winston expecting fifth child any day. Ordered lumber cut and delivered to help Winston rebuild his barn. Sending dairy cow to Winston farm. Savannah allowed to see John for the first time since his birth, but she's still too weak to hold him. Boy still small but thriving.

I pondered the roulette wheel of life. But for the luck of the draw, I could've been born in Josiah's world—thrust into a life void of the romanticism I had imagined those times to be.

Hollywood's idea of Camelot, with Kings of Cotton living on enchanted lands created by a loving God for their pleasure. Ladies-in-waiting gowned in silks and satins and bright happy smiles with the heirs of the kingdom mounted on golden steeds as Knights of the Round Table.

Portrayed as a time of chivalry and honor, in reality hardship and lack plagued most people regardless of skin color. Even the rich were pawns in destiny's heavy hand. Surrounded with the best money could provide, and a doctor dedicated to his profession, still the future of Josiah's family was questionable. I turned back to the journal in anticipation of the unfolding drama.

April 15, 1842

Little John Milton took a turn for the worse in the middle of the night. Dr. Thomas arrived from the Winston farm to attend him. Savannah is stronger today and insists her son be placed in the bed with her. Dr. Thomas is against this. Tempy is with her mistress and is able to calm her. What would I do without Tempy, I asked the God of heaven. Dr. Thomas will be staying the night.

With little sleep, the country doctor worked on. In my book, he's the hero of this story.

April 16, 1842

Trouble at the Winston farm. His wife is in labor. Dr. Thomas left early this morning after promising to return as soon as he can to check on John Milton who continues to decline. Dr. Thomas returned around midnight. Mrs. Winston was delivered of twin baby boys, but Mrs. Winston's health is suffering a setback.

No wonder the woman's health suffered. Too many kids. Mr. Winston needed to wear a sheepskin raincoat or abstain from sex for a spell. Damn, give the woman a break!

April 17, 1842

Sunday. Rain all day. Blessing from God. Two field hands injured in accident. Savannah relapsed with a high fever. Dispatched George to fetch Doctor. Tempy and Nance are at Savannah's side. I don't believe I can sleep with problems mounting.

And I thought I had problems running a beauty salon and keeping up with five employees and two sisters. In comparison, my life smelled like a bed of roses.

April 21, 1842

Bad news from Winston farm. Mrs. Winston's health deteriorating. Sent Nancy with food stocks for family. Dr. Thomas stopped in to check on Savannah and John Milton. Both doing badly. Spent the evening in prayer. Corn sprouting out. Potatoes doing well. George is my best gardener. James taken with a violent toothache.

Troubles kept piling up. What could go wrong next?

April 22, 1842

Tuesday. Mrs. Winston died this morning. Newborn Winston boys failing. Dr. Thomas brought them to Pineridge Plantation for wet nurse. Not hopeful children will survive. Savannah fretful all day. Still fighting fever. I question Dr. Thomas's advice to keep John Milton from his mother. Tempy agrees with me. What am I to do? Spent night pacing the floor and praying for wisdom.

I found myself praying for them and I knew the end of the story.

April 23, 1842

Black Wednesday. Tragedy has struck Pineridge Plantation. The weakest Winston twin passed away from unexplained complications. Dr. Thomas was in attendance. Savannah and John Milton are showing signs of improvement. Lord, bear the sorrows of our neighbor, John Winston. Amen.

Brushing away the tears from my eyes, I closed the journal. Even the knowledge that all the people in the diary had died and been buried a long time ago held no comfort. Death sucks in every century. Camelot had vanished beneath the embers of the Civil War. The South would falter under the punishing blow from the North and would never be the same again.

****

Bradford hadn't called me back by the time I left for work Thursday morning, so I called and left another

148

message on his cell phone and on his voicemail at the police station. Dixieland Salon's front parking lot spilled over with cars when I arrived at eight to find my appointment book overflowing with old and a few new clients for which I was thankful since that left little time for drifting thoughts. Josiah's diary had dampened my spirits, and I found myself desperate to regain my buoyancy; even if it meant listening to outrageous gossip.

"Nothing like a possible scandal to coax the curious out of the woodwork," I told my sisters when I had stopped for a mid-morning snack while a client roasted under a hot dryer. "Reminds me of Scarlett's unfortunate demise in the facial room. The sightseers came in droves for a peek at us."

"Gossip is flying for sure," Billie Jo agreed as she grabbed one of my crackers and popped it into her mouth. "Mr. Whitehead said the grapevine's a fire about Barbara's secret love affair with the fire chief."

"Why that's absurd," Deena scoffed. "Chief Alderman is twice her age and is married to the sweetest woman in the world. Where do these people come up with this garbage? Next we'll be hearing that Jolene and Daddy hired a hit man to do Theo in."

"And there you have it. First question Mrs. Sullivan wanted to know when she sat down in my stylist chair this morning," I said with a laugh. "I told her we tried but couldn't find anyone who'd do it for a dollar."

"You shouldn't say things like that," Deena admonished. "Mrs. Sullivan is one of the biggest gossips in town and would love to get something started."

"Lighten up, sis," Billie Jo said. "Jolene's joshing."

Deena swiped a wet cloth across the kitchen counter. "But does Mrs. Sullivan know that?"

I nodded. "Yes, she does. We shared a good laugh and then she dropped a bombshell in my lap. Were you aware that Herrington threatened to foreclose on Pineridge Plantation?"

Deena frowned. "More absurd gossip."

"Not necessarily," I countered. "According to Nancy, Redding opened his home to tourists because of a financial downturn, remember?"

"Meaning the rumor could be true," Billie Jo concluded.

Deena's lips pursed. "Could you please tell me why we're having this conversation? I find it distasteful to discuss other people's business in such a casual manner. It's rude."

"That it is, dear sister. Habit, you know, part of the profession. Well, I need to see who's next on my book." I drank the last of my fruit juice, put my dirty glass in the sink, and headed back to my station.

I was finishing a haircut and blow dry on a new client when Bradford strode through the front door and came over to my station. The usual hubbub of conversation died down. Bradford and I were the center of attention.

Switching off the hairdryer, I said, "Give me a minute, will you?"

He nodded. "I'll be in Deena's office. It's important that I speak with you and your sisters."

His voice, though quiet, had a predictive quality which spurred me to action. I grabbed up a can of hairspray, doused my client's hair, and ripped off the cape. "You're all done, my dear."

Her expression told me she wasn't happy with the results of my labor, but followed me up to the reception desk without complaint and paid her bill.

"Can you stall my next client, Holly? Something's come up," I said hurriedly.

"I'll swap Mrs. Brown's appointment with you to Ellie. You can take her afterward."

"Thanks, Holly. I'll be in Deena's office if you need me."

Billie Jo and Deena were already seated when I went into the office and closed the door. Bradford, who sat facing Deena's desk, got up and drew me into a light embrace. Leaning my head against his, I inhaled the faint scent of woodsy aftershave.

"I'm sorry I haven't returned your calls, but I've been wrapped up in another homicide. Would you care to tell me why you called last night, or can it wait."

His dour tone and tense body language distracted me. Something bad had transpired or he wouldn't have requested this private meeting.

"It can wait," I said, disengaging my arms from around his neck. "What's wrong? Why did you need to speak with us?"

He pointed to a chair. "Perhaps you should sit down."

I sat down in the chair beside his. "What's going on? Has there been an accident? Becky? Hannah? Are Mama and Daddy okay?"

He held up a hand to silence me. "I'm not here about an accident, although I need to speak with your parents as soon as possible. I'm here about the Herrington case. The official cause of death is cardiac arrest brought on by anaphylactic shock as you know. However, peanut flour and oil were found in two of the entries. Officially that makes his death suspicious since peanuts were on the list of ingredients not allowed."

Anxiety spurted through me. Bradford hadn't said so, but I knew he wouldn't be here if the contaminated entries hadn't belonged to Dixieland Salon.

Deena nervously clasped her hands together. "I don't understand, Sam. Why are you telling us this? And why do you need to speak with Mama and Daddy? We have nothing to do with this whatsoever."

Billie Jo gave a short, desperate laugh. "I believe he's inferring that the offending peanut flour and oil was found in Dixieland's entries, aren't you?"

"Unfortunately, yes. I'm going to need y'all to come down to the station to answer additional questions. I thought perhaps you'd like to call your parents and have them meet us there. They'll take it better coming from you."

"This is déjà vu all over again," Deena exclaimed. "This is the second time we've been hauled downtown for questioning in a suspicious death that we had no part of."

"Then you know this interview is routine," Bradford informed her. "No accusations have been voiced. However, your official entries tested positive for peanuts. Accidental or purposely added to cause harm to the victim is the pending question."

I felt a stirring of concern. My tongue stuck to the roof of my dry mouth. Loose bits and pieces of recent conversations tossed and turned over in my mind, drawing a distorted picture of murder. The dreaded word raced around the frontal cortex of my brain like a greyhound chasing a mechanical rabbit on a fast Florida racetrack.

Well, here we go again. Another murder investigation. Bradford hadn't said those exact words, but he didn't have to. Either a death is natural or it's not. Unnatural deaths tend to point to premeditated planning on the part of an unscrupulous person or party, and the finger of the law pointed directly at us. There was more than a teaspoon of suspicion in a pecan pie laced with peanuts.

"Jolene, stop scowling at me. I'm not arresting you or your family."

Bradford's sharp voice startled me out of my ponderings. Before I could question the wisdom of my actions, I jumped to my feet and blurted out, "I know who killed Theo Herrington!"

"You can explain it to me on the way downtown, Jolene." Bradford picked up his cowboy hat from the desk, and settled it on his head. "Your family can meet us there. You're taking a ride with me. We're gonna have a private conversation so you can tell me what's on your mind."

****

The tranquil scene outside the car window contrasted with my stormy emotions. A family of ducks bobbed for insects on the green-brown surface stirred by a brisk fall breeze. Joggers dressed in sweats side-stepped seniors and mothers with baby strollers on the crowded dirt footpath. Mother Nature had swept through overnight splattering the fiery hues of sunset throughout the trees and flowering bushes hugging the trail.

Bradford turned off the ignition, fixing me in a blue-eyed vise. "What do you know about the

Herrington case?"

We were parked under a towering oak tree overlooking Joggers Pond. I swallowed the lump in my throat. Now that the time had come for me to explain myself, I felt the sting of guilt for ratting out Ellie and Ryan, but better them than my family.

"I overheard a suspicious conversation yesterday between Ellie and Ryan which led me to believe they conspired to kill his father so they could be together."

Bradford frowned. "What exactly made you jump to a conspiracy theory? Marital bliss was their motive?" He sighed. "They could've been discussing a number of things that you misconstrued."

"I didn't misconstrue anything," I snapped back. "I know what I heard. They were talking about killing someone. Ryan said, and I quote, 'I didn't plan to hurt him. Things kinda snowballed out of control'. And then, bam, Herrington bites the dust. Put the pieces together, Bradford. I witnessed Herrington offer Ellie a fortune to walk away from the relationship. When she refused, he threatened her. If they wanted to be together, Herrington had to go."

"Everything you told me is circumstantial and hearsay."

I gave him a withering glance. "Do you doubt me?"

"No. I believe you heard something. What, I don't know. But I am trying to caution you before you make an unsubstantiated claim that may backfire in your face."

"And yet in spite of everything I just told you, I'm the one on my way down to the police station. And how could you believe that any member of my family would have anything to do with murder?"

"You're the one screaming murder," he said with a sigh of impatience. "His death is suspicious, but the investigation is ongoing. Jolene, please get out of the way and let me do my job."

Gazing out the window at the happy passer-byes, I allowed the silence in the car to lengthen. Bradford made a strong argument. Why did I continue to be so obstinate? At first, even I'd believed the idea of Ellie and Ryan murdering Herrington to be preposterous.

My family coming under suspicion had changed everything, and I'd storm Heaven and earth to protect them. Although I trusted Bradford, in the recent past I'd tangled with Detective Larry Grant, a dirty cop with a nasty disposition. With that thought upmost in my mind I made the decision to keep silent about my investigation. Bradford didn't need to know all my secrets.

"Given that you're a detective—and a damn good one—I concede the argument," I said. "But only if you'll hear me out on a few other observations I've made."

"We've been down this road before. I distinctly remember a blackmailing incident connected with Scarlett's murder investigation. Look me in the eye and tell me you're not repeating that folly," he warned.

I gave him a quick, wicked grin in response. "That *folly,* as you love to remind me, my dear darling detective, led to many hours of heated debate"—here I paused, raking my eyes down his body suggestively—"between the sheets. Unfortunately for you, blackmail is not on my agenda today. But I do want you to read over the notes I made last night after careful consideration of the incident. I'm hoping they'll assist you in your investigation and clear my family of any wrongdoing in Herrington's death."

Bradford ran a finger down my cheek. "If I'm not buried in paperwork later tonight, I'll come over and we'll debate the use of metal or plastic handcuffs on resistant offenders. You've worn both so you should have good insight on the subject."

"I like the way you think, Detective."

"Now, where are these notes you want me to read?"

"At my house," I said.

"Okay, let's get going. I'll wait in the car so we don't waste time. And leave your gun at home."

The drive to my house passed without comment. When we pulled into the driveway I jumped out and ran inside to deposit Mini Pearl and retrieve the notebook from my bedroom nightstand. In less than five minutes we were back on our way downtown.

Bradford parked in his assigned space, and I followed him into the station and back to the interviewing rooms. He introduced me to Detective Timothy Goodwin and left with the notebook promising to return after copying the pages I'd marked.

Detective Goodwin pulled out a chair. "Have a seat and we'll get started."

Scooting my chair closer to the table, I studied the young detective seating himself across the table from me. His face was all American with a boyish smile that set one at ease upon meeting. The eyes were green behind wired glasses, and his carrot-colored hair was cropped short, military style. The freckles sprinkled across his nose were especially appealing.

"I'd like you to tell me about the evening of the thirteenth. Please start from your time of arrival at the fairgrounds until Mr. Herrington's collapse," he instructed.

I took a sip of water from the glass provided and considered the question. "We arrived at the fairgrounds around four. First, we registered and were shown our working space by one of the staff members. Then we set up and received the list of instructions from another contest staff member."

Detective Goodwin glanced up from his notes. "That's when you received notice of ingredients not to be used? Did you read over this list?"

I thought back and tried to recall the paper of instructions left on the counter. "No, I didn't read over the list. But I'm sure Mama did."

"Were you aware of the victim's allergy to peanuts?"

"No."

"Okay, what happened next?"

"Nancy Chance showed up with the judges and a photographer for a photo shoot."

"And then?"

"Well, Mama forgot to submit our recipe to the officials when we registered so we had to take care of it before we could start baking."

"And who would we be?"

"My mother and sisters and me."

"And where was your father at this time?"

"We left him guarding the kitchen."

"Guarding the kitchen? What do you mean?"

I took a quick sip of water. "Mama was afraid someone would sneak over and steal her fresh pecans."

"And what happened next?"

"Well, Mama was furious when we returned and found Daddy gone."

"Any idea how long was he away?"

"Daddy said he went to the men's room and was gone about ten minutes. He ran into Victor Redding and they had a chat. Anyone could have come along and sabotaged our containers. They were on the counter in plain sight."

"So your father was left alone with the ingredients for how long?"

"I don't like what you're suggesting, Detective."

"Just answer the question."

"We were away for approximately twenty minutes."

"Which left him plenty of time to plant the peanut flour and oil in the containers without anyone being aware of his actions. Is that a correct assumption?"

My quick temper flashed, but I took a couple of deep, calming breaths and relaxed back into the chair. It wouldn't do to lose my temper at his attempt to twist my words.

"Someone had lots of time to frame us, Detective."

He paused over his notepad. "What happened next?"

"Deena went to register the official name of our entry while we started baking. You know the rest."

He handed me his card. "I may have additional questions later so stay available."

Bradford waited for me outside the interrogation room. He handed back my notebook. "I agree with your observations—but you're not off the hook yet. Please stay out of trouble. I repeat, stay out of trouble."

"Your automatic assumption that I'll get into trouble stinks."

"I'm telling you to stay out of my investigation, Jolene." He held up the copied notes. "Snooping leads to trouble—especially where you're concerned. Promise me this ends it."

I noted his reasonable request, but I had no intention of following through. "I promise."

He chuckled. "You gave in way too easy to be sincere."

"Take it or leave it. That's the best I can do on short notice."

"I have a feeling this conversation is going to come back to haunt me." His easy voice lost its gentle tone.

Looking over his shoulder for any possible other-worldly visitants out for a willing mouthpiece, I murmured, "Better you than me, Bradford. Better you than me."

Chapter Fourteen
Kiss My Grits

Lunch turned out to be a sober affair. The fearful atmosphere in Deena's office rivaled the oppressive heat of Georgia summers, stripping us of our usual healthy appetites. Daddy nudged his untouched plate away and stood.

"What I don't understand is how peanut flour and oil got into those containers," he said in a troubled voice. "My God, they suspect we had a hand in Theo's death. I don't like it." He smacked a fist into an open palm like the crack of a small pistol.

"Stop pacing. Sit down and eat your lunch, Harland." Mama's voice was full of entreaty, but Daddy didn't listen.

"I'm not hungry, Annie Mae. You know I can't eat when trouble comes knocking on the door."

Shoving away my half-eaten sandwich, I pushed up from the cushy office chair and joined him at the window. "Mama's right. Come eat your lunch and stop worrying. We've got to trust that the police will get to the bottom of this mix-up."

I purposely left out my intention of digging into the mystery on my own, not wanting to add to my parents worry. As soon as we were alone, I fully intended to draft Deena and Billie Jo into my investigative team. Whether they liked it or not.

This not being my first murder mystery, I hoped my limited experience would see me through until I could get the hang of it again. And perhaps I could even convince Scarlett into lending me a hand. Would she take me on as a client? Hmmm. That thought deserved further consideration, but Daddy patted me on the arm effectively drawing back my attention to the pursuing conversation.

"Sam's a good man," he said. "But sometimes fate has a different plan."

"But we're innocent. We don't have anything to worry about," Billie Jo declared.

"Don't be so sure. Innocent men are sent to prison every day," Daddy said.

"Y'all are jumping to conclusions," Deena said from behind her desk. "Sam's on the case and that nice detective said they were questioning everybody in connection with the contest. We weren't the only ones brought down to the station."

Daddy's brows drew down in thought. "Deena honey, I'm sure your confidence is well placed in Sam Bradford, but I'm bothered by the fact that circumstantial evidence can and has convicted innocent men."

"That's enough, Harland," Mama blustered. "We've been through hard times before, and we'll come through this."

Daddy and I returned to our seats and resumed picking at our food. I peeked at the clock on Deena's desk. 12:45. Fifteen minutes before my next client. I needed to hatch out a few things with my sisters, but not until my parents were out of the way. I classified them as a need-to-know basis and this they didn't need to know.

"Theo's funeral is tomorrow morning. I expect the staff to be there," Mama said.

"Maybe we should allow them to skip it. A few of them haven't gotten over the last one we forced them to attend." Billie Jo shivered. "God, sometimes I still see Scarlett's body tumbling out of that overturned casket, her mangled face in full view."

The day from hell. Forever burned in my memory. Scarlett, unhappy with her funeral had shoved her former employer, Robert Burns and his wife Cherry into her casket—sending it crashing to the floor, top open and her body hanging halfway out. The place erupted in chaos and funeral-goers scattered like roaches on a Raid commercial.

I picked up my plate and threw it into the trash can. "Well, it's time to get back to work. Mama, don't you have dress rehearsal over at the theater this afternoon? And Daddy, I'm positive you need to spend a few practice hours on the green before the golf tournament in the morning."

"Let's go, woman." Daddy leapt to his feet and tugged on Mama's arm. "A few hours on the green will calm my rattled nerves."

Mama snatched her arm out of his grip. "Hold your horses, Harland. You're acting like a crazy man."

"You make me crazy, woman, with all that yapping, now come on. Daylight's a fadin'."

"And your brain's smoking with all that helium gas knocking against your skull."

Daddy's answering grin showed his unconcern for her punishing remark. "My truck is pulling out of the parking lot in one minute." He ambled over to the door, pulled it open with a flourish, and disappeared through the doorway.

Billie Jo gathered up plates off the desk and threw them into the trash can. "I swear to God, Mama, y'all need a referee."

It was on the tip of my tongue to order Billie Jo to shut up and let Mama follow in Daddy's wake, but thankfully I was spared the confrontation. Mama picked up her shoulder bag and smiled warmly at each of us.

"I'd better be moving on, girls. Your father is gunning the motor again. That old car of his is single-handedly responsible for enough greenhouse gases to melt the polar ice-caps."

In the background, I could indeed hear the racing engine outside the office window and it was with much relief I watched Mama hurry out the door.

"Well, now that they're gone, I need to confess that I'm concerned about this police investigation," Billie Jo said. "We don't have the best track record with the victim and somehow the incriminating evidence ended up in our lap."

"As am I," Deena added. "Sam didn't say so, but I could hear the concern when I spoke with him at the station. Jolene, did he give you any indication of his thoughts on this?"

"I'm glad you brought this up," I said. "I didn't want to discuss this in front Mama and Daddy for fear of upsetting them, but someone planted the peanut flour and oil in our containers. The question is who and why? I've already started looking for answers, but I'll need help."

"I believe you're meaning us." Deena frowned.

"Who else?" Billie Jo said. "It'll be a cinch. Like

last time."

"That's a lie and you know it," Deena proclaimed. "Definitely not a cinch, and if I remember correctly she swore off investigating after that. What changed your mind, Jolene?"

"The incriminating evidence showing up in our pies changed my mind," I retorted.

"And you've got to admit last time ended well," Billie Jo boasted. "Jolene bagged the killer and Bradford in one night with our help. I'm casting my lot with her. I thought you were looking for some action?"

"I don't think that's the action she was hoping for," I volunteered.

Deena hunched her shoulders. "Okay, I give up. What do you want us to do?"

"Same as last time," I cautioned. "Keep your mouths shut and your ears open for any information and then pass it along to me. I'll take it from there."

"And where am I supposed to glean this information?"

"Deena, we work in a beauty shop," Billie Jo squawked. "What better place to gather juicy information than Gossip Central?

****

As fate decreed, I was on my own for the last tour of the day out at Pineridge Plantation. Mama had called at the last minute needing Deena's assistance at the Riverside Theater, and Billie Jo had driven out to Westgate Country Club to meet Daddy for a short round of golf.

Luck continued to smile down on me as I ushered the last tourist out the front door and into the deepening twilight as Victor approached me from the back hallway.

"I have a meeting with the mayor in thirty minutes and mustn't be late. I hate to impose on you, but Mr. and Mrs. Turnipseed are out of the mansion and won't return until later tonight. Would it be possible for you to secure the house before you leave?"

I fingered Josiah's key in the pocket of my gown, delighting in my good fortune, and allowed a huge smile to light my face. As much as I could figure, I would have an hour or two of undisturbed snooping.

"It's no imposition at all," I replied in a light tone. "I'll be here for a while. I'm beginning my sweep of the house for any mishaps the tourists might've left behind. You go on ahead. I'll lock up when I leave."

He tipped his head. "Thank you and good night. Oh, and please turn off all the lights, but for the lights in the front foyer and the mud room."

I locked the door behind him and made a beeline for the downstairs formal dining room hoping the built-in china hutch might hold the treasure I sought. The pullout drawers yielded heavy antique silverware etched with the family crest, but no locked boxes. Among the drawers in the sideboard I found an Empire-style cake basket, a tray, and candlesnuffer, a hot-milk pitcher, and silver goblets.

The dining room was a bust, so I made for the front parlor with its marble-topped ladies desk and bookcase used by Savannah Redding. A sweep of the room brought me no closer to the prize and after several minutes of searching, I switched off the table lamps and left empty-handed.

The shadowy hallway, filled with the flickering golden glow of electric candlelight, gave me the heebie-jeebies as the mansion came to life. For a long moment, I listened to the house whisper to itself in creaks and groans and noises I couldn't place. The walls closed in with evil fiery eyes. Faint footfalls stirred just beyond my vision, and the hair on my arms stood on end as my heart beat in an ever increasing rhythm like the voodoo drums on a Caribbean island.

Just as the thought popped into my head, Scarlett appeared in a flash of bright light nearly accelerating my entrance into the mysterious hereafter. Fortunately for me, I'd emptied my bladder earlier so I didn't pee my pants like I did the last time she'd pulled this stunt.

"Damn your black soul," I screamed as she swooped down beside me. "You scared the hell out of me."

"I announced my arrival as requested," she said, frowning. "I know you heard my footsteps—I was watching."

"You were watching me? That's creepy, Scarlett."

She gave me an exasperated look. "Get over it, Claiborne. We're always watching. Now, enough about you. Josiah is anxious for a report, and I promised him I would speak with you before heading out for Purgatory."

"Speaking of Theo Herrington, I might need your services," I said with a still shaky voice. "The police found incriminating evidence in our pies, and we're now persons of interest."

"Are we talking murder here?"

I sighed. "Yes, I believe so. The killer used the contest as the perfect opportunity to frame us. I need your help. You owe me."

"What about that gorgeous detective you're

sleeping with? Don't trust him to handle it?"

The question came out of nowhere and I hesitated. Trust had been an issue I'd struggled with since my twelfth birthday and Daddy disappeared out of my life. As hard as I tried, I couldn't fully trust a man to handle my problems. Daddy's return brought hope that in time I would conquer this flaw and learn to let go. "Leave Bradford out of this. Please answer the question. Can I count on your help?"

"My plate is full at the time, but I'll see what I can find out for you. We do work well together. What's the rundown on Josiah's case?"

"There's not much to report. I'm reading the ledger and his journal." I held up the key. "That's what I'm doing, now, searching the mansion while everyone's out."

"I'll let you get back to it," she said, then vanished from sight.

Cautiously, I proceeded with my search of the downstairs. Room by room, I peered into every promising nook and cranny only to come up empty-handed. The ballroom at the back of the house turned up nothing, as did the upstairs chambers.

Up until now I'd been confident that with sufficient time I could solve the mystery of the antique key. Now, doubts settled in. My fingers ached from poking and prodding into tight places, and I was ready to give up—at least for tonight.

Wearily I trudged back downstairs and changed out of my period costume into my street clothes. Moonlight and indigo shadows greeted me when I stepped outside with the garment bag slung over one arm. I locked the back door and moved over to my car serenaded by the welcoming night sounds of crickets chirping, frogs singing, and a lone owl hooting from its perch in the trees. As I struggled to unlock the back passenger side door I noticed a small circle of light flash behind one of the storage sheds and then the distinct sound of digging.

That odd light and sudden scrape of metal against rock set alarm bells ringing as the newspapers regularly reported trespassers searching the plantation for its infamous buried gold. Last month a man had been arrested for digging up Victor's prize azaleas looking for the legendary treasure. Someone was at it again.

A quick survey of the area showed Victor's vacant parking space so I knew he'd left for his meeting with the mayor long ago. Moving quietly, I stashed the garment bag in my car, reached inside my purse for Mini Pearl, and snapped off the safety.

With my gun cradled securely in my hands, I approached the side of the house closest to the large wooden storage shed and peered into the shifting shadows. In the stillness of the November evening—a night where sound travels a long distance, I could tell the trespasser labored somewhere in the vicinity of the rose garden.

I pushed my way through the hedge of boxwoods lining the back terrace and silently picked my way through the trees.

Careful not to alert the offender of my presence, I covered the remaining distance to the garden at a snail's pace. Lucky for me the moon peeked out from behind a cloud, and I spotted the outline of a man standing in a waist-high hole. He took another shovel-full of dirt and threw it onto the growing pile, exposing his face to the muted light.

Kiss my grits. Victor Redding. Hmm. Interesting.

His presence out here in the night sparked a number of questions. If the Confederate gold had been recovered as he'd said, then what was he doing under the cover of darkness digging a hole—an enormous hole, I might add. Where's his car? Why hadn't he parked in his usual space? And why hadn't he alerted me of his return?

Crouched down low behind a leafy bush, I continued to watch his quirky behavior. Victor's heavy breathing spoke of his determination to complete his task. Every few seconds a smattering of swear words colored the twilight.

My curiosity grew with each mound of dirt—fairly certain he wasn't adding another rose bush to his garden. The other alternative? A grave. The hole appeared large enough to be a grave of some sort. I pictured the stray cats hanging around the plantation. I shook my head, awful big hole for a dead cat. What about a dog? Although I hadn't seen or heard one around the property, they could be here somewhere. And dogs die at some point. A plausible explanation.

For a while, I lingered in the lengthening darkness, watching and waiting, scarcely daring to breathe in fear of alerting him of my nearby presence. Reluctant to be caught spying, and dead on my feet, I backtracked to my car and drove home—unsettled by the odd nighttime activity I'd stumbled upon.

****

After a long, hot shower, I changed into my pajamas and padded into the kitchen, Tango meowing under my feet. Starving, but not in the mood to prepare a meal, I popped a frozen dinner in the microwave, put on the kettle for hot herbal tea, and fed the cat all in that order. While the kettle heated, I flipped on the television for background noise and settled down at the kitchen table with my notes, determined to find the real culprit and clear our name. Even with limited experience tracking down clues, I knew it wouldn't be easy. Murderers hated the light of truth, and wouldn't like being exposed. As a matter of fact, they could get downright nasty when confronted.

I know this because I've been in that uncomfortable position before when Scarlett's murderer decided to take me out of the picture. I wasn't anxious to repeat it since I've a real affection for breathing.

The microwave dinged signaling my supper had been nuked to perfection. Getting to my feet, I set the table for one, fixed my hot tea, and sat down. The buzz of the television filled the kitchen with the muffled sound of human voices, but as I picked up my fork, loneliness swept over me.

A knot rose in my throat as I thought about my dysfunctional relationship with Bradford. Mama's words came back to haunt me. "Jolene," she'd said, "you've got a lot of love to give if you'd open yourself to its beauty."

Disgusted with my train of thoughts, I wiped my eyes dry on my napkin, choked down my supper, and got up to load a sink full of dirty dishes into the dishwasher.

Afterward, I mulled over my notes. I then decided to call Billie Jo, hoping she'd heard some useful gossip at the salon. Roddy answered on the first ring.

"Hello," he sang into the receiver.

I smiled at his cheerful tone. In all the years he and

my sister had been married I'd only heard him mad once. And that was the other night at the pageant when Lynette lost her crown to Kandy Herrington. Billie Jo had enough temper for the both of them.

"Hey, Roddy, is Billie Jo there?"

"My better half is looking at guns online. I'll get her."

Billie Jo came on the line. "What's up, sis?"

"Anything to report?"

"Hold on," she said in a low voice. "Let me change phones. I don't want Roddy to know what we're doing. He's not terribly fond of me putting myself in danger."

"I wouldn't exactly say listening to gossip is putting you in danger. Your exposure to danger is minimal."

"Well, in case someone gets the big idea to cause us trouble, my new .357 Magnum should put a damper on their criminal pursuits. When it gets here, let's you and me go out to the shooting range and try it out."

Her upbeat attitude had me smiling and glad I'd called. "I'd like that, Billie Jo. Now, tell me about your afternoon. Overhear anything helpful?"

"Not a thing. I spent most of my afternoon fending off questions about our involvement. Several of my male clients even had the gall to thank me for having a hand in his demise."

"Did these clients volunteer a reason for their complaint with Theo?"

"No one's volunteering anything. Hey, listen, I gotta go. Roddy's hot on my trail. Talk to you in the morning."

I disconnected the line and dialed Deena's number. Perhaps she'd had better luck than Billie Jo. Helping out at the reception desk most of the day put her in the perfect position to overhear several conversations at once. She didn't answer so I left a message on her voice mail and put a load of wash into the dryer while waiting for her to return my call.

When the phone rang, I rushed out of the laundry room to answer it.

"I'm sorry I missed your call earlier, but I was talking to Bill," Deena said. "He hates to be put on hold for me to take another call. Is there a problem?"

I wanted to say yes, but my resistance to the match would only add fuel to the fire so I opted instead to address the main reason for my earlier call.

"Other than the one we discussed earlier, no. Billie Jo had no luck. Did you hear anything interesting at the salon this afternoon? About Herrington?"

"I heard plenty," she said. "Mostly speculation. Oh, and Rachel Wesley stopped by. She said she didn't get a chance to speak with us the other night out at the fairgrounds with all the commotion."

"I didn't see her there. I'm sorry I missed her."

"Her father insisted they attend. He said that with everything going on at his bank, he needed to be seen supporting community events. His professional image has taken a beating, she said. Talking with her reminded me of the pictures I took of the event."

That made me grin. "Maybe you captured something on film that'll help."

"You think so? With so many people milling about, I'll be surprised if I managed to capture the scum in action. And we weren't even close to the kitchen when the ingredients were planted in our containers. It could be anyone."

"Where's the camera now?" I wanted to know.

"In my desk at the salon where I normally keep it."

"Have you looked at the pictures?"

"No, I actually forgot about them, but I will first chance I have in the morning."

"We've got Theo's funeral in the morning," I reminded her.

"I could get dressed and drive over there now if you think it's important. Or I could send Daddy. I'm sure he wouldn't mind."

I glanced over at the wall clock. "No, it's late and I'm closer so I'll do it."

"No, you won't. The desk is locked and I'm the only one with a key."

"Shoot, I'd forgotten about the break-in last spring. Okay, it'll have to wait. Keep your eyes and ears open at the funeral. There's going to be a lot of emotional folks and that means loosened tongues. I don't want to miss a thing, understand?"

I hung up the phone and made a notation in my notes of Roger Wesley's presence at the bake-off. Not really suspicious of him, but unwilling to leave out any viable suspect, I added his name to my list of suspects. Under motive I listed 'possible hostile bank takeover by victim'.

Finally, at ten, I put away my notes, turned out the kitchen lights, and headed for my bedroom, Tango leading the way. Still too wired for sleep, I grabbed Josiah's ledger out of the bedside table and read several entries before I laid it aside and reached instead for his journal. It was the chronicle of his life that drew me. I opened the cracked and faded cover and began reading.

Chapter Fifteen
Those Stinking Secrets

May 30, 1842

Monday. John Milton is thriving after a slow start at birth. He's steadily gaining weight and cries so loud when Sophie is late with his meal I fear for his health. Dr. Thomas assures me he's in no danger of a relapse. Savannah's health is also improving, and I have high expectations for her complete recovery. The weather was exceedingly hot for spring—crops suffering for want of rain.

June 1, 1842

Wednesday. Had a visit from Dr. Thomas today. He brings sad news of John Winston. The man must sell his farm and return to Ohio where Mrs. Winston's family resides. Dr. Thomas is agreeable with my suggestion that I purchase Mr. Winston's farm. Winston is agreeable to my terms. Purchased 100 acres, house, barn, and livestock. Settled the matter for a goodly amount.

June 4, 1842

John Milton is to be christened in the morning. The plantation is bustling as we prepare for tomorrow's party. Butchered calf laid to fire. The manor house cleaned and aired for guests arriving today. Nance moving my things back into my room. Savannah and I will share a bed again. Tonight I have a special gift for her. A diamond necklace from a jeweler in Atlanta.

Glancing at the clock, I smothered a yawn. Eleven. No wonder my eyes stung with fatigue. I needed sleep, but I couldn't put down the fascinating journal—perhaps a few minutes more.

June 5, 1842

Sunday. Went to church. John Milton christened. Named Henry and Alice Major as the child's godparents. Savannah's happy and well. Friends and neighbors joined in our celebration. Slaves given a holiday. The Majors will stay on before returning home to Lingering Oaks.

June 10, 1842

Sold Winston farm and furnishings to Mr. Greenfield for goodly profit. Greenfield to take immediate possession. Meeting of the Agricultural Society in Whiskey Creek. Discussion of weather and new insect prevention methods.

June 28, 1842

Tuesday. The hottest day I've ever felt, almost perspired to death. Crops and livestock suffering. Slaves brought in from the fields from the heat. Prayed for rain.

July 4, 1842

Monday. A heavy cloud commenced rising in the west around noon—got heavier and heavier. When the heavens released its burden, I got down on my knees and gave thanks to the Lord. Randall is frightened of storms. Hope the boy grows out of that before too long. The house girl, Cassie delivered of two healthy twin girls this night.

I must have dozed. The shrill summons of the phone blasted the quiet of the bedroom, waking me, the journal still lying open on my lap.

Mama. What was she thinking calling me at 11:30? The lateness of the hour could only mean she was either angry or upset. I dreaded picking up the receiver, but she'd keep on calling until I answered.

"What's up?"

"I just got off the phone with Billie Jo, and she told me what y'all are up to." Her voice cracked with strain. "Would you care to explain?"

Blindsided, I paused to consider my response. Deena was the snitch in the family.

"I can hear you breathing so I know you're still on the line."

"Did Billie Jo tell you everything?"

"Now, how would I know that? I only know what she told me; mostly about your impromptu meeting this afternoon after Harland and I left. Is there more? Give it to me straight."

My mind shifted into overdrive. In reality, I'd only asked my sisters to pass along any information they happened upon. In danger, they weren't. Mama couldn't object to that.

"Okay, here's the deal," I said. "Someone framed us to take the fall for Herrington's murder, and I intend to gather whatever information I can find to help the police. That's all. I asked Deena and Billie Jo to listen out for any gossip they hear in the salon. And I'm worried about Daddy."

"Why are you worried about your father? He didn't have anything to do with Theo's death."

"Did you forget about the salon full of witnesses that heard him threaten Herrington Monday night? You've got to admit it doesn't look good with the incriminating evidence turning up in our entries. Daddy was there. Even the police believe he had opportunity. All they need is a motive and then he's their prime suspect."

"That's hogwash," she huffed. "Where are you coming up with this murder stuff? I have half a mind to call Sam and see what he thinks."

"Do that and you'll shut down my operation faster than the speed of light," I told her. "Bradford's already warned me to stay out of his investigation. Don't you understand, Mama? There's a chance, Daddy could go to prison for a crime he didn't commit. You heard him say that circumstantial evidence convicts innocent men every day."

"Accidental death hardly points to murder, Jolene."

"Mama, didn't you hear one word I said? Traces of peanuts turned up in our containers. Did you put it there? Daddy? Me? Or Deena? Billie Jo was upset about Lynette losing the crown to Herrington's granddaughter so she could be the culprit."

"Don't be silly."

I sighed. "I'm trying to make you see a point. We're under investigation. All of us, but Daddy seems to be the main person of interest. Detective Goodwin questioned me about Daddy's whereabouts during the bake-off. He asked questions I couldn't answer."

Her gasp of fear rang loud over the line. "Good Lord, Jolene. I never considered things could get so out of hand at a pie bake-off. Next time the police want to question us, I'm going to contact our family lawyer. We should have done so sooner."

"Good idea. Listen, I need to ask you a question— and be truthful with me."

"What is it?"

"What did Theo mean about Daddy trying to put him under six feet of Georgia clay?"

"It happened long ago. A practical joke Harland played on him back in high school."

"What happened?"

"It was a practical joke, Jolene."

"Tell me anyway. It may be important."

"Back then, Harland and Theo were best-friends, but highly competitive with one another. Harland and I were going steady, and Theo asked me to the senior prom. Harland found out about it and swore he'd get even. Everyone in school knew about Theo's allergy to peanuts, but we didn't give it much thought. Well, Harland bribed a friend to slip Theo a corndog fried in peanut oil. The prank backfired, and Theo ended up in the emergency room. When the truth came out, Harland was suspended and not allowed to attend the prom. There's been hard feelings between the two ever since."

My nerves tensed as the story unfolded. Didn't Mama see the similarity between the incident from high school and the one that killed Herrington? If the story leaked out the police were sure to zero in on Daddy. They might theorize that Daddy had been planning his revenge all these years and had waited for an opportunity to finish the job.

"Who else knows about this?"

"That's impossible to know, Jolene. I doubt anyone remembers the incident. Most of our classmates have either moved away or died."

"Listen to me, Mama. You've got to warn Daddy to keep this under wraps. Not even Bradford can know. And whatever you do, don't tell Deena and Billie Jo.

Neither one can keep a secret."

"I don't believe it's a good idea to keep this from Sam. He's family and would do everything in his power to help your daddy."

"He's the law first."

"You're making a mistake, Jolene. If Sam finds out you've kept this from him, you could lose him. Sometimes love isn't enough to hold two people together."

A volcano of emotions assaulted me. Who'd said anything about love? Those words had never been spoken between us. I told her good-night and hung up the phone.

I lay awake, my mind refusing to shut down. Like a broken record, over and over the day's conversations with Detective Goodwin, Bradford, my sisters, and Mama kept repeating. And how could I forget Scarlett returning from the dead—again, or Josiah with his mysterious key. I guess I could be thankful Theodore Herrington hadn't put in an appearance...yet.

****

When the alarm clock buzzed at seven, I hit the snooze button and drifted back into a fitful slumber. Tired and cranky from lack of sleep, I needed the extra ten minutes of shut-eye. I hit the button two more times before rolling out of bed at seven-thirty to dress and shower for Herrington's funeral.

For the solemn occasion, and because a mild cold front had finally pushed through, I chose a charcoal gray, cable knit, sweater dress with matching heels. With my hair pulled into a loose bun at the neck, and makeup covering my discolored skin, I went into the kitchen for a light breakfast.

Tango, ever on my heels, settled down with his bowl of Friskies, and me with a steaming cup of black coffee and an egg sandwich. The morning news spouted nothing but worldly disasters so I switched over to the country music channel.

The funeral would take place at nine, but I wanted an up close and personal view of the bereaved when she got there, so when my watch read eight-thirty, I collected my purse, set the security alarm, and drove the several blocks to the red brick funeral home and parked out front. From my vantage point I could see every vehicle and its occupants arrive.

Minutes later, a silver Lincoln Town car with attached funeral home flags pulled up to the front entrance. A balding man exited from the driver's side and rushed to open the back passenger side door. I recognized Barbara's platinum curls peeping from beneath the black-veiled hat when she emerged. Her sister exited from the opposite side, joining Barbara at the white-columned entrance.

Staying a few steps behind the balding man, whom Barbara clutched with damsel-in-distress drama, I followed them into the claustrophobic interior of the funeral home, pausing on the threshold to suck one last breath of living oxygen. From the shadows of an adjoining room, a tall, skinny man appeared at my side, nearly scaring the wits out of me.

"Pardon me, ma'am," he said in a deep voice. "To which party may I direct you?"

"You're throwing a party?" I joked to lighten the mood. "If you are, I'd like an Irish coffee, please. It's chilly out there."

His face broke into a friendly grin. "A party isn't

such a bad idea in my opinion, and this is a perfect day for Irish coffee. However, my boss is strictly Southern Baptist and spirits are forbidden in this establishment." He offered his arm. "You must be here for the Herrington service. His widow and sister-in-law have arrived."

Knowing what I do about the dead, I'd bet my last dollar the spirits of the dead took devilish delight in haunting these rooms until something better came along. I cut my eyes toward my left where a blue coffin with silver handles rested on a pedestal as its ghostly occupant poked her head through the top of the casket, waving at me.

"Oh, God," I whispered. "Stay dead, stay dead."

"Miss, is there a problem?"

Feeling a mite silly and wondering if I'd left my common sense and discretion at home, I allowed him to steer me into a large room to my right. I signed the visitor's registry and went over to the small area dedicated to a photo montage of Theo Herrington. Pictures at varying stages in his life were posted on the board—his graduation from Whiskey Creek High, a blown-up shot of his and Barbara's wedding on a tropical island. There was a candid shot of him with his young son, Ryan, playing ball in some forgotten backyard, and a recent shot of the banking icon hugging his granddaughter, Kandy, the newly crowned Miss Pecan Festival Queen. Amelia Herrington, Theo's first wife, and Ryan's mother who'd died of cancer three years ago had failed to make the cut. Not a photo of the gracious lady in sight. Bummer. She'd played a huge role in the man's life and deserved a spot on the board. Spoke a lot about wife number two.

I took a seat in the back of the room where I could watch without drawing attention to myself. Barbara and her sister stood at Herrington's open casket flanked by flowers of every color and arrangement. Nearby a connecting door opened and an impeccably dressed young man joined them. Even at this distance, as Barbara lifted the veil away from her face, I could see that she hadn't done much else but cry.

I was entertaining the thought of making my presence known when a pink vapor twisted into the shape of a woman on the chair beside me. With luck like mine, I should've figured Scarlett couldn't stay away after all the fun she'd had at her own funeral.

"What is that smell?" I sneezed into a tissue.

"Cotton candy perfume," she said. "Too much?"

"Yes. Keep your distance. I don't want it to rub off on me." My watery eyes roamed over her pale pink cotton blouse, pink jeans, and pink snakeskin boots. A pink western-styled hat perched on shining bronze curls. "Odd choice of clothing for a funeral," I whispered.

She leaned closer. "Actually, I dropped in on the request of the deceased since he's unable to attend himself. He wanted to be sure his wife hadn't buried him in a cheap coffin. As soon as I leave here, I'm going trail riding with Clark Gable. The Galaxy Mountains are beautiful on horseback this time of year."

Scarlett had a way of making death sound enjoyable. I'm not ready to take the plunge or anything, it's just that, well, as a young teenager, Wayne Radcliff had offered me a ride on his horse. After settling me in front of him in the saddle, I discovered he'd grown six more hands. That year I learned what it meant to be 'felt up'. Since then horseback riding triggers pleasant memories for me.

"Herrington will be happy to know she spared no expense," I said with a smile. "That fancy oak coffin he's resting in is super expensive."

I glanced up to see the widow and her entourage standing a few feet from where I sat, staring at me. I flushed at their shocked expressions. Damn. They heard my comment about the expensive coffin. Damn, Scarlett for making me crazy.

"Well, now that I can deliver a positive report, I'll be off to greener pastures." Scarlett snickered. And then, poof, like magic, she vanished in a pink cotton candy perfumed cloud.

The sound of voices broke our stunned silence as the group continued to stare in horror at me. I turned with relief when Mayor Kent and his wife walked into the room and up to the group.

"My condolences on your husband's death, Mrs. Herrington," the mayor said. "One of our finest citizens. Yes, his leadership will be missed by the business community."

With them occupied, I slipped out of the chair and into the crowd making their way through the double doors.

"Jolene. Over here."

Deena stood at the photo montage with William Mahoney, my parents, and Billie Jo.

"I thought we decided to meet outside," Deena accused when I joined them. "We got tired of waiting in the cold so we came on in. I saw Ellie arrive with Ryan and Kandy. And Ted is here somewhere. He remembered to wear a suit and tie, thank God."

"Sorry, I forgot," I said, half-listening, tilting my head from side to side hoping to get a better glimpse of the funeral-goers.

"Looks like a nice crowd," Daddy said. "The service is about to begin. Shall we go in?"

"What I don't understand is why the service is being held here and not in church," Mama complained. "And not to have a reception in her home afterward? I swear I've never heard of such a thing. No self-respecting Southerner would stand for such a disregard of manners."

"Barbara is a Northerner. I'm sure they do things differently up there," Daddy told her. "And don't forget Theo also hails from upstate New York. He didn't move here until his sophomore year of high school. And he wasn't a church going man, Annie Mae."

"That's no excuse for his widow not to feed the mourners, Harland."

Bill Mahoney appeared uncomfortable with the conversation. Good. Time for him to get an eyeful of what membership in this family entails. If the thought of engaging in pre-marital sex with Deena freaked him out, boy would he be in for a shock if he married her. We're not a tame bunch.

Billie Jo and I trailed after the others. I heard one snide remark about 'the audacity of some people showing up at the funeral of the man they offed'.

"Ignore them," Billie Jo advised as I turned around to confront the offender. "Where's Sam this morning? He's joining you, isn't he?"

"He's busy with the investigation," I said. "He'll show up at some point, I'm sure."

Nancy Chance threw me a discreet wave as we passed by her chair, but I didn't stop to speak with her. There'd be plenty of time after the service to mingle. Mama and Daddy found a row of empty seats several rows from the front. Deena sat with us while William moved up to the front row since he would be conducting the 'y'all gotta get saved' portion of the service. Too bad the deceased failed to acquire this mandatory license to paradise living, since every good Christian knows you can't 'be saved' after you kick the bucket. I spotted Bradford squeezed in between two burly police officers several rows in front of me. After the service he cornered me out in the hallway.

"There's a bright moon tonight," he whispered into my hair. "I thought we'd saddle the horses and have a late supper under the stars."

Desire almost fried my brain. "A midnight ride sounds wonderful. Can we ride double?"

"Won't you be uncomfortable sharing the saddle with me? I'm not a small man."

"I have experience with this sort of thing," I said with a smile. "Remind me to tell you about Wayne Radcliff and his horse, Scout."

****

After our steamy meeting of the minds, Bradford reluctantly headed back to the station, and I went to the salon where a full appointment book waited to test my concentration abilities after our sexual fantasy bonanza. I'd just slipped an apron over my sweater dress when Holly seated my first client in my stylist chair.

"Good morning, Mrs. Sanford," I greeted, draping her diminutive shoulders with a plastic shampoo cape. "I see you've finally decided to let me give you a relaxer."

Hattie Sanford, Ellie's great aunt, had been coming to Dixieland Salon for years. Seventy years young, and full of grit and spit-fire, she'd advised me from the first day she sat down in my chair. She filled the salon with sunshine with every visit, and I loved her for it.

"You're in for a tough mornin' with this rat's nest, Miss Jolene," she said. "Leroy thinks he's in love with a woman on the television set. That's why I'm here."

"I take it the woman had straight hair?"

"As a poker. The old fool wants to run his fingers through my hair before he meets Jesus—his words. I'm a grantin' his last wish."

As I worked, time flew as Hattie entertained me up with stories of her fifty plus years of marriage to Leroy Sanford. If couples cultivated their marriages as they had, divorce would be wiped out and lawyers would have more time for their own families. I was finishing up with her chemical straightener when Hattie spoke up.

"Miss Jolene, I've got somethin' on my mind and I'd like to air it out with you if you don't mind," she said. "This thing's been buggin' me since Ellie took up with that Herrington boy."

I squirted conditioner on the section of hair in my hand. "He's hardly a boy, Hattie. Ryan's my age, and I'm hovering close to, well, I won't mention any numbers, but thirty-five is in the rearview mirror."

"Ellie's older than you, but she's still my niece's baby girl." She caught my eye in the mirror. "I've got a bad feelin' that she's gonna get hurt by that white boy."

I applied the hot iron to the last section of her hair, replaying Wednesday's conversation in my mind. Had

Ryan pressured Ellie into helping him commit murder? Did Hattie know about the conspiracy? Highly unlikely. Hattie, being deeply religious, wouldn't step over certain moral boundaries.

"Your face says it all, Miss Jolene. I'm sorry I said anything. I'll keep my own counsel."

"Oh no, Hattie," I said, not wanting to miss any information she might have, however minor. "Ellie's like family. I want to know if she's in trouble."

Hattie lowered her voice. "Now mind you, I'm not prejudiced when I say that Herrington is white and rich. But ever since Ellie took up with him, she's changed. And the past couple of days, they's been acting strange. Whispering with their heads together until you come into the room and then they scamper apart like they's don't want you to know what they's whisperin' about. Strange actin', that's what it is. Like they's got a secret. I don't like it one bit."

"Auntie, what nonsense are you spreading?"

I jumped at Ellie's outraged voice and nearly dropped the flat iron.

Hattie slumped down in the chair. "I'm concerned about you." Her voice cracked.

"Ellie, don't be mad," I butted in. "This misunderstanding is my fault. I pushed her to tell me what's bothering her."

Ellie snapped at her aunt. "You're just one more voice against us. I told Ryan it wasn't over. I'd better not hear that you've been talking to the police."

Stylists and patrons alike stopped to stare at us, but I didn't intercede between the two. The girl had something on her mind. Written all over her face. Overreacting big time. Not grief—she had no more love for Theo Herrington than I did. Guilt could produce anger. So could resentment. So could a lot of other issues I could name.

"You're holdin' a hard spirit, child," Hattie said. "We're family and we stick together. You remember that. But it ain't like you to raise a breeze in your workplace. Come tell me what's got you actin' this way." She got up from the chair and opened her arms wide.

Ellie's face crumpled, and Hattie caught her in a tight embrace. With so many prying eyes, I finally interceded. They needed privacy and Ellie was after all an employee. After removing the cape from Hattie's shoulders, I led them to the unused facial room, and closed the door behind them.

Deena motioned to me from the door of her office. "What's going on?"

"Ellie had a meltdown when she overheard a conversation between me and her aunt," I said when I joined her. "Hattie said Ellie and Ryan have been acting strange—like they're covering something up. Ellie misunderstood. Could be the stress getting to her. It's getting to me."

Deena closed the office door and sat down at her desk. "We're always stressed out. Tell me, how'd you get Ellie into the facial room? You know, she won't step foot in there since she learned a client died there. She says it's haunted. Nothing but nonsense, but she refuses to listen. We need to put some thought into utilizing that space. With Carla gone, we're losing money on an empty room."

Our former aesthetician, Carla Moody, had quit shortly after she'd unwittingly played a hand in

Scarlett's murder. Last we'd heard from her, she had moved to Hollywood. Taking acting lessons. Oh well, good luck to her.

I slid into the chair across from Deena. "It'll keep for now. We need to concentrate on proving our innocence. Have you had a chance to download those bake-off pictures?"

"Not yet, it seems I've misplaced the camera."

"Deena, we need those pictures. There might be something on them to help in the investigation."

"Give me time. It didn't walk out of here on its own." Her intercom buzzed. "What is it, Holly?"

"Nancy Chance is looking for you guys."

"Send her in... Oh, and Holly, is Ellie back at her station yet?"

"Not yet. Her next client is here. As is Miz Claiborne's."

"Send Nancy in, Holly, and prep Jolene's client. She'll be out shortly."

The office door opened and Nancy came in.

"I'm sorry I missed you at the funeral, but you'd already left when I broke free of Mr. Redding." She took the other chair across Deena's desk. "I have some exciting news to share with you. Where's Billie Jo?"

"Westgate Country Club with Daddy for the golf tournament. His caddy got sick so she volunteered." I laughed. "She doesn't know squat about golf or golf clubs."

"Poor Daddy had his heart set on winning too," Deena added with a laugh.

"Well, I guess you'll have to break the news to her later," Nancy said. "Mr. Redding has decided to keep Pineridge Plantation open for tourism for the foreseeable future. He's asked me to retain the volunteers until permanent tour guides can be hired." She clapped her hands. "Isn't this great news?"

Deena and I glanced at one another and then back at Nancy. Her face beamed enthusiasm.

"You'll stay on, right? The three of you are the best guides I have," she said. "Victor has great things to say about you, Jolene."

That surprised me. The few times I'd bumped into him, I'd been snooping around his house searching for clues to solve a hundred and fifty-year old mystery, or swiping historical objects from him. To help his ancestor, I might add, but he didn't know that. This news afforded me the extra time I needed to figure this out.

"We'll be happy to help out," I said.

"But only until he's hired replacements," Deena piped in. "We have a salon to run."

"Victor will be appreciative of any time you can give him. He's a businessman and understands your position," Nancy boasted. "As a matter of fact, he told me this morning that he's expanding the estate to include horse-breeding. Thoroughbreds, I believe."

"I don't understand," I said. "I thought the place was in the red. You yourself said so. That's the reason he opened it up to tourists—to help with the cost of the place."

Nancy nodded. "All true."

"Then where is he getting the money for this expansion?" Deena asked. "Stables and quality breeding stock won't come cheap. I can imagine it would cost upward of a quarter of a million dollars, or more."

Nancy smiled broadly. "He found an investor."

"Did he happen to name this investor?" I wanted to know.

"I didn't ask," she replied.

"Rumor has Theo Herrington's bank is foreclosing on the property," Deena said.

"And there's one going around that y'all killed Herrington, and we all know that's not true," Nancy countered.

Nancy left after promising to see us tomorrow at Pineridge Plantation for the re-enactment battle for Piper's Gold. Deena promised to continue her search for the digital camera. Hours later with no luck, she gave up the search. The camera had disappeared from the salon.

Chapter Sixteen
A Rose by any Other Name

When I arrived out at Pineridge Plantation later
that afternoon, I surveyed my surroundings with new
eyes. Pulling my car off to the side of the dirt driveway,
I noticed for the first time a general air of shabbiness
about the place. The wide expanse of landscape needed
maintenance. Overgrown flower bushes and trees
dotted the garden, and the magnificent house seemed to
crouch in shame of the peeling paint falling like snow
from its lofty heights.

Armed with the knowledge of Victor's monetary
windfall, I envisioned the plantation coming alive with
clean, precise gardens, a fresh coat of white paint on the
main house, a paved driveway, and new buildings in the
back acreage, white picket fences, and green pastures
overflowing with fat, sleek, horses. A dream come true
for Victor and, I for one, felt happy the plantation
would become a working farm once again.

A romantic mood had settled over me when I
finally pulled onto the crowded parking area at the back
of the house. Increased activity from the re-enactors
arriving could be heard as I climbed out of my car.
Leaving my garment bag and purse in the back seat, I
followed the sounds around past the back terrace and
into the rose garden.

Automatically, I gravitated to the spot where I'd

seen Victor digging the other night. Instead of a grave marker as one would expect when burying a beloved pet, a fully-grown rose bush had been planted in the spot. If I hadn't known exactly where to look, I'd never believed the plant hadn't been there for years. New red mulch had been scattered around the base of the plant giving the ground an undisturbed appearance. Puzzled by this development, I studied the other plants. With the toe of my shoe, I pushed away the mulch to discover freshly turned earth. Not being a gardener, I rationalized that there had to be a reasonable explanation for Victor working in his rose garden after dark. It was his property after all and none of my business.

Captured by the shouts of men, I picked my way to the far reaches of the garden and saw what appeared to be a soldiers' camp being erected in a neighboring grove of pecan trees by a dozen men or more in Confederate uniforms. Small white tents with burning campfires sprang up one by one as I stood watching behind a screen of rosebushes. There were no women in the camp, only men, and I could hear horses whinnying nearby.

I cast a quick glance at my shoes. Although I wanted to check out a true-life representation of a Civil War camp, my heels wouldn't fare well in the terrain. Making a mental note to bring an old pair of walking shoes to the reenactment tomorrow, I took one more sweeping survey around the camp, turned around to make my way back to the house, and screamed as a man stood in full Confederate uniform with a realistic-looking sword drawn and pointed at my chest.

"Mr. Redding, you scared the life out of me," I

accused. "I heard all the commotion and decided to take a peek. I'm not trespassing, am I?"

Victor sheathed his sword. "Women aren't allowed back here until tomorrow. Please respect the rules and stay away. Come, I'll escort you back to the house."

I turned to follow him back to the mansion when a half a dozen men in Union and Confederate uniforms burst through the bushes further startling me.

"We heard a woman scream." The man had a scraggily beard and roaming beady eyes.

"Everything is under control Corporal Rainey," Victor said. "Return to your duties."

The man saluted. "Very well, Major Piper." He turned to his men. "Men, we have a camp to set up. Sunset comes fast this time of the year."

I remained silent until the men disappeared back through the hedge. Time to fish for some much needed answers. "So you're playing the role of Major Piper? I figured you'd want to portray your esteemed ancestor."

A smile lifted the corners of his lips. "Ah, but I wanted to be dashing on the back of a horse, dear lady, in the uniform of the Confederacy. An honor for a Southern gentleman, I assure you. Samuel Bradford is playing the part of Josiah Redding."

"Yes, I'm aware of his part."

Placing my hand in the crook of his arm, he steered me back to the center of the garden, pointing to various varieties of roses, careful to explain how each came by their name and how the recent warm spell allowed them to bloom into November.

Our genteel stroll ended directly in front of the rosebush I'd been nosing around earlier. "This is a special rose," he said. "My mother planted it on the west side of the house thirty years ago."

"It looks like it's been here forever," I said, bewildered by his behavior. Why were we strolling in his rose garden like this was an everyday occurrence? And why point out this particular rose?

"Looks can be deceiving, Miz Claiborne. To the untrained eye, the plant looks healthy, but fools digging for Piper's gold damaged the root system. I transplanted it here with the others. The soil is richer and will have a better chance to survive. The weak must be pruned back so the strong can survive."

That sounded suspiciously like a cryptic message. Looks can be deceiving? The weak must be pruned back? A subtle warning to watch my step? I didn't think so. Victor Redding impressed me as the type of man who spoke his mind. A man who didn't beat around the bush with a small stick.

He patted me on the arm. "I can be such a bore when it comes to horticulture, dear lady. I never had children and I tend to lavish my attention on my roses."

I fingered a limp leaf. "It's not that I'm uninterested, but twice now, you've mentioned the gold's recovery. If trespassers are destroying your property, I'm curious to know why you perpetuate the rumor of its existence."

"Simple, Miz Claiborne. Tourists flock to the most mysterious sites. They want to experience the thrill of the unknown. They want to fantasize about finding lost riches. Without the legend of lost gold, the place is another relic from the past. Come let's get you back to the house. There's lots of work to be done before the battle and costume ball tomorrow."

Victor left me at the back parking area and

disappeared back the way we'd come. I proceeded to my car to retrieve my belongings. When I opened the back passenger door, I spied my purse lying on the floorboard, contents strewn around it.

All but Mini Pearl. While I'd been gone those ten minutes, someone had emptied my wallet and stolen my gun.

****

Mini Pearl's disappearance sent me into a major cussing tantrum. That's how Deena found me, I'm ashamed to admit. When she ran up to my car I was scrambling around in the back seat searching for my cell phone so I could call the sheriff's office to report the theft.

"Jolene, what's the matter?"

I backed out of the back seat with my cell phone in hand. "Someone broke into my car. I have to report this to the police."

"Sam arrived a few minutes ago. He'll know who to call."

Grabbing my purse and the garment bag, I followed her into the house. We found Bradford in the library with Nancy. A series of books were spread on the large desk. They stopped their work when we entered.

"Jolene, what's wrong?" Bradford asked with concern.

"Someone broke into my car. My money and gun were taken."

"A thief? Here?" Nancy's tone of voice echoed Bradford's. "The place is crawling with strangers, but the re-enactors have a strong moral code. I doubt one of them would've broken into a car to steal a gun. Not when they have their own."

"Nancy's right," Bradford said. "I know most of those men out there. I suspect a drifter happened by and found an easy target. Pineridge Plantation is out of my jurisdiction, but a couple of sheriff deputies arrived about the same time as I did. I'll give them a call and have one of them come up here and take an incident report."

"Jolene, we can change into our costumes while you wait for the deputy," Deena said. "The next tour starts in fifteen minutes. I can handle it alone until you rejoin the group."

With everyone in agreement, Deena and I changed into our period gowns. Deena went to meet the tourists, and I returned to the library. Nancy was still at the desk when I stepped in. Bradford was in deep conversation with one of the men I'd seen earlier at the makeshift camp. The deputy took down the information, warning me not leave my car unlocked in the future, and excused himself with a quick handshake with Bradford.

"I'll leave you two alone," I told them. "You have research to do on the re-enactment and Deena will be wondering what's taking me so long."

Bradford escorted me to the door. "Is seven okay to pick you up for our ride? I've got some paperwork at the station after I finish here." He dropped a kiss on my forehead.

"Seven's fine."

The buzz of excited voices led me upstairs to one of the many guest rooms where I found Deena pointing out the intricate stitches reputedly hand-sewn by slave women on the colorful patchwork quilt spread across the polished mahogany four-poster bed. The personal items left by some long ago visitor rested untouched on the dresser and night table.

For the rest of the afternoon, Deena and I shuffled tourists around the mansion and by the time four rolled around I was ready to call it a day, and lose the tight bodice. Deena, needed back at the salon, ducked out, leaving me to conduct the last tour which I did in record time. Grumbled complaints were muttered as I closed the front door behind the last tourist.

Silence blanketed the mansion as I leaned against the door, breathing in the contentment of finally being alone. My parched and scratchy throat begged for water so I headed for the kitchen.

Mrs. Turnipseed wasn't around so I found a glass in the cabinet and filled it from the tap. Refreshed, I rechecked each room on the ground floor for trash or debris left by the tourists. When I reached the library, it too was empty. Nancy and Bradford had returned the books to the shelves before leaving. Not a creature was stirring, not even a ghost or two. Amused with my parody, I rushed upstairs, ready to finish and go home and shower before my date.

Scarlett ambushed me on the top landing. "Whatever it is, it'll have to wait until tomorrow," I said. "I'm tired and wanna go home."

"You do appear haggard. Perhaps a rejuvenating facial would ease the puffiness around your black eyes."

"Knock it off, Scarlett. I'm not in the mood. What do you want?"

"Josiah thought you might want to poke through some old trunks in the attic. He and I stumbled upon them while we were waiting for the house to empty."

I heaved a sigh, not enthusiastic with the prospect of entering a dirty storeroom, but it wouldn't hurt to take a look. Attics were notorious hiding places. Every generation piled their junk up there. No stone unturned, even if it meant wading through years of dust and possibly encountering spiders. FYI—I hate spiders. "Okay, but I don't have a lot of time."

I shivered with dread, but followed her up to the third floor anyway. The door creaked open on its own and the waning afternoon sunlight filtering through the fan-shaped windows cast eerie shadows across the room. The overhead light fixture gave out a small amount of light, and I could see boxes stacked high upon each other. Dressers, wardrobes, and chairs piled with indiscernible objects, made navigating the small path in the bulky gown tiresome.

"I should've changed my clothes before attempting this," I told an amused Scarlett, who watched from her perch atop a wardrobe.

"Josiah said the trunks he wants searched are in the corner over there."

Squinting to better peer into the corner where she pointed, I cautiously picked my way around discarded toys, broken furniture, and musty clothes. The farther back I traveled into the attic, the older the junk. Each layer represented another happy generation of Redding's. If my assumption proved correct, the objects against the back wall had to be from Josiah and Savannah's time. Too bad Victor had never married and produced offspring. His layer of junk wouldn't make a dent in this accumulation.

"Where is Josiah? I can smell his cigar."

Scarlett floated over my head. "He's here

somewhere. Oh, there he is. Looking at that portrait against the wall."

Josiah acknowledged my presence with a brief nod, and I returned the gesture. Making my way around the junk, I finally maneuvered my bulky frame close to the trunks and lifted the lid. On top were musty old newspapers which smelled bad. The one on top dated back to December, 1864, the timeframe of Sherman's march to the sea. The ones underneath were hometown news of Confederate soldiers home on leave. The Redding name caught my eye so I dug them out, placing them with the one giving a firsthand account of the Union general's raid. I would return them in a couple of days along with everything else stashed at home.

Curious at what I might discover, I dug through several layers of men's clothing until I glimpsed a square metallic box at the bottom of the trunk. I reached for it, but snatched my hands back as if scorched when I heard my name being called.

"Jolene, are you up there?" It sounded a second time.

Crap. Nancy Chance.

Footsteps echoed on the hardwood floor. Now what to do? No way could I sneak past her with old, musty newspapers stuffed inside my dress. She'd hear, and smell me coming a mile away.

Could the box in the bottom of the trunk possibly be what I'd been searching for? For the first time, I felt positive about solving the riddle. If only Nancy hadn't returned!

Scarlett hovered over the open trunk. "Would you like me to get rid of her?"

"How do you propose to accomplish that? Nancy's never perceived you before."

"I'm getting the hang of it. At least let me try. I need the practice."

"Bad idea. Your stunt could spook Victor, and he might close down the house if he suspected something." I began stuffing the contents back into the trunk. "No, I'll have to retrieve the box, and the newspapers, later."

Josiah finally joined us. He had a few words with Scarlett then vanished through the floor.

"Tonight will be a good time for you to return," she said. "Victor's bunking out with his men in the encampment. The staff has the night off so you'll have the mansion to yourself."

"I don't know, Scarlett. I don't like being here without permission."

"Poppycock. A small matter. Besides, Josiah and I will keep a sharp lookout in case someone returns. I won't let anything happen to you."

"I've heard that before."

"Instead of rehashing the past, you'd better make up your mind. Nancy is closing in on your whereabouts. If you hurry you can lose her."

I needed no further prodding. "You'd better not let me down this time, Scarlett. Midnight at the back door. Be there."

Chapter Seventeen
The Night-Owl Belle

"Jolene, what are you doing?"

"If you have to ask then I'm doing it wrong." I breathed into Bradford's ear, my hands roaming intimately over his chest before slipping inside his unbuttoned shirt. "You're supposed to be enjoying this, not asking silly questions."

"We're on the back of a horse, and I'm limited in my response. I'm enjoying it, honey, it's just I think I'd have a better time if I was the one in back and my hands were wrapped around you instead of these reins."

His breathing quickened as the horse's gait jolted, plastering my amble boobs tight against his back. I freed one hand from his shirt to unfasten his belt buckle and zipper. "Shut up and enjoy it, Bradford. I've been thinking about what I'm going to do to you all day," I teased as my hand slid lower.

He gasped. "Holy moly, your hand is cold."

"I could blow on it or perhaps I could employ the old tennis ball in the hand trick." I applied pressure. "The repeated squeezing and releasing strengthens the muscles, and increases heat, wouldn't you agree?"

In my excitement I must've squeezed too hard. Bradford let out a yelp, gripped my hand, causing me to scream in surprise and tighten my hold. The horse, spooked by all the activity on his back, took off through the dark like a coon hound on the scent of injured game. I lost my hold on Bradford, and the saddle, and landed hard on the soft forest floor.

As I lay gazing up at the star-filled night through the swaying tree limbs, I swore off horseback riding forever. As God as my witness, I'd never climb on the back of that beast again. I tried to raise my hand to solidify the promise, but it hurt too damn much to move.

That's how Bradford found me several minutes later. Sprawled out like a fileted fish on a cutting board. Even the sound of approaching hoof-beats didn't get a rise out of me. I just lay there in my pine needle bed listening to the forest sounds around me and wondering how high my health insurance premiums were going to jump after tonight's trip to the emergency room.

Bradford knelt at my side, his hands roaming over me, probing and feeling for broken bones. My pleasure meter blipped a few times so maybe I wasn't as hurt as I'd first imagined.

"Are you hurt, sweetheart? Can you move your fingers and toes?"

His deep-timbered voice coaxed me to try. "Yes," I said, flexing my limbs. "Can you help me sit up? I believe something is crawling up my pant leg."

"Slowly," he directed.

With his arms supporting my back, I sat up, and then climbed to my feet, my head spinning with the effort. Bradford swung me up into his arms and carried me over to where General Lee stood tied to a small tree.

"Put your foot in the stirrup, honey."

"No way I'm getting back on that horse," I told him as he lifted me up to the saddle, which wasn't an easy feat seeing how I'm…uh, not skinny.

"You need to be checked out by a doctor, and we're a good distance from my barn. You have to ride back. It's too far to walk."

"Put me down. There's a bug crawling up my leg." I squirmed around in his arms, trying to dislodge it.

Bradford lowered me to my feet. Thankfully, the dizziness had subsided and I was able to stand still as he ran his hands up my leg in search of my creepy crawler.

"A Palmetto bug." He opened his hand to release the large roach he'd captured mid-way up my calf. "Now can we get you to a doctor?"

"No. I'm fine and want to stay. We haven't had our supper under the stars."

"The picnic basket is gone. General Lee bucked it off right after you. Whatever possessed you to squeeze me so hard?"

"It's a long story, Bradford. Remember this morning when I mentioned Wayne Radcliff and his horse, Scout? Well, this is their fault—kind of."

"Give me the shortened version."

So I did.

He untied General Lee's reins from the nearby tree. "Baby, let me show you how to do it correctly."

Under the canopy of moonlight, the night came alive, and I found myself spellbound by his wolfish grin. One suggestive smile from a fine-looking man in tight jeans and a cowboy hat had me breaking my promise.

That night I learned things on General Lee's back that had me hankering for a horse of my own, but all good things must come to an end and soon we turned back in the direction from which we'd started.

After fifteen minutes of further riding, the barn came into view. We dismounted and Bradford led General Lee inside. I waited outside on a bale of hay in the cool evening air reliving every delicious detail of our satisfying ride as he bedded down the horse for the night.

"Can you stay over?" he asked when he emerged from the dark barn a couple of minutes later.

I thought about my midnight rendezvous with my ghostly partners and shook my head. "Not tonight. I need to be at the salon early if I want to get finished in time for the re-enactment battle."

Bradford remained quiet on our ride into town. His small ranch on the outskirts of town was a good distance from my house on Pinecone Lane so after about five minutes of silence I got antsy.

"I take it you've got something on your mind? If so, spit it out," I finally said.

He reached across the seat for my hand. "I'm thinking about tomorrow."

"Are you nervous about portraying Josiah Redding?"

"No. Nancy and I spent a lot of time going over the accounts of the incident over the past weeks so I have a good feel for the part. The Redding library contains numerous histories written by the descendants of John Redding. He was the only member of the family to survive the war. Can you imagine such a loss of life in one family? And the tragedy repeated throughout many families in the South."

I knew all this, but he needed to talk and I to listen. Leaning back in the seat, I allowed his voice to wash over me.

"Those histories recount fascinating personal stories passed down through the years. I'm not sure I believe it entirely though. Most of it is family hearsay, and as a detective I can attest to the fallacy of a person's memory. Nancy mentioned a diary supposedly written by Josiah Redding around that time period, but we were unable to locate it. Too bad, a personal account leading up to the battle would be an invaluable tool in deciphering the truth."

I knew he referred to the diary stashed in my nightstand along with the plantation ledger I'd snatched, but it couldn't be helped. I would confess to my crime at the right time and not before. "Victor believes the history suggests Tempy betrayed his family."

"There's not enough evidence to draw a conclusion about her from what I've read. There was a spy in the household, but no one will ever know who tipped off the enemy about the gold. History can't be changed."

"Do you remember ever reading about the gold's recovery?"

He stopped for a traffic light. "You know, I do recall reading an article about Piper's gold, but that was years ago. They didn't mention the gold's recovery. Why do you ask?"

"Because Victor claims the gold's been found. I don't buy it. If it's true, then why doesn't he publicize it and stop all the trespassing on his property? But what if the gold hasn't been recovered and he's searching for it? That means there's a fortune buried out there."

Bradford shot me a frown. "Please tell me you're not searching for the gold. Redding won't be happy if you are. Hell, I won't be happy if you are. Don't go looking for more trouble."

"Calm down, King Kong. I'm not searching for gold. All I'm saying is I don't like lying to the public if I don't have to. And another thing, some trespasser looking for treasure stole my gun. What if Mini Pearl is used in the commission of a crime? My fingerprints are all over it. What then? I'm in deep doodoo, that's what."

"Now you're the one that needs to calm down. You're exaggerating."

We turned onto Dalton Road. We'd be at my house in a few minutes. The bright streetlights highlighted Bradford's serious face as we pulled into my driveway and parked.

"There's something I've been meaning to talk with you about, Jolene, but I got distracted."

I smiled to lighten the mood. "You're welcome."

He reached for my hand. "It's about the Herrington case."

"That's what's been bugging you. Give it to me straight up, Bradford."

"We're closing in on two persons of interest. An arrest is coming soon."

"And one of them is Daddy."

He swore softly. "I hate this part of my job. But yes, your father is a strong suspect. Better prepare your family for what's coming."

"But Daddy's innocent. Surely you don't believe he's a killer?"

His expression didn't falter. "Can't you trust me to do my job?"

Little pricks of unease danced up and down my

spine. Trust—a five letter word still haunting me to date. Perhaps the powers that be up there in the wide blue yonder were sending me a message to take a leap of faith and trust Bradford with Daddy's secret. Mama had wanted to tell him right from the start, but I'd warned her not to. Now, I balked at confession. I had a demon on my tail and no way of shaking him off.

****

Once inside, I wasted no time and changed into all black—jeans, T-shirt, and sneakers. Sweeping aside my mounting fears for Daddy's safety, I wrapped my braided hair coronet style around my head and secured it out of the way with bobby pins.

11:17. No time to spare. With car keys in hand, I headed out the door, fired up my Mustang, and backed out of the driveway. The non-existent traffic guaranteed a speedy trip to the plantation, and I arrived without incident. As soon as I turned onto the dirt driveway leading up to the mansion I killed the headlights and parked in the dense shadows of the tree line.

The mansion loomed dark, but for a few pinpoints of light from the downstairs windows. Muted masculine voices carried on the cool fall breeze from the direction of the re-enactors encampment. Sending a prayer heavenward that Victor and the Turnipseeds were still away, I made my away around the mansion to the back door. Slipping my key into the lock, I turned it, and bolted through into the adjacent mudroom.

My pent-up breath released in a whoosh. Plastering myself against the wall, I waited until my eyes adjusted to the semi-darkness. Out of the corner of my eye, I caught movement. Tempy stared at me from the threshold leading into the old kitchen.

"There be no peace here on this night."

I quaked inwardly from the psychic vibrations surrounding me, and the old slave woman's appearance hadn't helped matters. Spirits from past generations materialized through the walls and floor, surrounding me.

"Back off," I croaked, making the sign of the cross with my fingers. "Scarlett, get your ass down here like you promised."

As usual she failed to appear, but thankfully the *Others* faded back into the walls and floor from which they'd come. Spooked as General Lee, and poised to take flight, I flipped on my small flashlight and tip-toed into the kitchen, and then out into the main part of the house, stopping every few steps to listen for any signs of human life. Satisfied that I was the only living inhabitant, I climbed the stairs to the third floor.

The attic door stood open. I stepped inside and made my way through the maze of junk to the steamer trunks I'd explored earlier, extracted the newspapers on top and set them aside. As I pulled clothes from the box, another journal fell out to the floor. I placed it on top of the newspapers and kept digging until I reached my main objective: the box hidden at the bottom.

Placing it on top of a twin trunk, I tried the lid to find it locked, as expected. Reaching inside a jean pocket, I withdrew the antique key, clamped the flashlight between my teeth, and slipped the key in the lock.

Damn, it didn't fit.

Anger flashed through me. Where the hell were Scarlett and Josiah? After all, I was doing him a favor, not the other way around. I'd searched high and low trying to locate some mysterious box which continued to elude me. Feeling abandoned and pissed off, I took the key and flung it as hard as I could.

It landed with a clink somewhere in the dark recesses of the attic.

"Gracious, Jolene. You wear stupidity almost as bad as Deena."

Scarlett and Josiah materialized in front of me. If she hadn't already been dead, I'd have killed her on the spot—Josiah, too.

"You're late, and I'm tired of looking for clues to solve this riddle." I pointed my finger at Josiah. "And I'm tired of Blue Eyes here keeping me in the dark. It's like the blind leading the blind."

Josiah pointed at one of the bulky trunks. Scarlett nodded her head with understanding.

"Before you go, Josiah has a gift for you. It's in there."

I cut my eyes to the indicated trunk, but hesitated opening it. "Is this a bribe? Because if it is, it's not gonna work. I'm finished with the mystery of this haunted house."

"Josiah said you're much too smart to fall for such a trick," Scarlett said. "He's serious about the gift. Go ahead and look inside."

Pride held me rooted to the floor. Twice in one night I faced backtracking previously stated promises. Earlier, I'd said I'd never climb back on a horse, but at the first suggestion of personal pleasure, I caved like a sinkhole. And now, here I stood ready to commit my second about-face of the evening.

"Just a peep," I conceded, opening the lid, and shining the flashlight inside at a layer of yellowed tissue paper. Gingerly, I lifted the paper. Underneath lay a pale green gown of such extraordinary beauty I feared touching it, but ached to do so.

"Josiah said you'd be the belle of the ball tomorrow night in Savannah's favorite evening gown, Jolene, and I agree."

"Wear this gown to the ball? What if I ruin it?"

"It would bring back a lot of happy memories for him to see you in his wife's gown."

Propping the flashlight on one of the trunks, I lifted the gown free and pressed it against me.

"I wish I had a full-length mirror so I could see myself. Suppose it doesn't fit?"

"Don't worry, it's a maternity gown."

"Gee thanks."

"Touchy, aren't we?"

"Yeah, a little, but I'll get over it. Does he really mean for me to wear this to the ball?"

"He does. Are you accepting his gift?"

I twirled, delighting in the crisp rustle of the stiff silk. "How could I resist such graciousness?"

"There are accessories to match."

I tried to refold the gown, but the thin beam of light from my flashlight made it impossible. Turning on the overhead bulb wasn't an option as it would be clearly seen from the soldier's camp, alerting Victor, or anyone else, of my presence in the mansion.

"How am I going to get it out of here?" I asked Scarlett.

"Now where did I see that garment bag? Oh, yeah. Over there on the far wall."

I swung my small flashlight to where she pointed barely making out a clutter of objects leaning against the far wall. Weaving my way proved time-consuming, but finally I stood before the plastic-covered object.

A heavy blanket further covered what appeared to be a life-sized painting. Removing the blanket, I passed the small light over the portrait of the woman I knew to be Savannah Redding. Arrayed in a lovely blue gown of exquisite workmanship, she posed with her two sons, one older and dark like his father, and the younger, an adorable curly-haired strawberry blond with shining green eyes.

The woman glowed with happiness. Although not beautiful, she had an intelligent face that bespoke of kindness and patience. Her chin square, her smile enchanting, and dark hair and eyes finished the painting of the striking young wife of Josiah Redding.

"Savannah Redding with Randall and John Milton," Scarlett said. "Josiah had it commissioned just before Randall's sixth birthday. John Milton was four at the time, and Savannah was pregnant with their only daughter, Adelaide, at the time of the sitting. Asa Douglas was born four years later."

"He had a lovely family," I observed.

"It's a shame he can't join them on the Other Side. But of course, you already know this."

"I can't believe I let you bribe me with a gown."

Scarlett laughed. "Keep thinking Cinderella, girlfriend. Hey, I believe there's even a pair of glass slippers in the trunk."

I draped the canvas with the heavy blanket and stashed the gown and accessories into the plastic garment bag. With the rolled up newspapers and journal safely zipped away in an outer pocket, I slung the bag over one arm and started for the attic door when twin beams of headlights momentarily lit up the room.

"Hurry your ass. Someone's coming," Scarlett said.

"Can you stall them?"

"I'll try."

Being burdened with my latest haul, I fumbled down the stairs and into the foyer. My best shot of escape was through the front door as the Turnipseeds, and it could only be them, came through the back door. I waited until the headlight beams faded from view before slipping out onto the veranda and into the blackness of the night.

****

Deena had left a message on my cell phone which I retrieved when I finally made it back to my car. Exhausted and dusty from my excursion, I hung the garment bag in back, climbed in the driver's side, and listened as Deena's voice came over my phone. "Jolene, I've searched the salon numerous times and I still can't find the camera. I called Billie Jo and she hasn't seen it. Oh, and Daddy won third place in the golf tournament. I'll be up for a while so call me when you get this message."

My watch read one. Too late to return her call. It could wait until morning. My sisters and I needed to put our heads together and come up with a plan to rescue Daddy from the law. Reaching for the bottled water I'd left on the seat, I chugged it down, cranked up my Mustang and headed out.

As soon as I arrived home, I hung the dress in my laundry room to air out the scent of lavender. In the morning, I'd drop it off at the cleaners for a professional pressing, not trusting myself with an iron on such delicate material.

A hot shower followed next, and with Tango, who curled up with his long tail around him, I settled down on the bed with the fragile newspapers and the journal from the attic trunk. Setting aside the journal and the papers with the accounts of Sherman's march to the sea, I carefully leafed through several additions of the neighboring county newspaper until I found the story on the Redding son's promotions in the Confederate army.

The Whiskey Creek Register.
28 April, 1862
Promotions in 4th Regiment,
2nd Georgia Cavalry Company G
The following changes have taken place in the 4th Regiment, G Company:

Redding, Randall J. from the rank of 1st Lieutenant to Captain

Redding, John M. from the rank of 2nd Lieutenant to 1st Lieutenant

Smith, William E. from the rank of 1st Lieutenant to Captain.

The friends and families of these brave men will be pleased to hear their promotions to positions to which their talents and military experience so qualify them to adorn. As gentlemen and soldiers they stand high in Company G, and their advancement is evidence of the highest merit.

Josiah's sons were officers in the 2nd Georgia Cavalry, Company G of the Confederate Army. Reading the account of their promotions from the original print brought Josiah's predicament into focus. So far, I'd never seen any of his immediate family lingering on the plantation grounds. Only Josiah remained. Surely, the answer would be found somewhere in the personal items now in my possession. I picked up another paper.

The Whiskey Creek Register
20 December, 1863
Party to Honor Local Soldiers
Mr. and Mrs. Josiah Redding held a pleasant affair at Pineridge Plantation to honor their sons, having returned home for a short leave to recuperate from wounds incurred during the battle of Chattanooga. Captain Randall Redding and 1st Lieutenant John Redding, of Company G, 2nd Georgia Cavalry, were praised for their brave part in this vilest war. Mr. Josiah Redding is one of the most esteemed residents of our fair town.

I closed my eyes picturing the strands of holly embracing the grand staircase, a large evergreen tree decorated with homemade ornaments in the front parlor, and mistletoe hanging in strategic places to encourage romance. Holiday baking, laughter, dancing, and then tears when the celebration came to an end. A mother and father's heartbreaking sadness as they watched their sons ride off gallantly back into battle. Rubbing my tired eyes, I reached for one more addition. Tango voiced his objection with a loud meow and moved down to curl at the foot of the bed.

The Whiskey Creek Register.
13 July, 1864
Deserter at Large
Phillip Green, a member of the 4th Regiment, was arrested in Whiskey Creek, on Wednesday, on a charge of desertion. Green is suspected of ties with the Federals. Green, a desperate fellow, after assaulting a

police officer, was able to make a daring escape from his cell and is now being hunted down like the dog he is. Until captured, the residents are warned to keep watch for this man. He was seen heading north out of town.

I don't endorsed desertion, but I could understand how a man would want to escape the bloodshed of war. Walking into the face of blasting gunfire demanded the strictest discipline and bravery. Most men weren't cut out for that destiny and flee in horror. Phillip Green was one of those men. Wait, he had been spotted in the area around the time of the massacre. What if he knew about the gold? He was suspected of having ties with the Northern Army and could have passed the information on. Could he be the missing link in this mystery? I read on until I came upon the following article:

The Whiskey Creek Register
15 July, 1864
Soldiers in Town

Captain Randall Redding and 1st Lieutenant John Milton Redding, of the 2nd Georgia Cavalry, Company G, are home on leave. Sons of the prominent landowner, Josiah Redding of Pineridge Plantation, reached town on July 13th and received the welcome to which their manly, genial qualities entitle them. The Redding sons will be in town for one week before reporting back to Atlanta Headquarters where the fighting is fierce.

Stunned with the news of Randall and John's presence at Pineridge Plantation at the time of the massacre, I sat back against the pillows for a moment before re-reading the article. But how could that be? According to history, Randall Redding died in the battle for Atlanta on July 22, 1864 under Commander Joe Wheeler of 2nd Georgia Cavalry Company G. John Milton escaped harm in the battle and went on to surrender with General Robert E. Lee's Army of Northern Virginia at Appomattox on April 9, 1865. He'd returned home and the farm prospered under his tutelage, and he was buried in the family cemetery.

Digging into the past unearthed more questions than answers. I picked up the paper and leafed through the remaining pages looking for more information on the Redding brothers and the escaped deserter, but found none. Wide awake now, I folded up the newspapers, reached for Josiah's journal, and hoped it would eventually provide some of the elusive answers.

Chapter Eighteen
The Yankees are Comin'

July 15, 1864

The entire household is celebrating the arrival of my sons from the battlefield of Atlanta. Both men are suffering from exhaustion and exhibiting long-term effects from their previous wounds. I worry about their health if this war continues another planting season. We have so little time with them as they must return to their Company in four days. Savannah is planning a party for the eve of their departure and inviting all the young women in the county. She confessed she favors playing matchmaker, but I told her now was not the time for our sons to become enamored. Savannah wouldn't hear any of it, so a party we'll have in three days. I didn't have the heart to explain how hard supplies are to obtain in Whiskey Creek. Asa and Adelaide are restless with the return of their brothers. Tempy is silent and withdrawn. I contribute this to the added chores she must bear since three slaves ran off last week. Tempy is too old for such work. She refuses her freedom which I offered her this joyous day. Randall and I spent several hours discussing plantation issues, and my new updated will, after the others had retired for the night. It's time to share the burden of my secret with him.

Tell me already! Geez, if he didn't hurry up and

spill his precious secret I would explode, or fall asleep. My eyes stung with the strain, and I had a headache, but I had to know what happened next so I turned the page and continued to read.

July 16, 1864

Saturday. Another hot morning. Randall and John accompanied me on an inspection of the fields and the remaining field hands. This war has served to show me the folly of slavery and as soon as I am financially able, I fully intend to free every man, woman, and child. I will pay them a good wage for a good day's work. I expressed my wishes to my sons as we rode over our land. Randall is in full agreement, but John Milton warned me to refrain from such traitorous talk as it could prove to be my downfall. The young man is fiery passionate in his defense of the cause, but Randall is weary of the fight and sees the end coming, as I do. Perhaps tonight I'll find the courage to share my secret with him. One day all this will be his, but for the two sections of land I've set aside for John Milton and Asa Douglas.

Today, I presented John Milton with his inheritance; 500 acres of prime farm land. When he returns from the war, he will be given funds to construct a small house and barn as stipulated in my will. The rest is up to him.

I swallowed down a couple of aspirins and went right back to the journal. Close to finding out what terrible secret Josiah harbored, I couldn't stop reading until I knew.

July 17, 1864

The entire family went to church. John and I spent the better part of the day closed up in the library going over plans for his future. Randall took Asa Douglas riding and Adelaide is working with her mother on invitations for the party to be sent out tomorrow. All is well. Pray God, it stays that way.

Supper was a happy occasion. In the evening, a Confederate soldier arrived with a message for Randall from Atlanta headquarters. The threat of Union troops breaking through the line of defense has strengthened. A large cache of gold is being transported south to Thomasville by Major Travis A. Piper and his small band of specialized soldiers. They will cross Pineridge Plantation in approximately two days. A small band of Union soldiers has been reported fifty miles north of Whiskey Creek. Immediately, I sent for James and Lewis. These men have proved their trustworthiness. Preparations will begin tonight. When told, Savannah didn't show her disappointment, but hurried off to help with the preparations.

Finally! Here's what I've been searching for: Josiah's account of Major Travis A. Piper and his cache of Confederate gold. Mesmerized, I continued to read.

July 18, 1864

The plantation is in a flurry of activity preparing for Major Piper and his men. A pig and calf slaughtered to feed the additional mouths in an already lean time. Savannah came to me extremely upset. Tempy is missing. James and a group of men are searching the plantation. Savannah is adamant. Tempy isn't a runaway. Major Piper's unit arrived late this afternoon ahead of schedule. He and his officers, and the gold, will be housed in the manor. His men will set up camp behind the stables.

Good grief, on top of everything else, Tempy's

missing. Where could she have gotten off to? Does Phillip Green somehow figure into her disappearance? I gripped the book tighter and turned the page.

July 19, 1864

Tuesday. Another message from headquarters arrived today. My sons and I sat in on the meeting with Major Piper and his officers. Word leaked out. Reports of a renegade band of Union soldiers were spotted heading south. Secured the gold in an undisclosed location and a guard over it for as long as possible before retreating. Randall and John have been recalled to Atlanta. They are to leave immediately. Major Piper requested a private meeting with me. I am to hide the gold and create a map detailing its whereabouts. No one is to know about this, but the two of us. I am the only one to know its burial place in case he is captured and tortured. Tempy is still missing. I have sent Savannah and Adelaide away from the plantation. They will be safer with friends in Whiskey Creek. Asa Douglas refuses to accompany his mother and sister. God in heaven, protect us from this evil threatening to destroy us all. Amen.

****

Tango woke me an hour late Saturday morning, the journal still lying open in my lap. As much as I wanted to pick up where I'd left off, I had a busy morning scheduled at the salon so I called Deena to move my first two appointments to another stylist. Hanging up the phone, stiff and sore from being bucked off General Lee, I showered, and dressed in record time, fed Tango, set out for the dry cleaners, and then the salon.

"You look like a zombie," Deena said when I came through the back door twenty minutes later. She handed me a cup of steaming black coffee.

I took a sip. "Ah, thanks, I need this. I had a late night catching up on some reading."

"That must be an exceptional book to keep you up so late."

I ducked into the dispensary for my apron. "Sounds like a madhouse out there."

"It is," Deena said from the doorway. "But we have a problem. Ellie called after I hung up with you. She's been called back down to the police station for questioning. She didn't say why. Anyway, you'll have to take her clients until she gets here."

Bradford had mentioned two persons of interest. Although, he hadn't said Daddy's name per se, the fact that he brought it up could only mean one thing: Daddy topped the list. Could Ellie be the second? But what about Ryan? Shouldn't he be downtown answering questions with her? They were after all, partners in more ways than one.

"No way can I take Ellie's clients." I secured the sash around my waist. "I'm booked myself. What about the new girl? You hired her to pick up the slack."

"Throwing Lizzie to the lions on her first day is cruel and unusual punishment. She's fresh out of beauty school and libel to quit after one hour in that madhouse of demanding females."

"That's how I learned," I complained. "If she runs into a problem, I'll be here to help. You've got to get your license for emergencies like this one."

"I'll register Monday morning."

"Good. Now, did you find the camera?"

"No. I left a message on your phone last night. Why didn't you return my call?"

"Late date. Sorry."

"Have fun?"

"I'll tell you about it later," I promised. "I'm getting a late start, and it's all ready nine o'clock. The reenactment begins at two and if we're going to get out of the salon by one, I'd better get a move on."

Controlled chaos is the best way to describe the reception area when I rounded the corner to see every chair occupied and standing room only.

"Who are all these people?" I said to Holly as I slid behind the front desk.

Holly shifted her gaze from the computer. "Clients and walk-ins. Your client is shampooed and draped and waiting." The phone rang. "Dixieland Salon, how may I help you?"

I left Holly booking a Tuesday morning appointment and headed over to my station where Mrs. Humphries sat scowling into the mirror.

"Good morning," I chirped. "Sorry for the wait. The usual roller set today?"

Mrs. Humphries withdrew a handful of yellow silk flowers from a plastic bag in her lap. "I'd like something special today. Mr. Humphries and I are attending the costume ball tonight." She handed me the flowers. "An updo with these in my hair, don't you think?"

Speechless, I stared down at the bright flowers trying to picture how to fasten them into her short, tightly permed hair. An updo? Nope. Nothing to work with. Sometimes, I wondered what women see when they look in the mirror—because it's not always reality.

"My ball gown is to die for," she continued her prattle. "I found it in a vintage dress shop in Athens last week. You know, women back in those days were a lot thinner, but I found a seamstress to let it out a few inches and now it's a perfect fit. Hey, are you listening?"

"I'm multi-tasking," I said, setting the flowers down on my workstation counter. "But to be honest, an updo simply won't work with your hair."

"My heart is set on it, my dear."

I sighed. "There's a hair piece in the back close to your brown shade, but it's the finest human hair on the market and expensive. The piece is two hundred dollars."

"I'll take it," she said without blinking an eye.

Sold. I rolled her hair, put her under the dryer and went to the dispensary for the hair piece, and then cut and blow-dried my next client's hair.

A little while later, I finished with Mrs. Humphries' updo, and had taken my next client over to my station when Rachel Wesley burst through the front door, visibly upset. She made a beeline for my station.

"Can I talk with you privately?"

I draped the plastic cape around my client's neck. "I'll be right back, Cynthia. Pick out something from the styling book while I'm gone and see if there's anything you like."

Billie Jo was in the kitchen fixing a glass of iced tea when Rachel and I came through the door. She and Rachel exchanged polite greetings.

"Can we have some privacy, Billie Jo?"

She gave me a questioning look, but when I nodded my head that everything was okay, she left the kitchen.

"Have a seat, Rachel, and tell me what's wrong." I

went over to the cabinet and took down two glasses. I poured tea into them both and joined her at the table.

"Detective Goodwin showed up at the bank this morning with more questions for my father. Can you believe he's a suspect?"

"They suspect mine."

"How can you be so calm?"

"On the inside, I'm not. But I've got to keep my wits about me. How, I'm not sure. I'm as jumpy and restless as a cat in hell with no claws."

Rachel chuckled. "Feeling doomed, huh?"

I nodded. "Yeah. I'm afraid this is the calm before the storm, my crystal ball is out of commission, and Madame Mia is on vacation. The noose is tightening around Daddy's neck, and I have no way of stopping it."

****

By the time we arrived out at Pineridge Plantation most of the best viewing spots behind the roped off battlefield were taken. Lawn chairs dotted the landscape as well as brightly colored umbrellas shading families of every description who'd gathered to watch husbands, brothers, and friends participate in living history.

"What a crowd," Billie Jo remarked as we found a break in the line and jockeyed for a better position under the shady oaks and pines.

Mama opened up her lawn chair and sat down. "Roddy's portraying a Yankee soldier?"

"Yeah, he was so excited to be included that he didn't care which side of the Mason Dixon line he landed on," Billie Jo said. "I never knew he'd be so interested in this sort of thing. I had to promise him we'd research the possibly of joining the local chapter of re-enactors. He borrowed one of Sam's horses for the event."

Daddy pulled his chair closer to the rope line. "Hand me those binos, Deena. I think I see Roddy with his unit." Taking the binoculars, he focused on a group of men in dark blue uniform gathered near a clump of trees at the far end of the property. "Yep, there he is. Hey, Sam's got some mighty fine horseflesh if that buckskin is any example of what's housed in his barn."

I didn't say so, but howdy could I tell them what's housed in his barn—and I'm not talking about horses.

"Do you see Bill?" Deena craned her neck around the head of an observer. "He's their unit leader and should be riding a big black horse named Thunder."

Daddy handed her the binoculars. "I believe he's talking with a blonde over by the big magnolia tree to the left if I'm not mistaken. Probably his sister wishing him well."

"He doesn't have a sister," Mama said.

Deena lowered the glasses from her eyes. "Gina Glover's his former fiancée. I didn't know she was back. Apparently, Bill is and looks happy about it, don't you think? I wonder why he failed to mention it last night."

Victor Redding galloped by on a beautiful golden horse. "I think they're ready to start," I said, hoping to redirect Deena's attention. "See, Major Piper is joining the Confederates."

A cry went up as a loud gunshot boomed from the Union side of the battlefield, and the thunder of galloping hooves shook the ground beneath me. More shouting and gunfire sounded. Smoke covered the field as men fell to the ground clutching their chests and sides, writhing in mock pain. Some played dead.

"This is more real than I expected," Mama said.

"And louder, too," I shouted over the volley of gunfire.

The battle raged. Suddenly, the golden horse charged the black horse in center field, the men on their backs locked in a fierce sword fight. With a scream, Major Piper fell to the ground and lay still.

With a cry of triumph, William raced his horse toward the manor house. Josiah Redding, portrayed by Bradford, burst from the front door, meeting him on the front veranda steps, gun in hand. A shot fired out and William staggered backward.

Deena gasped. "God, if I didn't know better, I'd swear this was real."

Blue uniforms converged on the mansion, guns blazing. Not able to see the action clearly, I snatched the binoculars from Deena. "I'll give them right back," I said as she grumbled her complaint.

Although I knew the outcome of the final scripted attack, I cringed as Bradford toppled in a crumpled heap at the bottom of the veranda steps. William, now supported on each side by a Union soldier, led a battery of men into the house.

Several minutes passed before William and his men exited the manor, helped Bradford climb his feet, and joined the other soldiers, live and ghostly, on the field. Victor and all the "dead" soldiers got to their feet. The crowd went wild with applause.

Roddy rode up on his horse, swung down from the saddle, swooping Billie Jo into his arms. "Man, what a blast." He kissed her soundly on the mouth. "How would you like to be the wife of a Confederate soldier and do this several times a year?"

"Only if you buy me an RV," she answered with an indulgent smile. "I'm not sleeping on the ground with the ants."

He kissed her again. "Oh, and I'll need to buy a horse and all the equipment, and a horse trailer, too."

"This hobby sounds expensive," Billie Jo said with a serious tone. "We'll talk about this later, after the excitement has worn off. We have to think about Lynette's college fund, you know."

Roddy's smile faded, but looped his arms around her, lifted her to the saddle, and swung up behind her. "Whatever you say, babe. How about riding with me over to Sam's truck? I might need your help loading General Lee into the horse trailer."

Billie Jo giggled as Roddy's arms encircled her. "Nix the RV. We can buy extra soft sleeping bags and a mosquito-proof tent. I do believe I might like this idea of yours. Do you think Sam would sell his horse?"

"Go have fun, you two," I said, slapping the horse on the haunches. "But forget buying General Lee. He's not for sale."

"Well, we'd better be getting our stuff together," Mama said as Billie Jo and Roddy rode off. She stood up and folded her lawn chair. "Deena, are you riding back to town with William, or your daddy and me?"

From where she stood, Mama couldn't see the hesitation written on Deena's face but I could. Inside that sweet head of hers, a battle raged, much like the one we'd witnessed on the front lawn of Pineridge Plantation. Women everywhere had been fighting this problem since the dawn of time—to confront the old girlfriend or let it rest. Personally, I don't have a problem with confrontation. My philosophy is: if there's a problem with the cock, better to know before he takes up residence in the henhouse.

"She'll hitch a ride with me, Mama," I said, taking the lead. "You and Daddy go on ahead. We'll see y'all later at the ball."

We gathered our chairs and made our way back to my Mustang parked down the driveway. After stowing the chairs away in the trunk, Deena turned to me and said, "I've got to talk to Bill before tonight. Do you mind?"

My feet were killing me, but the pleading expression on her face stilled my complaint and we silently hiked back to the mansion.

She pointed to a group of men gathered on the front veranda. "There's William."

Spying Bradford in conversation with the mayor and his chubby wife, I excused myself and joined them. Deena needed privacy. Plus, I didn't trust myself to keep my mouth shut. Deena had to work this one out on her own.

Bradford, still dressed in period clothing, greeted me with a smile. "We were discussing the ball tonight." He placed an arm about my waist. "It's going to be quite a shindig I understand from Nancy. Her men are putting the finishing touches on the outside lights now."

"She's doing an outstanding job as festival coordinator," I told the mayor. "I'm sure you'll agree. We're fortunate to have her behind the wheel of such a large production. It would be a shame to see her ousted on some trumped-up charge brought by an anonymous complainant."

"Yes, everything's gone off without a hitch unless

you count the botched beauty contest which resulted in a disgusting display of violent actions as you and your father should well remember, Miz Claiborne," Mayor Kent said icily.

Mrs. Kent snickered behind a white-gloved hand.

My good mood vanished.

Bradford squeezed my hand. The tension eased from my shoulders. "Nancy's not to blame, Mayor."

"Well, there's Theodore Herrington's death to consider," he continued as if I hadn't spoken. "Upon his recommendation, the Board voted unanimously to fire Nancy. Her replacement is ready to take over whenever I say. I'm just sorry he's not here to see his efforts come to fruition."

Hmm. Interesting. One snap of the mayor's fingers spelled the end for Nancy's position as Pecan Festival director. She'd be devastated to lose the coveted title she'd held for so long. But would she kill for it?

"Nancy must've been furious when she found out Herrington had recommended her removal as festival coordinator." I voiced my thoughts. "She takes such pride in her accomplishments."

Mrs. Kent shuddered. "Pride is a dreadful sin. Pride filled Satan's heart and he fell from grace. He swore vengeance on God and used us as bait!" She clutched her husband's arm.

The mayor's taut navy blue suit strained further across his generous girth as he drew in a deep breath. "Now, Nelma, don't go gettin' yourself all worked up again." He patted her hand. "Let's go talk with Reverend Mahoney."

Bradford eyeballed me quizzically. "What's up with them?"

I shrugged, not answering, the implication of Mrs. Kent's statement rattling around my head.

By golly, she was right. Revenge is a powerful motive for murder. But I needed more than motive. I needed facts.

Chapter Nineteen
The Costume Ball

The ravishing creature smiling back at me from the full-length mirror in my bedroom looked damn good considering the cosmetic calamity of her face. Savannah's sea-green ball gown hugged my curves, and the off-shoulder neckline plunged daringly low, emphasizing the creamy expanse of skin pushed to its corseted limits.

My coiffure, a cobweb of dark gold ringlets piled high and secured with twinkling jeweled bobby pins, drew attention away from the slightly crooked shape of my broken nose.

"I feel like Cinderella," I told the vision in the mirror. Liquid brown eyes, heavily made up to conceal the black bruises, glowed with eagerness, and the red bouffant lips pouted becomingly. "Minus the glass slippers, of course."

Laughing at my silliness and embracing the glorious moment, I twirled around, reveling in the rustling sound of crisp crinolines. Losing the cage-like petticoat of the 1800s, instead I'd opted for today's modern synthetic material, it being more comfortable and easier to travel in. The antique slippers had pinched my toes so I sported a new pair of white satin heels.

"I must say, Jolene, you make a stunning belle in Savannah's gown." Scarlett, dressed in an equally magnificent ball gown of violet silk, sat perched on the side of my bed, watching me pose in front of the mirror with obvious delight. "Josiah will be pleased."

"Right back at ya, Scarlett. I see you raided Vivian's closet."

"Where else would I go in a pinch?" She floated to the bedroom door. "Oh, your hunky detective is here."

Musical door chimes echoed throughout the house.

"See you at the ball, Cinderella," Scarlett said and left as silently as she'd arrived.

Taking one last looksee in the mirror, I grabbed my clutch bag, lace shawl, and hurried to greet Prince Charming leaning on the doorbell. He whistled appreciatively when I stood in the opened threshold. His blue eyes bathed me in admiration.

I did the same. Bradford's clothes were simple but rich. Black tail coat over a low-cut black vest, white shirt and bow tie, black trousers, shoes, and a top hat.

"Why, Mr. Bradford, sir, you're the picture of a 1860s southern gentleman," I said in an exaggerated drawl.

He held out his arm in a formal manner. "And I, my dear will be the envy of every man. Shall we go?"

Climbing into the passenger seat of his pickup proved challenging with yards of billowing silk, lace, and stiff petticoats. Finally, Bradford packed me in good and tight and we were off to the party.

The long drive out to the plantation sped by as we chatted about today's successful reenactment of the battle, both of us avoiding the subject of the continuing investigation into Theo's death, mainly the suspicion surrounding Daddy, knowing that it would put a damper on tonight's event.

When we turned down the long driveway leading to the mansion, I couldn't believe what a few days of hard work had accomplished. Nancy and an army of maintenance workers and gardeners had transformed the grounds into a fairy wonderland straight out of the mind of Hollywood. Tiny white Christmas lights glittered everywhere, bringing to mind freshly fallen winter snow. They were strung through the ancient magnolias and pines standing near the house, and the neatly trimmed azaleas and clipped, boxwood hedges lining the neat brick path leading to the front veranda. Every long, rectangular window in the house itself glowed softly against the black velvet backdrop of the night like stars littering the heavens.

"Oh, Bradford, I've never seen anything so beautiful," I gushed. "Victor must be thrilled with the results. Surely, Mayor Kent will take note of Nancy's hard work and let her continue in spite of everything."

He reached for my hand. "Remember, tonight is about having fun. Things tend to take care of themselves when you leave them alone."

"You're a wise philosopher, Samuel Bradford," I said. "I like that about a man."

He rewarded me with a wolfish smile. "Philosophy isn't what I like most about you."

His bold gaze dropped to my breasts in a roving manner that kick-started my desire to explore the matter further as we pulled up to the valet parking attendant.

Bradford jumped out of the driver's side, handed the keys to the young man, and opened the passenger side door for me. With skirts held high, I delicately exited the truck, not wanting the yards of fragile silk to touch the ground until safely inside.

Nancy herself greeted us in the foyer, and I did a double take. She, like me, had gone whole-hog. Her gown of lilac silk with a fancy lace design on the skirt had a sash of white silk trimmed in black velvet, and tiny lilac rosettes adorned her hair.

"You look beautiful," I told her. "And you've done such a wonderful job with the grounds and mansion. The tree is the perfect crowning touch."

Sometime in the last couple of hours, a huge Fraser Fir had been erected in the large foyer, and decorated with old-fashioned handmade Christmas ornaments. The unforgettable scent of a fresh-cut evergreen permeated the room, triggering childhood memories of long-ago seasons when Daddy would take the whole family out into the countryside to cut down the perfect Christmas tree.

"How kind of you to say so," she said. "Most of the ornaments date back to Josiah's time. They're family heirlooms."

"Congratulations on a job well-done," Bradford added. "This festival week has been a huge success. So successful, in fact, that I don't know how you're going to top it next year."

"Thank you for your vote of confidence, Detective Bradford, but I'm afraid this may be my last year as Pecan Festival Director," Nancy said.

The front door opened and another couple waltzed in. Bradford and I left her to greet them and followed the soft strains of Big Band music to the ballroom at the back of the house. The moment I stepped into the grand room with its azure blue, satin window curtains, rich blue paper with gilt against dark hardwood floors, the magic of the evening swept over me.

On the dance floor, couples waltzed by in their various period costumes. Confederate and Union officers, complete with swords in scabbard, twirled their ladies with dashing abandon, the rainbow-colored gowns dipped and swayed with the swelling music.

Scanning the room, I saw Mama and Daddy, both dressed in period costumes, seated in blue silk damask "elbow" chairs lining the opposite walls. Deena, resplendent in white, stood nearby talking with a Union officer who could be none other than William two-faced Mahoney, as I now dubbed him. Billie Jo was a vixen in black, and Roddy had worn his Union uniform from this afternoon's reenactment.

One of the catering staff, easy to spot by their modern apparel, offered both Bradford and I a glass of champagne. With glasses in hand, we skirted around the dancing couples and greeted my family.

Deena studied me for a moment. "Jolene, my God, where did you find that gown?" She fingered the material. "The local vintage shop doesn't carry clothing of such high quality."

"A friend lent it to me for the night," I replied. "This good friend has connections in antique clothing."

"Wow, some friend," Billie Jo said. "So it's the real deal? I mean the gown is authentic?"

I squirmed under their scrutiny, feeling like a bad germ under the microscope, and snagged another wineglass from a passing server. Bradford eyed me questioningly, but didn't comment when I downed the champagne.

Roddy offered his hand to Billie Jo. "Let's dance, honey. You can badger Jolene any ole time."

Billie Jo took his hand, pausing when Deena said,

"Who's the woman in the stunning gown being escorted by Victor?"

All eyes turned to the handsome couple making their way into the room.

Barbara Herrington.

Theo's weeping widow literally waltzed in wearing a demure smile and Savannah Redding's blue velvet gown from the attic portrait.

I had the sense of something moving secretly just beneath the surface of my psychic vision, but my spiritual equilibrium kept shifting like loosened sand on a desert hilltop. With my intuitive knowing off kilter, I couldn't read the tea leaves, so I had no choice but to surrender to the moment until the static snow cleared from my celestial receptors and I could figure out what the hell Barbara Herrington was up to now.

****

The music died down, and the dancing faltered to a stop, as couples spotted the host and his partner sweep by. As much as I hated to admit it, they made a magnificent pair and I, like the others, couldn't take my eyes off them as they approached the bandstand.

A myriad of muted sounds...voices, murmurs, whispers of speculation, wrapped around me like water around a rock in a fast moving stream.

"She's taking her husband's death rather well, isn't she?"

"Lower your voice, Deena, before someone hears your unkind remark."

William Mahoney's critical voice left me frosty. Bradford must've noticed because he escorted me a short distance away from the pious-in-the-ass pastor and handed me another glass of bubbly.

"Ladies and Gentlemen," Victor said from the bandstand, "Because of the tragic circumstances, the winner of the pie bake-off will finally be awarded their winnings. It's my great pleasure to announce Barbara Herrington's gracious acceptance to attend tonight's gala in memory of her late husband, Theodore Herrington. In his honor she will now present the first-place prize to the winners of Tuesday's Pecan Pie Bake-Off Contest."

Light applause sounded around the room as he handed the microphone over to Theo's now teary-eyed widow.

Barbara smiled at the audience. "Thank you for your kind hospitality, Mr. Redding, and for the use of this authentic antebellum gown belonging to your great-great-great-grandmother, Savannah Redding. Whew, that's a lot of great grandmothers." She paused as laughter rounded the room. "At first, when the festival committee approached me with the idea of honoring Theodore in this manner, I turned them down. But after further thought, I knew my husband would've loved being here with you this evening. So without further ado, would the winner of Whiskey Creek's fifteenth annual Pecan Pie Bake-Off contest, Don Juan's Plumbing on Pine Needle Drive, please join me to receive your first-place prize of an all-expense paid trip to Disney World in beautiful, sunny Florida?"

"I'll be right back," I said over the ringing applause, and handed the empty wine glass to Bradford. "I need a refill."

Mama and Daddy had risen to their feet and were clapping in response as the winners joined Barbara and Nancy who'd stepped up with an envelope in her hand.

"That would've been us if someone hadn't screwed with our entries," Mama said as I slipped my arm around her.

"Now, don't get up a head of steam, Annie Mae," Daddy admonished. "It's time you start writing your cookbook."

"Daddy's right, we'll win next year."

Barbara congratulated the winners, and the presentation ended with a champagne toast to Theodore Herrington. Then the band struck up a waltz, and Victor led her out onto the dance floor with other couples following. Deena and William took to the floor, Mama and Daddy joining them.

Bradford bowed over my hand. "Dance with me, beautiful lady? The drums of war have sounded, and I long to hold you in my arms before the light of tomorrow's day brings destruction's blight upon Georgia soil," he said in an exaggerated southern drawl.

"Sir, I, too, long to be in your strong arms before the dawn's early light." I giggled, batting my eyelashes at him. "And to bestow a token of my affection upon you before Daddy runs you off the plantation for deflowering his innocent daughter."

We both dissolved into playful laughter, and Bradford swept me onto the crowded dance floor. Together, we waltzed with synchronized abandon among the dancers, our heads and bodies touching, swaying to the swelling music, our attention riveted on each other; up to the moment I caught hazy movement out of the corner of my eye. A few yards away, transposed over the press of bodies, a spectral couple danced—and then another, and another, until the whole ballroom crackled with the galactic luminosity of spirits haunting the plantation.

I could've stayed in my lover's arms all night, but after three dances in a pair of new high heels pinching my sore toes, I stumbled to a halt.

Bradford led me off the crowded dance floor. "Would you like another glass of champagne? It's damned hot in here." He removed his black tailcoat and draped it over a chair.

Fortunately for me, I'd had tied the antique silk fan I'd found in the attic trunk to my wrist. Snapping it open, I generated a cooling breeze around my face with forceful efficiency.

"I'd love a glass," I said, slipping off my shoes under the cover of my long skirt.

Deena and William were exiting the dance floor as Bradford strode in the direction of a group of waiters at the other end of the room. Deena caught my eye, stepped over to my chair, and sank down into the one next to me, recently vacated by Bradford.

"Whew, I'm exhausted," she said. "Where's Sam disappearing off to?"

"He's in search of cool refreshment," I replied.

"That sounds wonderful. William, would you mind?"

He nodded. "Two bottled waters coming right up."

Deena grabbed his coat sleeve as he started to leave. "I'd like champagne. Tonight's a special occasion."

"We've had this discussion before, Deena."

"Yes, Bill, I'm aware of your feelings, but I want a glass of wine."

The two stared awkwardly at one another for a moment before he nodded, and sauntered off.

"I hate to ask but what's got into you?" I asked her, surprised by her behavior. Deena rarely stood her ground. Perhaps, mine and Billie Jo's defiant nature had finally rubbed off on her. She could use some backbone once in a while.

She scanned the crowd. "I'm feeling rebellious. Gina Glover is here."

"Oh," I said, understanding perfectly. "What are you going to do about it?"

"What would you suggest?"

"Let her have him and find a man who's more suited to you," I suggested over the strings of the waltz. "I could ask Bradford if he has an available friend in the department."

She didn't respond. Bradford and William were making their way toward us through the crowd. Bradford reached me first and set the full wineglass on the table beside me. William arrived several seconds later with two bottled waters and handed one to Deena.

Slipping on my heels, I stood up and handed Deena my glass of wine. "Take me for a stroll in the garden, Bradford." I grabbed his arm. "I need a breath of fresh air." Escape afforded me the only means of saving Deena further humiliation and me another trip to jail when I nailed Pastor Putrid with my spiked heels.

Mayor Kent waylaid us at the terrace doors.

"A word with you, Detective." He gave me the once-over. "Privately."

Bradford tightened his hold on my arm. "I'm off duty, Mayor. Can't this wait for a better time? Jolene and I were headed for the garden."

"I'd prefer to speak with you now."

Impatience darkened Bradford's eyes but he turned

to me and said, "You go on ahead. I'll only be a minute or two."

Stepping out into the cool night air, I strolled down the terrace which ran the length of the house absorbed in the dazzling sight before me. As with the front lawn, tiny white lights twinkled against a brilliant backdrop of azaleas and white Cherokee roses, dogwoods, sweet gum, and pines. A three-quarter moon cast its silvery shine over moss-draped oaks towering beyond the peaceful garden, their shadows shielding lovers from prying eyes.

A nearby stone bench offered privacy in which I could slip off my heels and wait for Bradford to join me. Seated demurely, I breathed in the majesty of the night, and stilled my anxious thoughts. Several minutes passed with no sign of Bradford, and I wondered if perhaps he couldn't find me tucked here in the shadows. As I debated whether to wait or go find him, the mayor's tense voice drifted over to where I sat.

"This conversation isn't over, Detective."

"You've made your point, Mayor. The department is working overtime. What else would you have me do?"

"Make an arrest."

"I don't have sufficient evidence to make an arrest."

"What about Roger Wesley?" The mayor's voice rose.

"Roger Wesley has a solid alibi."

"Are there any other suspects that stick out in your mind?"

"Ryan Herrington for one."

"Theo's son! Ludicrous. Ryan is an upstanding

citizen. What about Harland Tucker? My wife's cousin heard him threaten Theo at the beauty parlor."

"He's a strong suspect, Mayor, but the evidence against him is circumstantial."

With an ache, I realized they were discussing Daddy. More than anything, I wanted to make my presence known, but that would spark an embarrassing scene so I sat frozen in place, forced to listen.

"You're dating Tucker's daughter."

"What are you getting at?"

"I'm wondering if your association with the family might color your perspective on the case, Detective. A fatal mistake which could cost you your job. All I'm suggesting is maybe you'd better rethink the relationship. At least until this case is put to bed."

"Be careful, Mayor, that sounds like a threat," Bradford snarled. "I won't railroad an innocent man no matter how much you want this case to disappear."

"Find the smoking gun and make an arrest, otherwise I'm going to call a close friend in the GBI and get them involved, understand?"

"Are you finished? I'd like to enjoy what's left of the night." The intensity of his lowered voice raised goosebumps over my body, and I knew the mayor had pushed Bradford into a corner. Not good for Bradford. The mayor smelled political blood and would bulldoze the police until an arrest was made. Not good for Daddy.

Retreating footsteps echoed on the stone floor. The distant chatter and lilting music of the ballroom once again intruded on my thoughts, but the magic of the night had vanished. Pushing myself to my feet, I moved woodenly toward the golden light spilling out the opened terrace doors and the merriment waiting inside.

****

Bradford found me draped around Daddy. Tired from a long day, my parents were leaving the party, and I, having inside information felt as needy and clingy as a young child.

Daddy disentangled himself from my clutches. "Jolene, what's up with you?" A handkerchief magically appeared in his hands. "Here, wipe your eyes. You're ruining your pretty face with those tears. Sam, what's wrong with my little girl? Y'all have a fight?"

"I believe she's had too much wine and excitement," Bradford said, hugging me close to his side. "I'm going to take her home and put her to bed. She'll be fine after a good night's rest."

Even though I disagreed wholeheartedly with his statement, I let it stand. Better my parents believing alcohol and exhaustion caused my roller-coaster emotions than the truth that Daddy topped the suspect list in Herrington's murder, and the mayor was out for his blood.

Mama gave me a quick peck on the cheek. "You do what Sam says, and I'll see you at church in the morning."

I gathered up my lace shawl and clutch bag and followed Bradford through the crowd. Billie Jo waggled her fingers at me from the dance floor as we passed by her and Roddy. Deena and Bill, nowhere in sight, probably had left since he had to conduct the early morning church service.

Outside the night had grown chilly, and the lace shawl provided little warmth. Seeing me shiver,

Bradford placed his black tailcoat around my shoulders as we waited for the valet to return with his Dodge Ram.

"Care to tell me what's got you teary-eyed?" Bradford handed me into the passenger seat, slid behind the wheel, and maneuvered around so we were facing the driveway.

"Just what you said, the wine and dancing went to my head," I answered above the soft roar of the diesel engine as we followed a line of taillights down the long dirt road.

"I'm sorry for lying to your father. A couple of glasses of wine and a little dancing won't cause those tears," he countered. "Did something happen on the terrace?"

I clammed up, not knowing how to respond to his question. With Bradford's job at stake, the game rules had changed. No more insinuating myself into his investigation and putting his job in jeopardy. No fessing up that I'd been privy to his conversation with the mayor. From this point onward, I'd keep my thoughts and suspicions to myself. An acute sense of loss assailed me when I realized what I had to do.

"Something did happen and I'm tired of hiding the truth from you," I confessed, keeping my gaze on the road and away from his handsome profile.

"From the tone of your voice, I don't believe I'm going to like what's coming."

My next words would nail down the coffin lid, but Bradford needed to be free of me. Or, as the mayor had so eloquently put it, until the case was put to bed. If there's a relationship left to restore after tonight, I'd give it my best shot, but for now I had to make the sacrifice. A proposition I'd made many times in the past for my sisters. One more thing I'm good at.

"It's over between us," I said. "It came to me while I waited for you on the terrace, and I knew I couldn't go on denying it any longer."

"Just spit it out, Jolene."

"Scarlett's back with a whole boatload of her friends." I kept my voice calm. "They were at the reenactment battle and danced alongside us at the ball tonight. Hiding my paranormal abilities from you is a burden I'm not willing to bear any longer. Since neither of us is capable of changing, well, I've decided to move on to greener pastures and spare you the ghost stories."

Silence filled the cab for several seconds. I stole a glance at him. Strong hands gripped the steering wheel like steel bands ready to explode.

"I didn't see this coming so I don't know how to respond," he finally said. "This is sudden. Are you sure this is what you want? Why don't you take some time and think about the consequences of your actions?"

Here's my chance to take it all back, to regain our footing, but I couldn't back down. Bradford loved his job and I wouldn't be the reason he lost it.

"Yes, I'm sure. We're not compatible." My voice sounded concrete and final even to my own ears.

His sigh almost unraveled my plan. "Jolene, you chase after your tail and wind up biting yourself on the ass. I'm tired and not in the mood for all this drama, so if this is what you want I'm not going to stop it. But I'm not happy about it. You're throwing away a good thing."

He's right, my heart whispered back. I pressed my lips shut and in silence, we completed the trip to my house. Once there, I practically fell out of the truck in my haste to escape him. Bradford caught me in his arms before I could harm myself.

Every fiber of my being burst into flames at the sudden contact of his hard body, I tried to resist but couldn't. Our gazes locked. Blue eyes flared with raw desire. My defenses weakened.

His mouth crashed onto mine, his tongue exploring the recesses of my mouth. Somehow we were at the back door. I stood on trembling legs as Bradford fished the key out of my bag. Again, I found myself swept up into his arms and deposited onto shaking limbs in the semi-darkness of my kitchen.

"The alarm," I managed to say.

I stood in limbo for several seconds as he disarmed the security system, and then I was back in his embrace, his mouth on mine. Hungry hands roamed over my breasts and hips, pushing the material away to expose my fevered flesh. Desire burned so hot in my veins a fine sheen of perspiration covered my body.

And then, as soft as a whisper, his lips left mine. He stepped away and I tottered unsteadily.

His husky voice cracked when he spoke. "Goodbye, Jolene. If you change your mind, you know where to find me."

The door slammed shut behind him. I collapsed into a chair, and bowed my head into my hands. For a long time I sat there in the darkness listening to the hum of the refrigerator and the cat purring at my feet in the quiet kitchen.

Chapter Twenty
Daddy's Arrest

In the early Sunday morning pre-dawn hours I gave up any pretense of sleep, reached over and turned on the bedside lamp. Tango uncurled himself at the foot of the bed, blinked sleepily in my direction, and yowled in strong protest at being disturbed from his rest. With four hours to fill before dressing for Sunday school, I pulled out my notebook and poured over each notation for any nugget of information to take this investigation in a new direction. After church, I'd check in with Deena to see if she'd found the missing camera. Secondly, I'd check to see if she or Billie Jo had picked up any fresh gossip at the event last night.

The silver lining in my breakup with Bradford was the freedom to pursue any and all leads without the worry of prying eyes watching my every move. However, it also meant he wouldn't be there to extract me from any trouble I might stumble into. From this point, I'd have to be vigilant for any sign of danger and protect myself if the need arose.

And my third goal was to buy a gun since some rat had stolen Mini Pearl.

Satisfied with my progress thus far and with more time to burn, I put away the notebook, grabbed Josiah's journal, and turned to the last page.

July 20, 1864

Wednesday. I am writing this with a heavy heart. I, James, and a few trusted men, buried the cache of gold in an undisclosed location. The map I created has been hidden away as well. Randall and John are gone. Major Piper and his men are ready for action. James and the remaining slaves have taken up arms to help defend the plantation. Thank God my wife and daughter are safe in Whiskey Creek with friends. Thankfully, Tempy returned unharmed but with devastating news of a Union spy in the camp. To keep Asa Douglas safe, I have sent him this night to his grandparents in Savannah to travel with them to France for the remainder of the war. Tempy told me the name of the betrayer, but I can't bear to utter his name. May my son burn in hell for the evil he devised, but I bear the responsibility for it all. God forgive me for the evil I have done. Truly a man reaps that which he sows.

Well, shut my mouth! One of Josiah's son betrayed the Confederacy. But which one? I wanted to throw the journal against the wall as I was no closer to knowing Josiah's terrible secret than I was to finding the culprit guilty of Herrington's murder. But at least now the mystery of Asa Douglas Redding's disappearance had been brought to light, and the family history could be correctly rewritten. If Asa Douglas had grown to adulthood and produced children, Victor had extended family somewhere out there in the world. Hopefully, he'd be happy with the news. Curious about the possibilities but not to the point that I wanted to add genealogy to my already full plate, I decided that if Victor wanted to know the rest of his family, he'd have to do the research himself.

With the clock reading eight, I slipped out of bed

and padded to the kitchen to make coffee and feed Tango. As the coffee dripped, I showered and dressed in navy dress slacks and a white silk, long-sleeved blouse. After breakfasting on toast and coffee while reading the newspaper, at 9:45 I grabbed my Bible and left for church.

Deena waited for me outside our classroom in the crowded hallway. Dressed much the same as me, but in shades of peach, she appeared well-rested after our late night. I wished I could say the same, but the mirror didn't lie. Tired and grumpy, which I was.

"I'm glad I caught you before you went in," I said, before she could comment on my appearance. "Have you located the missing camera?"

"No, I must've misplaced it, but don't worry it'll show up."

Our teacher stuck his head out the door, saying he wanted to start the class on time. We joined the other singles and spent the next forty-five minutes debating the life lessons Jesus taught in the Sermon on the Mount.

****

After class, we joined the rest of the family in the sanctuary. I passed Bradford on the way in, but thankfully he didn't see me in the group coming in the side door.

"Isn't that Sam up on the front row?" Billie Jo asked me after I'd scooted down the pew for her and Roddy. "Don't y'all usually sit together?"

"Sam and I broke-up," I mumbled with my head downcast.

"Oh, good Lord, I'm beginning to think that's a good thing. Y'all are on and off like a light switch.

Have you told the others?"

"I'm planning to after church."

The choir took their seats in the loft. Music swelled from the pipe organ and piano as Reverend Inman climbed the steps of the platform and sat down in his big throne-like chair facing the congregation. A solemn-faced Bill Mahoney occupied the smaller throne beside him. A holy reverence settled over the sanctuary as the organist launched into "Amazing Grace" and the choir stood to their feet, lifting their voices in praise.

That's when Scarlett showed up, dressed in a long, flowing, white gown, with giant angel wings fastened to her back. With no regard for the sanctity of the moment, she zipped over the heads of the choir, unsettling their sheet music, which scattered in every direction, and headed straight for me, wings unfurled.

And wouldn't you know it, some young, budding medium in the congregation pointed at her, all the while screaming, that we were being visited by heavenly angels. Naturally, repercussions followed. Declarations such as this were strictly forbidden by the ruling powers that be and weren't to be tolerated. Outraged gasps and cries for the boy's immediate removal sounded the alarm.

Beside me, Billie Jo fished inside her purse, withdrawing the small black gadget I recognized as one of her ghost-hunting tools. She flipped it on.

"Don't, Billie Jo—"

My warning fell on deaf ears. Standing to her feet, she swung the meter in an arc, the high-pitched beeping blaring like a trumpet, red lights flashing. That, added to the cries of the boy being dragged out of the inner sanctum by his distraught parents, and the infuriated bellowing of the pastor, completed the pandemonium occurring around me.

"Hey, smart kid. I'm playing the part of the Christmas angel in the manger scene," Scarlett said, floating transposed over the woman's head in the pew in front of me, her face inches from mine. "I beat out Gabriel for the part. He's not happy, but I told him two thousand years was a long enough monopoly on the part. Heaven's ready for fresh talent."

"Leave me in peace for one day," I whispered.

"I'm delivering a message from Josiah. He wants to see you, ASAP."

Nodding my head in acquiesce, although I had no intention of driving out to Pineridge Plantation today, I agreed just to get rid of her.

Roddy shot to his feet. "Turn it off," he shouted over the noise.

Billie Jo shut off the EMF meter and together they sank down on the pew. Stunned silence filled the sanctuary as all eyes swung back to the front where Reverend Inman stood clutching the podium as if it were about to take flight. Anxiously, I glanced at Mama. Her lips formed a tight line, but Daddy, sitting next to her, seemed amused, while Deena bore a startled-fawn expression.

Scarlett's brief visit must've taken the wind out of the Reverend's sails. After twenty minutes of preaching, he wrapped it up and handed the service over to the worship leader, who seemed just as ready for lunch as the rest of us.

I caught another glimpse of Bradford after the last amen. He plunged into the already-dispersing crowd and out the doors. Billie Jo and Roddy headed out the side exit, promising to meet us out at the farm for dinner as soon as they changed into comfortable clothes. The rest of us followed at a more sedate pace. As soon as we stepped out into the noon sunshine, two men in black suits headed in our direction. By their grim looks, I guessed government; probably Georgia Bureau of Investigation.

Mama's hand groped for mine, and I gave it a reassuring squeeze.

The taller of the two men flashed his badge. "Mr. Harland Tucker?"

"Yes, that's me," Daddy said, stepping closer. "What can I do for you?"

"We need you to accompany us down to the police department," the man answered in a non-threatening voice.

I let go of Mama's hand and stepped up beside Daddy. "What's this about, sir?"

An audience of churchgoers gathered. Diane Downey and her gaggle of hens, a couple of singles from my class, Reverend Inman, and most of the choir gawked nearby.

"The Georgia Bureau of Investigation has been called in at the request of Mayor Kent," the second agent, a middle-aged, balding man spoke up, handcuffs in hand. "Additional evidence has come to light that we'd like for you to clear up, Mr. Tucker. We have a warrant for your arrest."

With a pang, I realized I had made a fatal mistake by keeping Daddy's secret from the police. Apparently, someone had their sights on Daddy taking the fall for Theo's murder, and I, by foolishly miscalculating their desperation, had all but helped them deliver his head on a silver platter.

****

Bradford appeared magically at my side. Heat flooded my face as last night's encounter seared my memory cells like bacon on a hot skillet. His gaze swept over me to the GBI agents.

What's going on?" He extended his hand to the tallest agent. "WCPD Detective Samuel Bradford. And you are?"

The agent shook Bradford's hand. "GBI agent Andy Stillwell, and my partner, Ian Farmer."

Bradford shook Ian Farmer's hand. "Care to tell me what you're planning to do with those." He pointed to the handcuffs dangling from the agent's hand.

My hands balled into fists. "That cockamamie mayor followed through with his threat and called in the GBI. They're arresting Daddy."

Bradford grasped me by the shoulders and led me several feet away. "Stay calm and let me handle this."

"But, Bradford—"

"Trust me for *once*, Jolene. They have an arrest warrant. Your father must comply. I promise not to leave his side. But I need your cooperation. Do I have it?"

Hating the vulnerable feeling coursing through my blood, I agreed. Relinquishing control wouldn't be easy, but the matter had been taken out of my hands.

Bradford pointed to the handcuffs. "Those aren't necessary. I'll escort Mr. Tucker downtown in my car. You can follow."

"Sorry, Detective Bradford, but we handle these matters by the book."

After handcuffing and reading Daddy his rights,

the GBI agents allowed him to kiss Mama, and then me and Deena goodbye, his strong voice urging us not to worry. Promising to keep an eye on Mama, we watched in horrified silence as they led him to their unmarked car and placed him in the back seat. Bradford tailed them out of the church parking lot.

Tears welled in Mama's eyes. "Jolene, drive me over to the police station."

"Daddy wants us to get you home, Mama," Deena said before I could answer.

"I know what Harland said but he needs me."

Diane Downey headed straight for us. I grabbed Mama's arm and propelled her toward my car. "Get in, now," I directed. "Deena, are you coming with us?"

She held up car keys. "No, I'll follow in Daddy's car."

Jumping in, I gunned the motor, shot out of the parking lot onto Main Street, and headed for the farm.

"This isn't the way to the police department," Mama complained as I passed the traffic light.

"Bradford made me promise to stay away from police headquarters. See if you can get ahold of your lawyer and have him meet them downtown. We'll wait for word at the farm."

Mama pulled out her cell phone and punched in a number. "I've got him on speed dial for emergencies."

I accelerated as I reached County Road 41. "Well, this qualifies as an emergency."

Mama had a long conversation with the attorney. She snapped her phone shut. "He promised to get right down there."

"That's good. I'm worried about this new evidence Agent Farmer spoke of."

"What do you suppose it could be?"

Slowing down to make a left turn onto Nelms Road, I turned to her. "I'm guessing it's the high school incident. The one I advised you and Daddy against admitting."

"I told you it was a mistake, Jolene. It never pays to lie."

I smiled at her observation. "And you would know that from firsthand experience, Mommy dearest. I remember—"

"Never mind about my past sins," she said as I turned onto See More Lane. "Between Sam and my lawyer, Harland's in good hands."

Not having the heart to dash her enthusiasm, I vowed to keep quiet about mine and Bradford's breakup. At least until Daddy returned home. Then I'd break the news.

Deena pulled into the driveway behind me, and the three of us went inside together. Mama headed straight for the walk-in pantry and the apron hanging on a nail on the inside door jam. She came out with it on over her dress and a box of cornmeal in her hand.

"I'm going to mix up some cornbread to go along with the pot of chicken and dumplings. Jolene, turn the burner on under those greens and how about whipping up that pistachio fruit salad with the miniature marshmallows Harland loves. You'll find all the ingredients in the pantry and refrigerator. Deena, set the table."

Deena and I exchanged glances, knowing what came next. Mama would spend all day cooking as a way of dealing with the stress. There were times throughout the hard years that I'd seen the dining table so laden with food I feared it'd buckle under the weight. Hopefully, today wouldn't be one of those days because if the truth be told, my appetite had fled at the appearance of those two GBI agents.

Billie Jo, Roddy, and Lynette arrived shortly after Mama slipped the pan of cornbread into the oven and hauled down her baking pans for a chocolate cake she suddenly had to have.

"Um, it's smells so good in here, Mama Tucker," Roddy said when he came through the back door. "Where's everybody? I told Billie Jo to hurry up and change or we'd be the last to arrive."

"Harland's been detained—"

I heard the catch in Mama's voice and rushed over to take the cake pans out of her drooping hands.

Billie Jo hung her shoulder bag on the back of one of the kitchen chairs. "What do you mean detained? A slight frown marred her brow.

"We got ambushed by the GBI when we were leaving church. They took Daddy to jail," Deena said, stirring the greens on the stove.

Lynette glanced up from texting on her phone. "Big Daddy's in jail? Bummer." She threw up her hands as five pairs of eyes fastened on her. "What?"

"Go into the den while your mother and I find out what's going on with your grandfather," Roddy ordered. "And don't publish it over the air waves."

After Lynette disappeared into the den, shutting the door behind her, Billie Jo and Roddy sat down at the kitchen table with me and Mama. Deena replaced the lid on the greens and joined us. In bits and pieces the story unfolded. Finally, we sat in silence, staring at one another.

Daddy and Bradford came in an hour later. Deena saw them first. Her screech of jubilation as she shot out of her chair, launching herself at Daddy brought tears to my eyes. Smiling, Mama pushed herself to her feet and ambled over to the stove, humming a gospel tune as she stirred the pot of greens. Billie Jo, like Deena, fussed over Daddy while Roddy stood waiting his turn. The noise must've drawn Lynette out of the den because I observed her linked arm and arm with her father.

Bradford caught my eye. He indicated by the motion of his head that he wanted to talk with me in private.

"Sam, you're not leaving?" Daddy asked when Bradford started out the kitchen door.

He paused with his hand on the doorknob. "I need to get back down to the station. You enjoy dinner with your family and I'll be in touch soon."

Amid cries of protests for him to stay, Bradford excused himself and stepped outside. I followed him to his unmarked police, car parked beside my Mustang.

"I wanted to speak with you without causing any more of an uproar," he said in a serious tone. "Hire your father the best criminal attorney your family can afford. I procured his release this time but I'm not sure how long it'll last. You see, I've been removed as lead detective in this case by my superiors on grounds of conflict of interest. The detective replacing me is young and hungry and looking to take my job."

His words sucked the breath from me. "Mama sent her attorney down to the station."

"Mr. Swanson practices business law, not criminal. He's no match for what your father is facing."

"What's this additional evidence Agent Farmer

spoke of?"

"A reliable witness came forward with knowledge of an incident that took place between Herrington and your father when they were in high school. Herrington told this witness that Harland Tucker purposely tried to kill him with peanuts."

"A practical joke," I protested. "Bradford they were teenagers!"

"So you had prior knowledge of this incident before today?"

"Mama told me on Thursday night before Herrington's funeral."

He leaned against his car, arms crossed against his chest. "And you failed to mention it to me. May I ask why?"

I shrank from his hurtful expression, at a loss for words to explain myself without causing him, and myself, further pain.

"According to your father, your mother wanted to tell me, but you didn't trust me with the information."

"I was protecting Daddy," I said in defense. "Who is this reliable witness?"

"The name is being withheld until the incident can be verified. Listen to me, Jolene, I've already gone out on a limb for your father, but I'll not further jeopardize my career so you can bungle this investigation. I'm off the case. However, there's more."

"More?" I groaned. "How can it get any worse?"

"It did. One of the employees at Golden King Peanut reported that your father purchased a five-pound bag of peanut flour and peanut oil the day before the bake-off."

"For me and Billie Jo! Not to knock off

Herrington, for God's sake. Damn, the loose tongues in this town."

"Just doing their civic duty, Jolene."

I wagged my head in agreement. "Yeah, I know, but can you at least tell me what became of the information I gave you about the conversation between Ellie and Ryan?"

"Yeah, but you're not going to like it." He laughed. "They were talking about euthanizing Ryan's sick cat, not killing his father."

I listened with bewilderment, not entirely believing what I'd heard. "That's their story? A sick cat? It sure didn't sound that way. Ryan said he didn't mean to hurt him, but the situation snowballed out of control."

"Again another reasonable explanation. Evidently, the cat attacked Ellie. Ryan overreacted and swatted the cat across the room, breaking its leg which led to the cat being put down."

"So that means they're free and clear and Daddy's the prime suspect?"

Bradford pushed himself off his car and opened the driver's door. "For once take my advice and stay out of it. Leave the investigating to the professionals. I can't keep riding to your rescue."

"And leave Daddy's fate in the hands of that young upstart who's out to make a name for himself? Not on your life! And I can rescue myself, thank you very much."

He slid into the driver's seat. "Oh, and one more thing. Your father has been ordered not to leave the county. If he doesn't comply he'll be arrested again."

Watching Bradford's car disappear down the drive, I bounced around several ideas in my mind on how to best break the news of Daddy's restrictions to the rest of my family. Keeping him here in the county should be doable. Mama could handle that assignment since they were practically glued at the hip anyway.

However, at the rate Daddy's future spiraled downhill, it might be a good idea to locate a strong suit of armor in case I had to rescue myself since my knight had just ridden off into the sunset without me.

****

"I asked y'all here tonight to give an update on our current difficultly," I said, pouring steamy cocoa into three cups. After my earlier discussion with Bradford I decided to call an impromptu meeting at my house for me and my sisters to ramp up our investigation before we were fatherless again. Daddy had already given Mama a condensed version of his visit with the police so I didn't have to reiterate the importance of his restricted boundaries.

"I'm not sure what else we can do," Deena said from across the table. "I'm willing to give it my all if it'll save Daddy from jail, but is it wise to exclude Mama? She's got inroads in places we could never enter. We need her help."

Billie Jo set down her cup. "Her hands were shaking."

"What do you mean shaking?" Deena demanded.

"When we were eating dinner I saw Mama's hands shaking. And she laid down right after dinner. When's the last time she's done that? She's stressed out. It's either stress or she's hiding something from us. You know how she hates to worry us."

"So on top of everything that's going on with Daddy, Mama's health is breaking down? Why haven't

I noticed?" I fumed at my ignorance.

"Maybe she's extra tired," Deena said. "I wish she'd sell the farm and move into a smaller house in town."

"Mama's bull-headed about the farm," Billie Jo said.

I opened up the notebook on the table and pulled out a sheet of paper. "Which means we have both our parent's lives hanging in the balance. This is a list of suspects I've put together. They are: Ryan Herrington, Barbara Herrington, Ellie Malone, Roger Wesley, and Nancy Chance. Daddy is the prime suspect."

Deena reached across the table for my hand. "We were all sorry about you and Sam breaking up."

"As I said when I told y'all, Deena, this isn't the first breakup I've gone through and probably not the last so let's not dwell on it, okay?"

"Mama and Daddy hoped you and Sam might get married," she went on as if deaf.

"Shut up, and let Jolene continue," Billie Jo piped in. "I'd like to know what she's got in mind before midnight. Like why Nancy Chance is on the list of suspects."

"Right, sorry." Deena picked up the cup of hot cocoa and cradled it in her hands.

"Because Herrington did his best to have her ousted as festival coordinator," I said. "She said that if he succeeded in his quest, she'd be gunning for him."

"And why's Roger Wesley on the list?" Deena asked between sips of cocoa.

"Because Herrington targeted his bank for a takeover," I answered. "Deena, find that camera. You might've captured the culprit in action. Also talk to

Rachel about the night of the contest. Roger Wesley has an alibi and I want to know what it is. Billie Jo, I want to know about Ryan's trust fund and his true relationship with his father. Track their whereabouts before the contest. And ask Ellie about Ryan's cat."

Billie Jo frowned. "What's a cat got to do with any of this?"

"Maybe nothing," I said. "Just do it."

"And what about you?" Deena asked.

"First thing tomorrow, I'm going to pay the widow a visit and see what I can learn. Nancy has an appointment on Tuesday so I'll sound her out then. Okay, that about wraps it up for now. Keep this between us, and we'll talk tomorrow."

They left and I cleaned the kitchen before Tango and I padded back to my bedroom. The clock struck ten when Tango let out an enraged bellow, taking off like an orange streak as Scarlett arrived in cinematic fireworks that threatened to set my bed on fire.

When the spots in my eyes finally died down enough for me to make out shapes and colors, I could see her standing hands on hips in the center of the room, her usual soft golden aura pulsating like a blinking light bulb. Thankfully, she'd lost the angel wings and had dressed sensibly in a gorgeous cream colored cashmere dress and heels.

"Could you turn off the strobe light?" I rubbed my eyelids to soothe the burning.

"You ignored the summons." Her silky voice held a challenge.

I released a tired sigh. "It's been a rough day, Scarlett. Tomorrow's soon enough for a man who's been dead for one hundred and fifty years. What's got his panties in a wad?"

"He remembered a vital piece of information. You have to come now."

I stifled a yawn. "Not tonight. I'm dead on my feet and couldn't possibly drive out there without ending up with a one-way ticket to the Great Beyond." Without waiting for an answer, I switched off the bedside light and closed my eyes against the resulting flash. "Scarlett still knows how to make a dramatic exit," I told Tango as he leapt back onto the bed and settled at my feet.

Chapter Twenty-One
Peach Cobbler for the Widow

Early Monday morning I parked my car at the curb and rechecked the address I'd written down against the one on the mailbox in front of the house listed for Theodore Herrington. Surprised by its simplicity, I had pictured the bank president and his society bride living in an expensive over-the-top mansion, not the muted red brick, two-story house with black window shutters and fancy wrought-iron railing running the length of the upstairs balcony.

Stepping from the car with a warm dessert dish in hand, I started up the brick pathway to the front porch. As I waited for someone to respond to the doorbell, I leisurely surveyed my surroundings. The stately home nestled under a canopy of massive pine and oak trees appeared meticulously cared for by a loving hand. The boxwood hedges were neatly trimmed, the yard manicured to perfection. Not a leaf in sight. Dogwood trees resplendently clothed in autumn foliage stood waiting for nature's signal to carpet the ground in scarlet.

The sound of soft footsteps on hardwood let me know someone was on their way, and I glimpsed a maid in uniform pass by the floor to ceiling glass sidelight. The lock on the front door scraped as it retracted, and the door swung open. A middle-aged woman in a blue uniform and starched white apron stood filling the threshold.

"May I help you?" she asked in a reserved, yet courteous voice.

"I'm here to see Mrs. Herrington." I held out the dessert dish. "I thought she might enjoy my homemade peach cobbler."

She opened the door wider and stepped back. "Please come in, Miss." Her lips pressed together in not an altogether friendly gesture.

"Tell her Jolene Claiborne is here to see her," I supplied, stepping inside the spacious foyer.

The maid led me to a formal living room with modern contemporary earth-toned furnishings. "If you will wait here, I'll see if she's receiving visitors."

Left to myself, I made a quick sweep of the room before settling down on a soft brown swivel rocker near one of the front windows. Several minutes passed before Barbara and the maid entered the room.

"Ms. Claiborne, what an unexpected pleasure." Theo's widow smiled a welcome.

I presented the dessert dish to her. "I hope you like peach cobbler," I said, giving her the once over. Barbara had shed her widow weeds in favor of a candy apple red jumpsuit which set off her fair coloring to perfection. She positively glowed.

"Thank you for the kind gesture." She took the dish from me. "Won't you join me for mid-morning tea? It will give us a chance to get to know one another better."

Pushing back the twinge of guilt, knowing that I was there to ask questions more than offer comfort, I gave my hostess a quick nod. "I don't want to impose,

Mrs. Herrington, but of course, if you insist I'd love to visit with you."

She turned to the maid. "Charlotte, please see that this is on the tea tray with the lemon loaf you made this morning. We'll take refreshments in the sunroom."

Charlotte bobbed her head and disappeared out of the room, dessert dish in hand.

I followed my hostess to the sunroom at the back of the spacious house. The room certainly lived up to its name. Pale yellow sunlight spilled in through large plate glass windows, pooling on the hardwood floor. The wicker furniture with colorful cushions and potted green plants gave the room a tropical feel that invited one to laze away the winter hours surrounded by the indoor warmth while blustery winds blew outdoors.

Following Barbara's lead, I sat down in one of the chairs opposite her. "Your home is lovely, Mrs. Herrington."

"Please call me Barbara. Mrs. Herrington sounds so stuffy."

I gave not a hint of surprise at her request. The woman sitting across from me seemed different from the woman who'd slugged me just days prior. Perhaps her husband's death had softened her. Death tends to change people—sometimes for the better.

"And you must call me, Jolene," I reciprocated, one eye on her and the other on Charlotte as she wheeled in the tea tray, then arranged the cups, saucers, and desserts on the table between us. I watched as Barbara poured tea in both paper thin china cups, and then mirrored her actions as she added cream and sugar to her cup.

"Your sister must've been heartbroken to return to

New York without you," I said, hoping to jumpstart our conversation.

Barbara peered at me over the rim of her teacup. "Yes, she's not fond of the South I'm afraid. She never understood why Theo wanted to remain here. Of course, I didn't share Theo's ties here to the South. I did not learn of it until recently."

"Yes, Mr. Herrington's parents moved from New York State to Whiskey Creek some years back." I nibbled on a small slice of lemon loaf.

"Oh, I'm talking about much, much, later. My husband found a family connection to before the Civil War. He became obsessed and joined one of the local genealogy clubs to trace his lineage. Theo wasn't pleased at first at what he found."

"How fascinating," I said. "What changed his mind?"

"Some old family papers he unearthed while going through his mother's possessions after she passed away last year. He spoke once of writing a book about the information contained in those papers. He even rode out on one Sunday afternoon not long ago to speak with Victor about his findings. Would you like more tea, Jolene?"

I didn't, but needed the conversation to continue so I held out my teacup. "Did Mr. Herrington share with you what he found?" Had Theo stumbled onto a connection between his family lineage and Asa Douglas Redding who disappeared out of history on July 20, 1864? If so, he would've headed straight for the one person who might have the answers: Victor Redding.

"I never asked him, not being interested in genealogy, or the Civil War." She lowered her tea cup.

"The few times he mentioned his mother's southern connections, I paid little heed to the conversation, I'm sorry to say, because Theo's obsession destroyed his health. Well, enough about that. Would you like a tour of the house?" She set her cup down with a clink.

Without being told that this was her polite way of ending our visit, I followed her out of the bright sunroom and into the darker recesses of the house. She had just finished showing me the beautiful built-in teakwood cabinets in Herrington's office upstairs when the phone rang. Seconds later, Charlotte stood in the doorway.

"Telephone, ma'am. It's the call you were expecting."

"Would you excuse me for a moment?" Barbara turned and hurried out of the room.

Left alone, I hastened to the large desk. Digging through each drawer, I rustled through every loose paper. Nothing. The bottom drawer was locked, but luckily I had a fingernail file in my purse. Several seconds passed as I juggled the file in the lock. Finally, the lock clicked and the drawer slid open as smooth as butter.

The deep drawer contained accounting ledgers and old checkbooks, and underneath the pile I discovered a file folder stuffed with old newspaper articles dating back into the nineteenth century, a faded family tree, personal papers, and a large faded photo of a family in late 1800s period clothing.

These had to be the family papers behind Herrington's obsession. Not sure if I'd gain any useful information by studying them, and not having the time to do so now, I decided to borrow them in case they proved to be insightful. How I'd return them without being caught, I'd figure out later.

Stuffing the folder into the oversized purse I'd brought for this purpose, I carefully replaced the other items and closed the drawer. When my hostess failed to appear after several more minutes of waiting, I made my way back down the hallway toward the front part of the house, hoping Charlotte cleaned nearby. The housekeeper could deliver my excuse for leaving to her mistress and I could make my escape.

At the top of the stairs Barbara's raised voice stopped me cold in my tracks.

"This is unacceptable, Mr. Howard. As the beneficiary of my late husband's life insurance policy, I'm entitled to the five million dollar payout. I expect your company to honor the policy and issue a check immediately."

Five million dollars! Translation: Five million reasons for wanting your husband dead. No wonder the weeping widow's tears had dried up. This information I could use. Cautiously, I tiptoed closer to her opened bedroom door and pressed my body against the wall.

"What do you mean your company is investigating?" Barbara's low voice whipped like steel.

A stair creaked.

I glanced over my shoulder.

Charlotte, holding an armload of plush towels, stood glaring at me from the top stair. If looks could kill I had a one-way ticket for the hairdressers union in the sky.

****

The door slammed shut as Charlotte unceremoniously kicked me out of the house. A first for me, but worth the embarrassment of being caught eavesdropping when I came away with a good motive for murder.

My cell phone rang as I unlocked my car door and slid in behind the wheel. "Hello."

"Have you spoken to Mama or Daddy this morning?" Deena's strained voice cracked over the line.

"No, I've been busy. You wouldn't believe what I found out during my visit with Barbara Herrington."

"Not now. I'm worried about our parents. They're not answering their phones and I've been trying to contact them for three hours."

"I wouldn't worry overmuch. They'll return your call when they're ready. Did you find the camera?"

"I'm at the salon now. Hey, I'm getting another call, talk to you later."

"But—"

The line disconnected so I hung up, dug the file folder out of my bag, and shoved it under the driver's seat. Satisfied with my morning's investigative work, I headed out to Pineridge Plantation. Light traffic made the drive pleasant and soon I turned down the dirt road leading to the plantation and pulled around to the back parking area, easing in the space next to Victor's BMW.

For peace of mind, I dialed Mama's cell phone and left a message asking her to call, then repeated the process with Daddy. The strong urge to read Theo's file challenged my will, but it'd have to wait until later. First things first.

In the back bedroom of the main house I changed into my period costume and went to meet the next tour awaiting me in the front foyer. My good luck took a nose dive. Scarlett waited for me with the others. The instant her blue-green gaze lit on me, she swooped down from her perch on the chandelier.

"I'm running out of patience," she complained. "Josiah is waiting for you in the library, so please hurry."

I gave her a quick nod and then, smiling at the group, apologized for my tardiness, and proceeded with the tour of the house. Two hours later, my shift over, I ducked into the library and shut the door. Scarlett, lounging on the sofa, leafed through a magazine, and Josiah paced the floor like an expectant father.

"Okay, I'm here. What's up?"

Josiah frowned at me from the fireplace. "He's upset," Scarlett said from over on the sofa.

I flashed him my best smile. "Sorry. Now what's the emergency?"

"He wants you to locate any descendants Asa Douglas might've had," Scarlett informed me.

"I'm not a genealogist, Scarlett. I wouldn't know where to begin."

Josiah floated over to his roll-top writing desk. "He wants you to go over there," Scarlett said.

I went over to his desk and slid the top back displaying the tooled leather writing surface and six small storage drawers. Nothing stood out as important.

Josiah pointed at one of the small storage drawers. "Remove that small drawer and tap on the back where he indicated," Scarlett directed.

Placing the drawer on the floor beside me, I tapped on the back section of wood and watched with amazement as it slid back to reveal a cloth-wrapped item within the enclosure. I reached inside and withdrew it, carefully placing it on the leather writing surface.

"Stash it under your dress," Scarlett admonished. "That nosey housekeeper is headed this way."

Footsteps echoed on the hardwood. Hastily, I restored the drawer to the desk, slammed down the lid, and shoved the mysterious document under my skirts.

"This is getting redundant," I muttered. "Every time I come into this house, I'm stuffing something under my petticoats."

I had picked up a stack of magazines from the table when the door swung open. Victor halted in the doorway when he noticed me over by the sofa.

"I thought I heard voices in here." He took in the empty room. "Talking to yourself again, Miz Claiborne?"

Flushing, I carelessly blurted out, "No. Ghosts this time!"

"So it's true that you can communicate with the dead?"

"Sometimes," I responded cautiously.

"See any of my ancestors hanging around?"

"Are you looking for anyone in particular?"

He joined me by the sofa. "The old man interests me the most. He built this house and tamed the land. I've a lot of respect for the grit and discipline needed to accomplish such a feat. He lost his life defending his home. Then there's Randall and John Milton. Both men loved the Confederacy and fought hard to keep the Yanks from destroying their way of life. Unfortunately, only John Milton survived to carry on the family name."

As I listened to Victor, the impression that Josiah

wasn't ready for me to share the family secrets imprinted itself in my consciousness so I clammed up about what I'd uncovered about the Redding history. The subject utmost on my mind happened to be Theo Herrington's possible family connections, but again the impression to keep my mouth shut possessed me. I decided to wait until I'd thoroughly gone over Herrington's papers. Perhaps in a day or so I could sit down with Victor and share with him his up-to-date family history. For now, I'd gloss over my paranormal abilities and let myself off the hook.

"I wish I could tell you differently, but your family hasn't made an appearance. Now, if you'll excuse me, I've gotta scoot."

Casting a sidelong glance at Scarlett still lounging on the sofa, and one at Josiah at his usual stance in front of the fireplace, I ambled toward the door and out into the hallway. Once clear, I dashed over to the bedroom, removed the cloth-covered document, and stashed it into my oversized purse. Changing into my street clothes, I left the mansion and went out to my car. Once inside, I turned on my cell phone to check my voicemail. No return message from my parents, only Deena's frantic voice ordering me to meet her and Billie Jo out at the farm ASAP. *Mama's missing!*

****

"You're sure her things are gone?"

My sisters and I were standing in Mama's kitchen. Nothing seemed out of the ordinary. The kitchen sparkled with cleanliness as usual giving no indication of its last usage.

"Come see for yourself," Billie Jo urged. She grabbed my arm and dragged me down the long hallway to the master suite at the back of the house. "Her overnight case is gone along with the usual items she'd need for a trip."

"I stopped by my house and some of Daddy's things are missing, too," Deena interjected. "Neither will answer their phones. We need to call the police and file a missing person's report."

"Deena's right," Billie Jo agreed in a hollow voice. "We should call the police."

Walking around Mama's bedroom, apparently in the same spotless condition as the kitchen and the rest of the house, I scanned for any sign of foul play. Finding none, I surmised that Mama had left of her own free will.

"Calling the police is a bad idea," I told them. "They might assume our parents are on the run. Only guilty people flee from the law. No, for the time being, we'd better keep this to ourselves."

Deena sank down on the bed. "You don't suppose that's what they're doing, do you? I mean running from the law."

"Mama and Daddy aren't Bonnie and Clyde," I said. "Pull yourself together. We've got to trust that they know what they're doing and will get in contact with us soon."

My cell phone rang. I dug through all the junk in my bag until I located it.

"That might be them now. Hello?"

"Jolene?"

The voice didn't register at first. I shook my head at my sisters to indicate the caller wasn't our parents.

"Jolene, this is Diane Downey. I'm trying to locate Annie Mae. She's late for the ladies church meeting, and I've been unable to reach her. As president it's her responsibility to preside."

My gaze remained locked on my sisters. "Mama ran into a slight detour this morning, Mrs. Downey. She asked me to call you and beg upon your kind assistance to conduct the get-together in her absence and it slipped my mind. Please accept my apology."

"Is she sick?"

I hesitated. If I answered yes, she and the entire Ladies Auxiliary would be on Mama's doorstep within the hour, and that wouldn't do under the circumstances. My mind snapped to attention. Come on, girl. Put on your lying cap. What believable lie would gain us time to track down our wayward parents and get them home without anyone the wiser of their absence? Ah ha. I had it!

"No, but Jimbo White came down with the flu. He's the farmer that's leasing the farmland. Daddy's helping out in the peanut fields, and Mama's lending a hand with the children," I explained.

"Annie Mae can't break loose for one hour? She's needed here."

"Mama said you preached Christian charity above all else and that's why you'd understand if she dedicated herself to practicing what you preached."

"I, uh—" Her voice held a note of uncertainty and I pounced on it.

"Thank you for calling, Mrs. Downey. I'll tell her of your generosity." I hung up smiling. "Well, that ought to hold us for a while."

Deena shook her head disapprovingly. "She's going to know you're lying when she takes the time to think about what you told her."

"How so?" I questioned.

"Daddy can't be working in the peanut fields. Everyone knows they lie fallow until spring."

"You've got a point, but I'm sure Diane doesn't know squat about peanut farming. I bought us some time so let's see if we can't figure this thing out."

"Let's do it in the kitchen," Billie Jo said. "I'm hungry."

In the kitchen, Deena and I sat down at the table while Billie Jo fixed three glasses of iced tea and opened a bag of Fig Newtons.

"Any word on the camera, Deena?"

"I forgot to tell you in the excitement that I finally located it in my office," she answered. "But we still have a problem."

"And that would be?" I asked.

She sat down her tea glass. "The memory card has pictures of Hannah on it. Becky must've borrowed the camera and forgot to replace the chip with the one she took out when she finished. I've called several times, but her phone goes directly to voicemail."

Becky's my only child and Hannah, my granddaughter. Like me, my beautiful seven month old granddaughter is blessed with the gift of sight. Daddy and I share this secret. Telling the rest of the family will be tricky as most still don't understand my gift, and now Hannah's. But there's plenty of time to prepare them for the chaos that's sure to happen. Hannah's too young to spill secrets. But the clock is ticking. She'll be talking soon.

"What about Roger Wesley's alibi? Did you have time to check it out?"

"I talked with Rachel on the phone this morning,"

Deena said. "She and her father were at the bake-off, but they didn't arrive until the second phase of the contest. Some kid backed his car into Mr. Wesley's Mercedes in the parking lot, and they had to wait for a police report. There's no way he could've planted the peanut flour and oil in our containers. Sam's right, they have a solid alibi. Sorry."

I turned to Billie Jo. "And you? Any luck?"

"Ellie seemed eager to chat this morning when I called her," she said. "You'll never believe the news she told me. Ryan proposed last night. They're officially engaged."

Mine and Deena's jaws dropped opened.

"Same reaction as mine," Billie Jo continued. "Once she started talking, I couldn't shut her up. Ryan does have a substantial trust fund and is a wealthy man without his father's money. He loved Theo, but couldn't abide his prejudice toward Ellie and that led to a break in the family. She's truly in love with Ryan and is even willing to sign a prenuptial agreement. They were with Kandy in an official capacity from the time they arrived out at the fairgrounds until the bake-off started."

I sipped my tea. "What did she have to say about the cat?"

"Evidently, Ryan's cat hated her almost as much as Ryan's father. Ellie said Butterscotch scratched and bit her every time she tried to handle him. One day the cat went berserk and took a chunk out of her leg. Ryan got upset and reacted in haste. The cat had to be euthanized."

"That's the same story Bradford told me. Anything else?"

"Oh, yeah, she gave her two-week notice. Ryan is setting her up in her own nail salon."

"Deena, I trust you signed up for those classes at the Beauty Academy?" I asked.

She nodded. "I'm enrolled for the spring semester. Until then, I'll call over there and put an ad on the message board for graduating nail techs. We can snag one or two before Ellie starts looking for employees."

"That's a good idea," Billie Jo said. "Ellie has big plans for her business. She plans to employ five to seven nail techs at first and build from there. Ryan's sinking a lot of money into her business."

Deena downed another cookie. "Jolene, I cut you off this morning before you could tell me what you'd found out from Barbara."

"Well, my visit with Theo's widow turned up a piece of vital information. She received a call from the insurance company. There's been a delay in paying the five million dollar death benefit and the beneficiary wasn't pleased."

Billie Jo whistled. "Five million dollars! Wow, that's a lot of money."

"My sentiments exactly," I voiced. "And a strong motive for murder, wouldn't you agree?"

Deena sat forward, her face furrowed. "I hate to throw a wrench at your head, but if Theo's estate was worth millions when he was alive, doesn't it stand to reason that Barbara, as his wife stood to inherit millions upon his death without his life insurance? If he's as rich as rumored, the five million dollars would be a drop in the bucket."

Billie Jo and I shared a knowing look. "The will," we cried in unison.

"You said something a minute ago about Ellie signing a prenuptial agreement, Billie Jo. What if Barbara signed one before marrying Theo?" I pointed out. "And what if his will states that if she breaks it, she gets squat? His estate would pass to his son and granddaughter. Did Ellie mention Herrington's will?"

"No, she didn't mention a will. But she said money does grow on trees."

"That changes the game," I said. "Without knowing who stood to inherit Herrington's millions, or if Barbara had signed and broken a prenuptial agreement, we still don't know who had the strongest motive for killing Herrington."

"So we're back to square one," Deena said.

"Not necessarily. Herrington's murderer is one of two, possibly three, people. His widow, his son, and his son's fiancée. We have to figure out which one."

"And how do you propose we do that, Jolene?"

I drained my glass of tea and got up from the table. "That's the million dollar question, Deena. Do you have any suggestions on how to bag a killer?"

"I thought that was your specialty," she replied.

"At the moment, I'm fresh out of ideas," I said from the sink. "But I've got plenty to think about, and sooner or later I'll come up with something. For now, y'all keep quiet about Mama and Daddy's absence. That information in the wrong hands would bring the police down on our heads and land Daddy in jail."

Chapter Twenty-Two
The Honeymooners

A strong cold front brought cooler temperatures Tuesday morning so I dressed warmly in a yellow turtleneck, brown corduroy jeans and boots and started out for the salon earlier than usual. Restless and fidgety from lack of sleep, I pulled in behind the shop, parked next to Deena's Buick, and went inside to find her making coffee in the kitchen.

"You're up early," I commented, removing my leather jacket and draping it on the back of a chair. "I don't suppose you heard anything from our missing parents?"

"Not a word," she said. "But Billie Jo called. She's on her way in. And Becky finally returned my call."

"Does she have the memory card?"

"Yes and no. She misplaced it, but promised to call when she finds it. I stressed the importance of her locating it as soon as possible."

At the refrigerator, I pulled out the cream and set it on the table along with the sugar bowl. "Well, hallelujah for some good news. I spent most of the night driving around town checking hotel parking lots for Daddy's car."

"Why didn't you phone the hotels and see if they're registered?"

I sank down in a chair across from her. "I did. No

luck. Then I got to thinking. They could be using another name other than Tucker. We know they're in Daddy's car so I thought I might spot it.

"Where do you suppose they are? This isn't normal behavior for them, and I'm worried."

"We'll find them, I promise." I rose from the table to pour two cups of steaming coffee.

The back door of the salon opened and closed. Billie Jo came into the kitchen. "Any word?"

"Nothing," Deena said. "You?"

Billie Jo plopped down at the table. "The same."

I poured her a cup before resuming my seat. For a few minutes we sat staring down into our coffee.

Deena broke the silence first. "Bill dumped me in the middle of Stop and Go last night."

Inside I wanted to shout for joy, but outwardly I showed no reaction to the good news. Instead, I patted her hand. "I'm sorry. Would it make you feel better to know that Bradford and I have called it quits too?"

"Not really. You and Sam are perfect for one another," she said. "You should give him a call and patch things up."

"Deena, why don't you tell us about it," Billie Jo encouraged.

A momentary grimace crossed Deena's face. "I had stopped for gas on the way home from Mama's last night. Bill just happened to come in and catch me cashing in my latest scratch-off tickets. He started making a big deal out of it. Then to make matters worse, he brought up Jolene's and Daddy's fight with Theo. He even shouted out for all to hear that Reverend Inman had questioned his association with me."

"Mister Holier-than-Thou is at it again," I said.

"I'm not all that upset about it."

Billie Jo asked, "Then why the long face?"

"It's because of what I did in retaliation."

I grinned. "What'd you do?"

Deena cracked a weak smile. "I think I'm more like y'all than I ever imagined. I called him a hypocrite in front of a store full of witnesses and went on to tell him that he preached one thing, namely purity, and then, when we were alone on my couch with the lights out, his hands were in all the wrong places. Not that I minded, I told him, I am alive after all."

Billie Jo and I burst out laughing. "Oh, sister, I bet he didn't like hearing that," I said.

"Oh, he didn't. But he liked it less when I told him that he was right to break up with me because I wanted a real man, not a sanctimonious hypocrite. Then I collected my winnings and exited as gracefully as I could."

I squeezed her hand reassuringly. "Deena, honey, I always thought you were looking for love in all the wrong places. You don't go to a graveyard to find a live man. Even Jesus said that."

****

The morning passed without word from our parents. By mid-morning, I tottered on the verge of calling the police to report my missing parents, but I held back, hoping they'd walk through the front door and scold us for worrying. For the hundredth time, I glanced over in that direction.

"Jolene, you're burning my hair."

Nancy's voice penetrated my thoughts, and I unwound the curling iron from the section of singed brown hair. After soothing a drop of silicone oil through it, I reapplied the curling iron to reset the curl.

I smiled ruefully. "Sorry. My mind is a million miles away this morning." I apologized for my mistake.

"Completely understandable under the circumstances," she said. "I heard about the GBI accosting your father after church services. Your mother must be sick with worry."

"She is," I agreed. "When this is over, we're taking them on vacation."

"That's nice, honey. And I hate to add to her worries, but I received a phone call from the director over at the Whiskey Creek Playhouse—well, with *Arsenic and Old Lace* opening tomorrow night, he can't have one of his leads missing dress rehearsal, and your mother isn't returning his calls."

I hesitated. Obviously, I couldn't tell her the truth so I repeated my earlier lie.

"Nancy, you're right about Mama being sick with worry, but if there's any way possible, she'll be at the rehearsal tonight," I assured her in what I hoped was a convincing tone of voice.

"Boyd will be relieved," she remarked. "According to him, your mother is a good actress."

"Oh, she's an actress all right," I said, then changed the subject. "I bet you're glad the Pecan Festival is coming to an end. All the work."

Her face mirrored conflicting emotions. After a moment, her eyes met mine in the mirror.

"It has been a difficult week," she admitted. "And I'm as exhausted as I look, but it's worth all the hard work. It's my one claim to fame in this small town, and I can't imagine giving it up."

"What about the complaint Herrington filed against

you? You were upset and threatened to go gunning for him."

She waved her hand in the air. "A minor imposition. Mr. Big Shot Herrington had everyone jumping hoops on that Board. He had them ready to replace me with his wife. Said she'd held an important position on the Macy's Day parade committee and could do a much better job as director than me."

"Do you believe he created the diversion at the pageant to further his wife's chances of getting your job?"

"That's part of it. And his granddaughter acing the Miss Pecan Festival title iced the cake. Yes, that and all the other fabricated crap he brought before the Board. Fortunately, I still had a few friends left and kept my position. With Theo's influence gone, the threat is gone."

"So with Herrington dead, your claim to fame is safe?"

She went silent at the question. I smoothed down the teased curls with my comb, pinning them into place, avoiding her reflection in the mirror. Several seconds passed in tense silence. Finally, I lifted my gaze to the mirror.

Her eyes stirred from hurt to anger. "Are you implying that I had something to do with his death?"

A pertinent question for sure. Even to my ears it sounded as if I'd accused her of killing Herrington to hang on to her trivial position in the community. Shame washed over me at what I knew she perceived to be a betrayal of sorts, but desperation robs a person of logical reasoning. And mine had fled with my parent's disappearance.

"Nancy, I'm only pointing out an obvious assumption based on your own words. I'm not accusing you, just stating that you had motive for wanting Herrington removed."

"I wanted him removed from the festival board's sphere of influence, not from life!" Ripping the cape from her neck, she bolted out of my stylist chair.

"Wait, I'm not finished with your hair," I said, instantly contrite. "Please let me explain."

She held up a quieting hand. "Yes, you're finished with my hair, *Miz* Claiborne." She slammed a twenty-dollar bill on my work counter and stomped out the front door.

Deena rushed up to my station. "What's wrong with Nancy? I've never seen her so angry."

A dozen interested eyes gawked nearby. "I insulted her," I answered in a low voice.

"How so?"

"By implying that she had a motive for killing Theo."

"Oh, Jolene, you don't seriously believe she's responsible for murder, do you?"

"I'm willing to believe anyone is responsible for Herrington's murder but Daddy. Nancy had motive and opportunity." I picked up my cell phone lying on my workstation counter.

"Who are you calling?"

"Bradford. It's time to start trusting him with the truth…and to file a missing person's report."

****

I placed the call too late. I had just left a message with Bradford's office when Detective Goodwin pushed through the front door, jingling the bells. I frowned at the petulant expression staining his boyish face. Geez. Did he lose his favorite toy?

"Ms. Claiborne, perhaps you and your sisters can help me with a problem. Seems a car matching your father's description was reported leaving the county. He's not answering his cell phone so it's imperative he come back down to the station and clear this up."

Worry came full circle. I forced myself to settle down, not wanting to show the detective the slightest sign of agitation and shot Deena one of my be-quiet-and-let-me-do-the-talking looks.

"Detective Goodwin, I think it'd be best if we moved this conversation into the privacy of the office." I motioned to Billie Jo, and the four of us made our way through the curious stares and audible murmurings to the office.

"Now what's this about?" I questioned once the door shut behind us.

"An APB has been issued for your father," he replied.

Billie Jo bolted out of her chair. "That's for criminals. Daddy's not a criminal, however—"

A knock sounded at the door. Bradford pushed it open and let himself in. "Holly said I'd find you in here, Jolene." His glance bounced from me to my sisters and then landed on Detective Goodwin. "Something going on I need to know about?"

His relaxed attitude had a calming effect on everyone in the room except the young detective.

"This is my case. I'll have no interference from you," he warned, half-seriously.

Bradford took an empty chair. "I may no longer be personally involved in this case, but let me remind you that I'm still your superior, Goodwin."

Detective Goodwin's cell phone buzzed, and he stepped away from us to answer it, giving me the opportunity to speak with Bradford. I scooted my chair closer to his.

"Bradford, Mama and Daddy are missing," I whispered. "That's the reason for my call."

"What do you mean missing?" he inquired in an equally low voice.

"Their personal items are gone. Overnight case, clothes, toothbrushes, that sort of thing," Deena whispered.

"And we haven't heard from either one of them since Sunday night," Billie Jo added.

"We're getting awfully worried. And then this turkey shows up." I flipped my head in Goodwin's direction. "He's put out an APB on Daddy."

"Yes, I'm aware of it," he said.

I frowned at him. "You could've given us some warning."

"There's no time to quibble, Jolene. Did you hire a good criminal attorney like I advised?"

The snap of a cell phone closing ended the conversation. Detective Goodwin stepped back over to Deena's desk. Bradford climbed to his feet, facing him.

"Harland and Annie Mae Tucker have been pulled over by a patrolman on Hwy 82," he informed us, a smug smile lighting his face. "They're on their way to the station now so I'll take my leave."

As soon as the words were out of his mouth, I bolted to my feet. "I've got to get down to the station. Deena, you stay here and reschedule my appointments. Billie Jo, you get on the phone and see if you can hire

T.J. Pickens. He's the best criminal lawyer in the tri-county area."

Detective Goodwin disappeared out the door, and I turned to Bradford, my hand on his arm. "I know I have no right to ask but can you beat him to the station and watch out for Mama until I get there? She'll be frantic."

"I have a better idea," Bradford said. "You ride with me."

"What about your job?"

Bradford picked up his cowboy hat from Deena's desk. "Let me worry about my job. Are you coming or not?"

"Go on ahead," Deena added her voice to Bradford's. "We'll take care of the rest and meet you down there as soon as we can.

Not needing any further convincing, I ran over to my station, retrieved my purse, and dashed out the door.

Bradford drove with his lights and siren on and five minutes later we pulled into his assigned parking spot behind the station. I reached for the door knob, but Bradford's strong grip halted me. I turned back to him.

His square jaw tensed visibly. "Are you carrying a gun in your purse?"

I shook my head. "No. I haven't had a chance to buy a new one."

He let go of my arm and swung out of the car. I followed suit and kept close behind him as we entered the station. I could hear Mama's frustrated cries as we drew close to the holding cells.

The first thing I saw when we rounded the corner was Daddy, handcuffed, and Mama standing nearby. Her arms flailed about as she complained bitterly to a female officer about their treatment. How I wished

Officer Diamond Presley could've been the one with Mama and not the hard-faced woman restraining her.

Once again Bradford's strong grip kept me in place. I started to protest, my first inclination to rush to Mama's side, but he cautioned me to stay out of the way until he could speak with the arresting officer. Only then would I be allowed to speak with my parents before Detective Goodwin arrived and whisked them off.

Mama spotted Bradford the instant he walked up. I could see her visibly relax when he gave her a quick nod of acknowledgement before turning back to the officer.

As the minutes ticked off, I grew antsy. Daddy had been escorted from the room by the tall officer Bradford had spoken with. I wrung my hands at the delay. Finally, after speaking with Mama, Bradford stepped back out into the corridor and to my side. I practically latched onto him.

"Tell me what's going on with Daddy. Where's that officer taking him?"

"He's fine, Jolene. Settle down. They've taken him to the interrogation room. He'll see a judge in the morning. We'll have to wait until then to see what happens next."

I tried not to frown at him. "What about Mama? Is she under arrest?"

"No, as a matter of fact, Officer Ballard is escorting her to my office as we speak. Boy, has she got some news for you." He motioned and I followed him.

Mama bolted out of her seat and was at my side the second we entered the room. Bradford excused himself and shut the door behind him.

"Jolene, honey, you wouldn't believe what your daddy and I've been through. I tried to explain that to the overzealous officer when he stopped us that it's all a big misunderstanding. Harland and I weren't trying to flee. We were on our way home when we were pulled over."

I steered her over to one of the chairs flanking Bradford's desk. "Mama, where have y'all been? We've been worried sick."

She stuck out her hand, pointing to a diamond wedding band. "We've been honeymooning at a friend's cabin in the woods."

I collapsed into the chair beside her. "You eloped? Mama, how could you and Daddy get married without us? Deena and Billie Jo are going be happy of course, but disappointed, too. We could've had a nice ceremony at the house."

"Harland and I couldn't wait to be together again. We've both been celibate too long. The Bible says it's better for a man and woman to marry than to burn with passion, so we took that advice and got married. However, it was a mite uncomfortable for me after thirty years, never imagined I'd be as dry as a bone."

Heat flooded my face. "Whoa, Mama. Way too much information."

She gave me a funny look. "Sex isn't just for the young, you know. It's like finely aged whiskey. Better with age."

Thankfully Bradford saved me from any further sexual revelations Mama wanted to share when he came through the door and seated himself behind his desk.

"You'll be happy to know, Jolene, that T.J. Pickens has been retained as Mr. Tucker's counsel. I've spoken with him, and Mr. Tucker's arraignment is scheduled for nine o'clock tomorrow morning. Until then, there's nothing else you can do here."

"But I want to see Daddy."

"He's with Mr. Pickens at the moment, and your mother looks tired. Your sisters are probably waiting on word so go home and get some rest."

Mama started to protest, but Bradford cut her off with a gentle reminder that her husband would be fine with the accommodations. Reluctantly we left with Officer Ballard, who'd been drafted into giving us a lift back to the salon. On the drive through town I kept Mama occupied with plans for a lavish reception, never voicing aloud the dreadfully real possibility that the honeymoon had ended with Daddy's arrest.

Chapter Twenty-Three
X Marks the Spot

Just as I predicted, my sisters were ecstatic when Mama and I arrived back at the salon with the good news of our parent's remarriage. However, they didn't relish the bad news of Daddy's temporary incarceration. To soothe rattled nerves, we began planning the reception for the newlyweds after our current difficulty resolved itself.

As we sat together in Deena's office, we hatched out a plan. Roddy and one of his employees could swing by and pick up the keys to Daddy's car and drive it out to the farm. In the meantime, Deena would pack an overnight bag and stay with Mama. Billie Jo and I would remain at the salon and finish out the day.

In the midst of making plans, Becky called to report the camera memory card had been found on the floorboard of the family car. However, the car and my son-in-law, Jacob, were in Athens on a business trip, but he promised to drop it off at my house when he returned home later tonight.

Leaving Deena and Mama to contact Boyd with the news that a replacement would have to fill in for Mama at the theater, I returned to my workstation and the client waiting for me in my stylist chair.

The rest of the afternoon passed quickly. News of Daddy's arrest became common knowledge by the time five o'clock had rolled around. Billie Jo and I were relieved to shut and lock the door behind the speculative looks we'd received throughout the afternoon.

Ellie Malone, in particular.

Several times, I'd overheard her bragging about her new business enterprise and offer an incentive to lure the client away from Dixieland Salon. I'm not against free enterprise, just opposed to an employee sticking a knife in the literal back of my business. Years of hard labor had gone into building this salon, and I'd not sit back and allow Ellie to waltz out the door with my client list. When I confronted her, she stomped out.

Billie Jo cocked an eyebrow at me. "Now that Ellie took a hike, who's gonna pick up the slack? We're out a nail tech, and I don't do nails."

"Lizzie's new and doesn't have a full appointment book yet," I said. "And I guess I'll have to pitch in and help."

"That sounds reasonable, especially since you're the reason why Ellie left before finishing her two-week notice."

Following Billie Jo back to the laundry room, I dumped a load of dirty towels into the washer while she withdrew clean ones from the dryer and started folding them.

"I heard another interesting piece of news this afternoon about Nancy," she said.

"Oh?"

"She put her house up for sale a couple of days ago."

I grabbed a towel to fold. "That's odd. She didn't mention it this morning."

"Nancy stepped down as Pecan Festival Director to accept a teaching position in Fort Lauderdale," Billie Jo continued. "She's leaving tonight on a house-hunting excursion. My client said that Nancy seemed anxious to get out of town."

"Why would she up and leave before the Pecan Festival is over? She loved being the director."

"Deena said you accused her of killing Herrington."

"I didn't, not really. She must think I'm a monster for questioning her motives."

"Did she have a motive for killing Herrington?"

My mind quickly reviewed my notes. "Nancy's position certainly gave her opportunity to plant the peanut flour and oil. And, in anger, she did say she'd be gunning for Herrington if she lost her position as director of the Pecan Festival because of ridiculous trumped up charges, but I don't believe she's a killer. One of the Herrington's did him in."

Billie Jo stacked towels in the overhead cabinet. "Well, we won't be getting any more insider information from Ellie, because you ran her off. How are we going to find out about the contents of Herrington's will? Or if Barbara had signed a prenup? Or who had the most to gain from his death?"

"I don't have all the answers to your questions, Billie Jo, but have faith. We've been through too much to give up now. Today hasn't been all bad. Our parents are no longer missing, and Mama has a shiny new diamond ring on her finger and a brand new old husband."

With a lighter note, we finished cleaning the salon and left for the day. On the drive home, I stopped for a burger and fries and chocolate shake, and spent the evening going over my notes.

At eleven, Jacob dropped off the memory card. Popping it into my laptop, I studied each picture until I spotted the thing that'd been bugging me from the beginning of the bake-off. The picture, taken in our kitchen space with the judges, showed Barbara Herrington wearing a dark blue pantsuit with an oversized matching shoulder bag. It caught my eye because the purse bulged as if it held a bowling ball.

Printing out the picture, I set it aside and continued my perusal of the remaining photos. Once again, an odd photo popped up. Deena, in her never-ending pursuit of the perfect scrapbook, had captured Theo's widow coming out of the ladies restroom. Unaware of the surveillance, Barbara had paused outside the door with a deflated, smudged purse. Somehow flour had spilled all over it and she'd hastily wiped it away.

Could she have been the one to plant the flour and oil in our containers? Just maybe, this could be evidence the police couldn't ignore, thus, possibly giving Daddy's defense reasonable doubt. I printed up the rest of the pictures and put them in chronological order on the kitchen table, and then dialed Bradford's number.

"I know you're off the case," I said when he answered, "but you're the only one I could trust with this. I have something here at my house that you need to see."

His heavy sigh echoed over the line. "You promised to stay out of it, Jolene." When I didn't offer a reply, he continued. "Okay, I'm in your neighborhood. I'll be right over."

He pulled into my driveway a couple of minutes later, climbed out of his unmarked cruiser, and met me at the back door.

"Okay, I'm here. What's up?"

"Take a look at these and tell me what you see."

As he studied the snapshots laid out on the table, I mulled over my notes in silence. Finally, he said, "I see why you called me. These are interesting enough to bring Barbara in for further questioning."

"There's something else I need to share with you,' I began. "The other day I overheard a conversation between her and the insurance company. The five million dollar death benefit would be delayed until the insurance company completes their investigation. That news made her plenty unhappy. And there's plenty of gossip flying around the salon about an affair. Did you check to see if she signed a prenup before marrying Herrington? What if the rumors are true and he threatened to divorce her? Maybe he even threatened to disinherit her and she killed him before he could follow through."

He started gathering up the pictures. "Interesting theory. I'll take it from here."

The wall of separation between us stayed firmly in place in spite of his generous praise. As much as I wanted to confess I'd been wrong to call off the relationship, the case hadn't been wrapped up and put to bed. Bradford's job could still be in jeopardy, so I'd have to bide my time for true confessions.

Bradford left with the evidence, and I called both my sisters, relaying the good news. Deena promised to tell Mama when she woke. Relieved with the progress, I showered and climbed into bed for a much needed rest. I reached over to turn out the light noticing my purse hanging on the bedpost and thought about the document stashed inside.

Curious, I fished it out and carefully unrolled the cloth to find what appeared to be Josiah Redding's original will, dated several days before his death. The legal jargon blurred before my tired eyes. The thick document contained pages of the faded script that would be hard to read even in the best of circumstances. So I rewrapped the will, returned it to my purse, and turned out the lamp—confident that tomorrow would bring to light the name of Herrington's killer and Daddy's release from jail.

****

Barbara Herrington's arrest dominated the morning news. Sitting at my kitchen table with a cup of coffee and the newspaper, I listened as the news anchor detailed Barbara's late night detainment. The voice of Detective Goodwin sounded from the TV, "In light of this new evidence, and additional evidence obtained from the defendant's house, we are following every lead to build a solid case. All charges have been dropped against Harland Tucker, and he has been released."

"Whoopee!" I shouted, heaving the paper into the air. A streak of orange fur zoomed from the kitchen—Tango fleeing in terror from my boisterous demonstration. Another successful investigation and my parents were free to rebuild their lives and marriage.

Scooping up my cell phone, I punched in Mama's number. Deena answered on the first ring.

"Is Daddy home yet?" I asked.

"He and Roddy just came in the door. They're

going to start moving his belongings back home after Mama fixes them a big breakfast. Oh, Jolene, you should see her." Her voice caught. "I've never seen them so excited to be together."

"What time did you receive the call?"

"Around five this morning. Sam said you'd earned a good night's rest and not to wake you right then."

"I'm glad it's over and we can get our lives back to normal."

"Me, too. Are you coming out to the house this morning?"

I glanced at the clock on the kitchen wall. "I won't have time. My first appointment is at eight. Give Mama and Daddy my love and tell them I'll be over this evening after I finish with my shift at Pineridge Plantation."

"Sounds like a plan. Will you and Billie Jo be able to handle the shop without me for a while? I'd like to hang out here, but I'll be in later."

"Of course. See you then."

Forty minutes later, I'd showered and dressed in a rich royal blue knit dress and heels to match my buoyant mood and left for the salon. Parking my Mustang in the empty back lot, I unlocked the rear door and turned on the lights. Peace and quiet greeted me, and I breathed in the familiar scent of toxic chemicals and styling products.

The morning flew by without a single disturbing incident. Feeling cheerful, relaxed, and invincible, I finished my appointments and prepared to leave for my afternoon shift at Pineridge Plantation. With Theo's murderer safely behind bars, and my parents reunited, I could concentrate on solving Josiah's problem, and thereby set him free to join his loved ones on the Other Side. After that? Well, who knew? Perhaps I could put my sleuthing powers to work and discover a couple of good-looking men to spice up mine and Deena's sorry love lives. After her disastrous relationship with the saintly pastor, perhaps she'd consider exploring the fascinating attributes of one of the bad boys in town. Nothing criminal—just sexy bad. There's something to be said for the unexpected!

The drive didn't seem as long in my greatly enhanced mood, and I pulled around to the rear parking area behind the mansion and parked beside Victor's BMW. Noting the time on the dashboard clock, I realized I had a few minutes before my shift, so I settled back down into the driver's seat to enjoy the autumn scenery.

A memory nagged under the surface of my mind, but I couldn't put my finger on the disturbance. I stared out the car window at the unparalleled natural beauty of the fall countryside, allowing my mind to choose the path of least resistance.

And then it hit me—the file folder hidden under the driver's seat! In the excitement of the last two days, I'd forgotten the Herrington family papers. Reaching under the seat, I withdrew the folder and opened it in my lap. Leafing through the paperwork, I set aside the photos, his mother's family tree, and newspaper articles until I touched the stiff papers at the bottom of the thick file.

Scanning through them, they appeared to be patient notes of a Doctor Thomas dating back into the 1840s. Recognizing the name from Josiah's journal, I found the date of April 10, 1842 and began to read. Fifteen minutes later, I stuffed everything back inside the folder, allowing the realization of what I'd learned wash over me. How could decent men perpetrate such a fraud?

At least now I knew Josiah's dark secret. Only a desperate man would have committed such a terrible crime and then attempted to cover it up with the help of another desperate man. Once upon a time, I'd thought Theodore Herrington could've possibly been the long, lost descendant of Asa Douglas Redding. Wrong. Big time wrong. However, a connection existed between the two families.

Digging out the Thomas family tree, I located Herrington's mother, Sylvia on the branch and traced the line back to Doctor Thaddeus Thomas, the country doctor spoken so highly of in Josiah's journal. Joining what I'd learned from Josiah's journal with the knowledge obtained in the doctor's papers, the pieces of the puzzle fell neatly into place. I now had a full understanding of the connection.

A terrible tenseness settled in the pit of my stomach as I pondered what to do with the information I'd uncovered. Josiah had altered his journal to hide his hideous action and paid another man to go against his principles. The implications of such action were unthinkable.

Could this be the reason for Theo's Sunday afternoon visit with Victor that Barbara mentioned? Did Herrington drive all the way out here to discuss his explosive findings with Josiah's descendant?

More importantly, what did he do with the information? Theo Herrington had a reputation as a cutthroat and it wouldn't surprise me to learn that he'd sunk to blackmail. But why blackmail Victor? Did

Theo harbor a secret desire to possess Pineridge Plantation? To search for the lost gold?

Which made no sense. If Herrington had wanted this land all he had to do was sit back and wait for Redding to default on his loan. Herrington's bank would foreclose and he could snap it up for a song, and then he could search for the gold until hell froze over.

What would happen if I made this information public at this late date? The act had taken place over a century ago. And where did this leave Asa Douglas's descendants in the legal scheme of things? If this story ever saw light, would they stand to gain from the estate?

All these questions were giving me a headache, so I decided to keep this news to myself until I could figure out a gentle way to break it to Victor. He deserved to know that his world had taken a major change. Besides, Theo's murder had been solved. Only one mystery remained—the name of the son responsible for betraying the Confederacy and causing the slaughter of innocent civilians.

Grabbing my things out of the back seat, I climbed out of my car and headed inside. The time had come to confront Josiah with the truth of his terrible secret and free him of the guilt binding his soul to this turbulent, blood-soaked land.

****

My last tour of the day turned out to be Mrs. Reynolds third-grade class from the local elementary school, and by the time we'd reached the old kitchen my patience had worn thin with the chatting, hyperactive children who couldn't keep still.

After picking up the shattered pieces of a broken

vase one of the little *darlings* had knocked over, I conducted the group out of the front parlor and into the connecting music room where an 1850 Steinway-Webber rosewood piano took center stage.

"Don't touch the instruments," I ordered as several children darted forward, heading straight for the antique cello and violin standing upright in their brass stands. Several pages of yellowed sheet music fell to the floor as they skidded to a halt mere inches of crashing into them.

Mrs. Reynolds wrung nervous hands. "Children, must I remind you to behave? We don't want another accident," she admonished in what I'd describe as a totally ineffective voice for this rowdy bunch.

Over the uncontrolled sounds of children talking echoed a rapping noise no one seemed to notice other than myself. Scanning the room for the source, my eyes focused on the white mist gathering over the surface of the piano. I nearly swallowed my tongue when Scarlett materialized wearing a black-sequined dress designed for an anorexic lounge singer. I flushed hot when she caught me staring at her boobs spilling out of the plunging neckline of the skin-tight dress.

A wicked smile creased her lips. "A certain someone I won't name is taking me dancing so shut up and listen. Meet us in the attic after you dump the kiddies," she said, fading away into nothingness.

Excited at the prospect of answers, I finished the tour in record time, and ushered Mrs. Reynolds and her group of yapping piranhas out to Mr. Peabody who waited on the veranda for his next outdoor tour. God help the man.

As soon as the door shut behind them, I bolted for

the attic where the ghostly duo waited for me in the semi-darkness. Josiah appeared out of the shadows and stood before me, his eyes reflecting the pain of his tortured soul.

"You know my crime," he said.

Startled to hear him speak, I hesitated for the briefest moment. "Yes, I know. But I don't understand why you defied your beliefs. You're a good man, and I'm sure you meant no harm. I don't condemn you for failing. Only God can be your judge."

"I fear His judgment."

"Your fear and guilt ties you to this house," I told him. "If you ever hope to join your family, you must let go of the past and forgive yourself. Trust that the truth will set you free."

"Trusting comes hard for me."

"Me, too," I confessed with a chuckle. "I'm a neurotic control-freak."

The beginning of a smile tipped the corners of his lips. "You and Scarlett have a lot in common with a remarkable young woman of my acquaintance. Rosie Greenhow was a brave and courageous spy for the Confederacy. You, in particular, would've made an excellent addition to her network of female intelligence gatherers."

His comparison pleased me. Rose O'Neil Greenhow had been fearless in her pursuit of Union secrets using all means and opportunities to extract them from her targets. All means, if you get my drift.

"And speaking of espionage, can you remember anything more about the night of the Union raid?" I asked. "Your diary stopped short of naming which of your sons betrayed the Confederacy. Is it possible that

Randall found out what you'd done and resented sharing the plantation with an adopted brother? Or perhaps John Milton found out and wanted to silence the threat of the truth leaking out of his true birthright? His father was after all a poor farmer. Pride goeth before the fall and that kind of thing."

The ghostly smile faded. "Savannah and I enjoyed a perfect life for many years," he began with a heavy voice. "Randall's birth brought more happiness than we could've ever imagined, and when she found out she was pregnant a second time, our contentment knew no bounds. After a hard labor, John made his entrance into this world, and I feared he wouldn't survive being so small and sickly. For days I prayed God would spare his life, but his health continued to deteriorate. Then Mrs. Winston died and her twins were brought here. When John Milton died, I feared for Savannah's mental stability so I turned to Dr. Thomas."

"And persuaded him with ten thousand dollars to go along with your plan," I added.

He shook his head. "I'm not proud of my actions but, yes, I persuaded him with the only means I knew. Winston couldn't offer the boy the life I could, so I buried my misgivings and swapped one of the healthy infants with my dead son. Savannah never knew the truth and raised the boy as her own. John Milton had every advantage. He followed in Randall's footsteps and graduated from West Point Military School. Savannah and I had high hopes for our boys. When the war started, our dreams crumbled. At fourteen, Asa Douglas spoke of joining his brothers on the battlefield. I couldn't take the chance of losing another son. I sent him to France with his grandparents."

"So with Asa Douglas safely out of the way, you and your most trusted slaves buried the Confederate gold. Then you hid the map? Tell me why you sent for me."

"You hold the key to the strongbox where I hid the map."

Excited and aggravated, I blurted, "And you didn't think to tell me this sooner? Wait… Victor said the gold had been recovered."

"The gold remains untouched in the grave. Every generation hopes to recover the wealth." He indicated the creaking floorboards beneath his feet. "The strongbox is here."

I dug into my pocket only to find it empty. "Oh, damn, I threw it away."

Scarlett withdrew the key from the plunging neckline. "I picked it up after your temper tantrum."

Going down on both knees, I tapped the wood with my knuckles for the telling hollow sound of space between two floors. Pressing fingers to the boards, I pried several loose and set them beside me as I peered down into the dark cavity and withdrew a small, silver strongbox.

In the semi-darkness of the attic, I inserted the key, turning clockwise until a soft click sounded. With trembling fingers, I threw open the lid and withdrew a stiff, yellowed parchment. Squinting in the dim overhead light, I studied the document in silence for several minutes. Recognizing the layout of the plantation, and the huge black X marking the spot in the deteriorating graveyard adjacent to the house, I concluded that I'd found the authentic map detailing the exact location of the legendary Piper's Gold.

Chapter Twenty-Four
Theodore Herrington to the Rescue

Staring down at the valuable document with amazement, I pondered the best way to approach Victor Redding with my discovery. Legally, the map belonged to him, and the money from the recovered gold would secure the future of the plantation.

I climbed to my feet, and searched the darkening room for my ghostly partners. Not seeing them, I decided to share the good news with Victor. Dusting off my period costume, I went downstairs to the small bedroom to change and clean up before locating him.

Dressed again in my blue dress and heels, I searched the mansion until I found him having tea in the front parlor. Hesitating on the threshold, I cleared my throat to gain his attention and waited for an invitation to enter.

"Ah, Miz Claiborne, do come in." He set down his china cup and saucer on the table before him. "I'm having a late afternoon snack. Mrs. Turnipseed made her delicious raspberry bars. You must try one. I insist."

Afternoon tea is not my forte. At this time of the day, I want a couple of glasses of chilled Sangria to take the edge off after a long day on my feet. Yet, his graciousness made it easier for me to accept his entreaty. I took the chair across from him and waited in silence as he poured a second cup of tea.

He handed me the cup of steaming liquid. "I'm surprised to see you here. The others left some time ago."

I set the tea cup down on the table. "I'm here to disclose a delicate matter. It's likely to change your life forever."

His eyes widened with interest. "Then perhaps we should retire to the library where we won't be disturbed."

I followed him to the library and perched on the edge of one of the chairs flanking Josiah's desk. Now that I was on the verge of divulging secrets, nervousness set in and I found something daunting about the sudden click of the closing library doors.

"We're alone and won't be disturbed, and I'm especially interested in hearing about this life-altering situation," His easy smile put me at ease.

Once I'd opened my mouth I didn't stop until I'd told him everything I'd learned. Asa Douglas's whereabouts on that fateful day, of Tempy's innocence, John Milton's true identity, finding Josiah's will, one of Josiah's two sons betraying the Confederacy, and finally the discovery of the map.

Victor leaned back and fit his hands together. "You've been busy, my dear. Everything I've heard about you is true."

His calm attitude kept me from being spooked, although my danger meter kicked on. "You don't seem surprised by my discovery."

"Because I've known most of what you've disclosed for some time now." His gentle face screwed up in a scowl. "I discovered John Milton's personal papers years ago. In them, he discloses his murderous rage at finding out his father's duplicity. In revenge, he betrayed the South. However, I'm curious to know what you intend to do with the information and the price for your silence."

His warped reasoning nudged my heart-rate higher. "I don't understand, sir."

For a second, his arrogant face froze. "Oh, come now, don't play me for a fool like Herrington tried to do. That blood-sucking Yankee showed up on my doorstep one day with his ancestor's tale of switched babies and demanded I share the gold with him—that I would never do."

"You're the brains behind his murder," I stated with false calm.

One corner of his mouth twisted upward. "I don't mind taking credit for it now since you'll never be sharing this confession with anyone, but yes, I planned every step to end his pathetic existence. I seduced his gullible wife and convinced her, after sufficient time had elapsed, I'd marry her. Of course, I never planned to do so. Barbara is a beautiful woman, and an enthusiastic lover, but no Yankee will ever be mistress of this plantation."

My danger meter let out a silent beep-beep. "So we were pawns in your game of murder?"

He nodded. "Part of the plan, my dear. For days, Barbara fed her husband trace amounts of ground peanuts, each day increasing the amount until it pushed him over the edge."

"And you planted the damning evidence so we'd take the fall."

"Yes. Barbara carried the flour and oil in an oversized purse—a gift from me—and your father leaving provided her with ample time to add the ingredients to your containers with none the wiser. A simple, brilliant plan, wouldn't you agree? Until you decided to blackmail me."

Well, it didn't take a genius to know I faced serious obstacles getting out of here without wearing a body bag. Easing open my purse, I fished for Mini Pearl, my heart sinking to my toes when I remembered my gun had been stolen.

"You misunderstand me," I hedged, rising from the chair, my purse pressed to my side. "Blackmail is the last thing on my mind. I know how to keep my mouth shut."

Uncertainty clouded his expression briefly, but then he scowled again and reached inside the top drawer, withdrawing a gun. "Please resume your seat, my dear. I can't let this get out, and although you seem like an acceptable person, you're no different than Herrington. I've been watching you and I knew sooner or later Josiah would lead you to the map."

Déjà vu swept over me. My mind flashed back to the last time I'd stood staring down the barrel of a gun. Panic bubbled close to erupting. "I seem to have a terrible sense of judgment about people," I said with false calm. "I believed you to be a true southern gentleman."

The gun inched closer to my face. "Hand over the map."

"Shooting me will draw attention."

He stood to his feet, cocking the gun. "I said hand over the map."

Nerves at full stretch, I threw the map onto the desk. "You won't get far."

He motioned with the gun in the direction of the back library wall. "Get to your feet. Walk in front of me."

My mouth dried up like old cotton. "Where are you taking me?"

"I believe Lake Seminole will be the perfect resting place for a woman of your talents, my dear."

With the gun pressed into the small of my back, I inched toward what appeared to be a seamless paneled wall, and caught my heel on the edge of the rug and purposefully stumbled to the floor.

This was one of those moments I was glad of spiked heels. Rolling over to my side, I jerked off my shoes and rose to my feet in one smooth roll, heels in hand. I pitched both of them at him. Victor howled in pain as one struck him in the face, splitting open one cheek and splattering blood down the front of his suit.

I tried to make it to the door, but slipped on the polished hardwood floor in my stocking feet and went down in a crumpled heap. Victor, one hand pressing a handkerchief to his bloodied cheek, pointed the gun at me. "Get up or I'll shoot you where you lay."

Scarlett, help me, please!

From my peripheral vision, at the bookcase, a white mist twisted into the shape of a man and a woman. A book sailed across the room, striking Victor in the back of the head. His gun crashed to the floor.

"Grab the gun," Scarlett urged.

Staggering to my feet, I dove for the gun and crashed into Victor. His hands closed around my throat, cutting off my breath. Black spots danced in front of my eyes, and I gave one last desperate shove, dislodging him.

He rolled over and reached for the gun, but found instead a broiling mass of black fog. Anger radiated from Theodore Herrington's ghostly form. I froze as a surge of strong energy burst from his mouth in a maniacal laugh.

Victor screamed, leapt to his feet, babbling incoherently.

Gathering my strength, I grabbed the gun, cradling it securely in my hand. Suddenly, the library doors burst open admitting Bradford and Detective Goodwin, weapons drawn. Detective Goodwin ran to handcuff Victor. Bradford knelt down beside me.

"Are you all right?" He pried the gun out of my shaking hand.

I nodded. "I thought you were off the case."

"Chief wasn't happy with the progress so he put me back on it a couple of days ago."

"I'm glad to see you. What took you so long?"

His mouth curved into a lop-sided smile. "It takes time to break a stubborn woman."

"Sometimes never." I took the offered hand and climbed unsteadily to my feet.

Bradford cocked a knowing smile. "Women are like horses. After a steady diet of hay and oats, a little sweet feed looks mighty good. Barbara jumped at a chance for a lesser charge. She gave Victor up about an hour ago."

I clung to his hand as I wobbled over to the desk and sank down. "Thank God. I thought I was a goner. And let me say that not every horse will fall for a little sugar. It takes a smart cowboy to throw the rope before she smells the trap. Some horses you can't tame."

He chuckled. "Just doing my duty, ma'am. Now,

let's get your statement so you can get out of here."

Bradford stepped over to have a word with Detective Goodwin, leaving me alone to catch my breath. Minutes later, backup arrived and Victor, whimpering about ghosts and flying books, was escorted from the room by several uniformed officers. Detective Goodwin had a short chat with Bradford before nodding in my direction and exiting from the library.

I gave Bradford my full statement, minus the ghostly antics, and soon found myself deposited in the driver's seat of my Mustang.

"Take care of yourself," Bradford said as he shut the car door. "An officer will follow you home and pick up Josiah's will and items you *borrowed* from the plantation."

My heart gave a little squeeze at our non-emotional parting. In the rearview mirror the image of Bradford staring after me replayed in my mind during the long drive home.

****

The next few days jumbled together as our lives returned to normal. Business spiked at the salon, thanks in part to the avidly curious who'd read of my part in Victor Redding's arrest for the murder of the late Theodore Herrington.

Of course, the newspaper exaggerated my courage and valor under fire. For them to call me the modern day female equivalent of *Sherlock Holmes* was pure fiction. I had been, after all, making a beeline for the door when the slick floor tripped me up. If it hadn't been for my ghost-partners, and Theo, of course, I might at this time be fish food. However, for the sake of propriety, I'm making an effort to be humble in the presence of so much praise.

Pineridge Plantation was closed to all tourists while the authorities investigate Josiah's will and decide how to proceed. The Turnipseeds are staying on as caretakers until then. For their sake, I hope arrangements are made to keep them permanently in residence as they've cared for the place for years and are dedicated to its preservation.

I'm delighted to report my parents continue their love fest. One would think by the way they're acting that marriage the second time around is better than triple chocolate brownies topped with Butter Pecan ice-cream. Mama scored a hit as Aunt Martha in the production of *Arsenic and Old Lace,* and Daddy's remodeling one of the bedrooms into an office for her writing project. Vanessa van Allen has taken her under her wing, and the cookbook's projected release date is late summer or fall—just in time for next year's Pecan Festival—much to the dismay of the First Baptist Church Ladies Auxiliary who'd hoped to upstage their former president with their own collection of recipes. Diane Downey swore to beat her at her own game. I guess that means the church ladies will be gunning for Mama.

The biggest change came from Deena. Out of the blue, yesterday, and with no explanation, she had me cut and highlight her brunette hair. And just this morning she bounced into work in an outfit which emphasized her cute figure. The biggest surprise, though, came in the form of a tiny diamond nose stud she acquired during her lunch break. Underneath that sensible head lived a vibrant, sexy woman.

"Jolene, did you hear what I said about hiring Kim Blackwood?"

Deena's voice broke through my pondering. "She'll make a great addition to the staff."

I gazed in wonder across the desk at her. "Billie Jo and I want to know what prompted this sudden make-over. We love the new you, but you know what they say about curiosity killing the cat."

Deena cocked a haughty brow. "And y'all are almost dead with curiosity?"

"Pretty much," Billie Jo said from the chair beside me. "I want to know where you had your nose pierced. If it doesn't hurt much, I'm thinking about gettin' one."

The loud roar of a motorcycle drew my attention away from Billie Jo and her desire for a nose piercing.

"Billie Jo, please warn your client not to race his engine," I said over the pop-pop of the engine. "Our older clients are going to complain."

"That's Ryder. He's here to see me," Deena said from the door.

We emerged from the office to see every woman in the place, and a few men, plastered to the plate glass windows overlooking the parking lot.

"He's a hunk," I heard one woman say.

"Sexy as hell," said another.

"I'd do him if I were alive."

I knew that voice well and peered over my shoulder to see Scarlett leaning against the reception desk, a mischievous smile lighting her ghostly visage.

I joined her at the desk. "Haven't seen you for days."

"I've been busy with Josiah. He's about to cross over."

"What's keeping him?"

"He's anxious about that unfinished business of the other day in the library. And then there's that other thing. Any word?"

"Everything is under control. I haven't been able to complete the one task yet, and the other item may take a week or so longer."

"Josiah's waited this long, a couple more days won't hurt him." She faded from view.

The bell over the door jangled again, and my parents hurried in to join Billie Jo and the man with his arm around Deena's waist. The group started toward her office, but Deena hung back.

"Where'd you meet him?" I asked her when she joined me at the reception desk.

"At the Stop & Go. Buying scratch-offs when I walked in. Our eyes met and it was love at first sight."

"That only happens in fairy tales, Deena."

"Yeah, I know." She sighed. "He's my Prince Charming and Beast all rolled into one delectable bite."

"Hmm. Sounds interesting. He does look yummy in leather."

"And without it."

We cracked up laughing and several of our older society regulars shot us disapproving looks from the sofa.

"Have you heard from Sam?" Deena asked in a lowered tone.

"No, I broke up with him, remember. Besides, he can't get past my problem."

"What problem?"

I shrugged my shoulders. "Talking to ghosts for one. Not minding my own business for two. And he did mention a lack of trust."

"What are you going to do?"

"I've already started working on the lack of trust thing."

"What about the other two?"

"That's the kicker. Some horses you can't ride."

"Huh?"

I took her by the arm and together we headed to her office. "Never mind, Deena. Come introduce me to that good-looking man you picked up at the Stop & Go. You reckon he might have a single brother or friend he could introduce me to?"

****

The letter arrived ten days later. After a lot of pushing and pulling with the authorities, a small private party had been arranged at Pineridge Plantation for a few limited guests. Fortunately for me, Deena's new boyfriend, Wheeler County Probate Judge Ryder Matheson, handled the legalities and made the gathering possible.

Most of the guests were unaware of the reason I had gathered this particular group of distinguished citizens here at the historic mansion. Present were Mayor Kent and his wife, Whiskey Creek Police Chief and Wheeler County Sheriff with their wives, the city and county commissioners and their spouses, Samuel Bradford, and my family. Nancy Chance had declined the invitation, but sent her best wishes.

Now, gathered in the ballroom, my VIP's mingled unknowingly with celestial visitors from another time. Tapping lightly on the side of my champagne glass with a spoon to get everyone's attention, I waited until the murmur settled down before stepping up to the front of the room.

"I want to thank everyone for coming out here tonight, especially with Christmas looming. As you've read in the papers, I've been compiling a factual history of the Redding family. The present day account is inaccurate. John Milton Redding wasn't the natural son of Josiah and Savannah, but instead was adopted from a local family. The account of Asa Douglas, their youngest son, his disappearance and possible death on the night of the massacre is also incorrect." I waited until the chattering abated before continuing. "Through research, I uncovered the true account of that fateful night. Josiah, knowing a Union spy had alerted the Federal troops of the Confederate gold's existence, feared for his youngest son's life and sent him to his grandparents in Savannah under the care of Tempy, a trusted slave. Asa Douglas survived the conflict, married a local girl and produced a daughter."

I held up the letter. "In his will, Josiah stated that his greatest desire was for his natural prodigy and their descendants to inherit the estate. Randall Redding died in the war but John Milton survived, returned here, and produced a son. Victor Redding comes from that line. Here, in this envelope is the name of Asa Douglas's direct descendant through his daughter, Isabella. She married a man by the name of James Mowery and had a son, Robert. Robert had a son, Malcolm. Malcolm married and had a daughter, Susan in 1942. Susan Mowery married William Bradford and had a son, Samuel. Chief of Detectives Samuel Bradford is Asa Douglas's great-great-great-great grandson, the direct descendant and rightful heir of Josiah and Savannah Redding of Pineridge Plantation."

Gasps filled the room and every head turned to watch Bradford's reaction at my announcement. From where I stood, I could see the shock registered on his face and realized I should've alerted him earlier of my findings. Practical, level-headed, Samuel Bradford abhorred surprises and had warned me numerous times to forego the drama.

"If you would join me up here, Detective Bradford," I said with a motion of my hand. "I would like to present to you a copy of the Redding family tree certified by Hoskins Genealogy Agency in Atlanta."

Light applause broke out as Bradford made his way through the crowd to stand stone-like at my side. Taking the envelope from me, he hesitated before addressing the onlookers.

"I'm sure most of you would agree that Jolene has a way of springing surprises on the unsuspecting and this one is a doozy." Laughter erupted at his statement. "Learning of one's heritage is a lasting gift I'll carry with me for the rest of my days so I'm grateful for her hard work and dedication to the project. My mother would've been overjoyed to walk the hallways of this great plantation manor house and bask in the stories of her family's struggles and triumphs. Like her brave ancestors who fought against the horrors of the Civil War, she fought a long battle with cancer before succumbing to the terrible disease last year. May they all find rest and peace. Thank you."

Another round of applause sounded as he stepped back into the crowd, envelope in hand. Slaps on the back and hearty congratulations echoed as well-wishers jockeyed for positions at his side.

Watching the merriment from the edge of the

throng, I perceived a subtle change in the atmosphere, a shifting of cosmic matter crackling with electricity. From my peripheral vision, a golden shaft of light curled into the form of a woman.

I recognized Savannah Redding from her attic portrait. Tears gathered in my eyes as she and Josiah came together in a lovers embrace. Together, hand in hand, they floated toward the terrace doors when Josiah suddenly turned and waved. Smiling, I returned the gesture and watched as they faded away into nothingness.

Scarlett materialized beside me. "Josiah and Savannah wished me to convey their heartfelt gratitude. Because of you, they are together again. Did you take care of his last request?"

I patted my jean pocket. "Tell him his secret is safe."

"For your eyes only, don't forget," Scarlett admonished. "Oh, and one more thing. Your guardian angel put in for a transfer." She laughed.

I didn't see the humor. "I fail to understand the problem."

"Too much drama for an angel nearing retirement."

I chewed on that a minute. "I suppose I am a handful at times. Tell him I promise to do better if he'll stay on the job."

"No promises, Claiborne." Scarlett adjusted her crooked Fedora.

Bradford broke from the crowd and joined me on the sidelines.

"So what do you think?" I asked him.

"You mean about my connection to the Redding's and Pineridge Plantation?"

"Yes, I'm sorry for springing it on you like I did. I know how you feel about surprises."

He shrugged. "What's done is done. I'm more scared of the prospect of inheriting this white elephant than being offended by your high handedness."

"Why would you be scared of inheriting this historical landmark?"

"It's a huge liability, Jolene. I'm a cop, not a gentleman farmer. I'm not even sure the will can be probated after so many years."

"True, but what if it can be?" I questioned. "Ryder Matheson is reputed to be the best probate judge in the state and it's in his jurisdiction."

"Like I said, to me this place is a liability. Let the state have it."

"So you don't care about the lost Confederate gold? It's worth millions."

"Redding babbled about a map down at the station, but one wasn't found on him or in the library—where he said *you* gave it to him."

I avoided his questioning gaze by admiring my new lime green heels. "Map? What map?"

He chuckled. "Just as I thought. Well, I'm glad it will remain a mystery. Greed always follows wherever there is a legend of wealth."

I lifted my eyes to his. "You're right. Piper's Gold is a dream from the past."

"Hey, I hate to butt into an interesting conversation but I'm outta here," Scarlett announced, exploding into a shower of cosmic sparks.

Bradford jumped back, flinging an arm to shield his eyes from the brilliant flash. "What the hell?"

"My liability," I said with a sigh.

He gave me wary look. "Please don't say I saw a ghost."

"I won't."

"What about us?"

"Nothing's changed, Bradford. I see dead people, and you can't accept it."

"Maybe in time, but for now I need time to digest everything,"

"Take all the time you need."

He dropped a quick peck on my check. "See you around, Jolene."

"Right back at you," I whispered, silently questioning whether or not we'd find our way back to one another and turned my attention away from his departing figure. Ghostly couples waltzed across the ballroom to a silent melody only they could hear.

I stayed until the last guest left. Turning off the lights in the ballroom, I made my way through the silent house to the third floor attic. Once again I pressed fingers to the floorboards, prying several loose, withdrawing the small, silver strongbox. Taking the faded yellow parchment from my pocket, I placed it inside, relocked it, and lovingly eased it back in its hiding place. With a satisfied smile I pitched the antique key into the far reaches of the musty attic.

With slow, lingering steps, I traipsed down the majestic staircase to the foyer, pausing for one last sweeping glance of the historic house. The mystery of Pineridge Plantation had been solved, bringing peace to a troubled family and forever silencing the ghosts of the past. Although the future of this grand house remained hidden in the shadows of tomorrow, somehow I knew the abiding love of history would assure its continuance.

Outside, the cold night had grown still under the pale light of a rare blue moon, and on the edge of the stone pathway a snowy camellia bloom lay crushed and forgotten. I stopped and cradled the frail petals in the warmth of my hands. Inhaling its sweet fragrance, my gaze swept over the thriving landscape recalling that from the ashes of tragedy, hope springs eternal in the red soil of this unconquerable Dixie land.

Penny Burwell Ewing

Annie Mae's Utterly Deadly Southern Pecan Pie

3 eggs
1 cup light corn syrup
1 ½ cups of fresh pecans, chopped
1 cup granulated sugar
1 teaspoon vanilla
2 tablespoon melted butter
2 tablespoons of fine Kentucky bourbon

~

Blend ingredients together and pour into a single homemade pie crust, or store-bought frozen deep dish pie crust. Bake at 350 degrees for 60 to 70 minutes until set.
Cool, and serve with whipped cream or ice cream.
Makes 8 servings

Penny Burwell Ewing

And for a sneak peek at the 3rd book in the Haunted Salon Series to find out what Jolene gets into next, just flip the page!

A Dead Pig
in the Sunshine

by

Penny Burwell Ewing

The Haunted Salon Series,
Book Three

Chapter One
Halloween Hoedown

The trouble began on Halloween. I awoke that morning with a keen sense that my world was, once again, about to change. The initial signs pointed to an all-out frontal attack from the Great Beyond. A black, hazy film skirted across the October sky, reminding me of the old classic Hitchcock film, The Birds. Static electricity buzzed through the walls of my red, brick home, causing Tango, my orange tabby, to prowl about the house screeching like a banshee. His fur standing on end like an angry pufferfish gave me cause for concern. And then, the undead started arriving shortly after my first cup of coffee with threats of retribution over unfinished business among the living.

With the creep factor off the charts, I didn't linger long over breakfast and hurried off to a full appointment book at my beauty shop, Dixieland Salon—where the day spiraled downhill from there. Strange incidents plagued the shop, and I suspected the undead shadowed me and had taken up residence in the facial room. By the end of the day, one frazzled hairdresser had packed her implements and stormed out, and there were several threats of lawsuits from disgruntled clients with fried hair.

By evening my patience had taken a hike when I ran out of trick-or-treat candy and a couple of loveable demons in the neighborhood toilet papered my front yard and smashed my jack-o'-lanterns all over the front porch steps.

Halloween. A rent in the veil between the living and the dead, and once my favorite holiday. Not anymore. That sentiment had died a quick death when the dead made a startling appearance during my mid-life crisis. People might call me a psychic, seer, a medium, or whatever the most popular term at present would be. I actually prefer "ghost coordinator". The term makes me sound hip, cool, even slightly normal.

Which I'm not.

Daddy says I was born this way and not the result of some tragic event in my life. Since my childhood had been chaotic at best, I tended to believe him. For a time, Mama scoffed at the idea that her eldest daughter could see departed souls, but after several visitations from friends and acquaintances that had met with violent, premature deaths, she began to explore the possibility that perhaps she'd been wrong in calling me crazy.

The first time had been when Scarlett Cantrell, a local television celebrity, had been murdered in my beauty salon with a facial mask, of all things. Sound crazy? Well, the crazy part happened later when her ghost showed up threatening to take up permanent residence in Dixieland Salon if I didn't help solve her untimely demise. Owning a haunted beauty shop in the Deep South wasn't a prize to be desired, so I tracked down the killer and before long, Scarlett zoomed off to that fabled golden city in the sky.

The second time happened in the midst of the fall Pecan Festival. While conducting tours out at Pineridge Plantation, I stumbled upon a ghost with a terrible secret that kept him bound to the blood-soaked land. Before I could high-tail it out of there, I had an ancient key that would unlock a century-and-a-half old mystery involving lost Confederate gold and murder. Of course, to make my life a living hell, Theodore Herrington keeled over dead during the pecan pie contest and the finger of suspicion pointed directly at Daddy. I solved that case, too. Well, with Scarlett's help, of course. She describes herself as an overworked heavenly private eye who hires her services out to the dearly departed.

It sounds like a child's tale, but believe me, I'm not making this stuff up. But thankfully the evening finally calmed down, and at the moment I find myself ghost-free. Of course, with it being Halloween, and the evening still young, I'm keeping my fingers crossed that I'll make it through the night without all hell breaking loose on my quiet, sleeping hometown. Little did I know, Halloween was to herald in one of the biggest mysteries I would ever encounter.

I was finishing up the last touches of my Halloween costume when the doorbell rang. I glanced over at the digital clock on the bedside table, noting that my date had arrived several minutes early. Settling the mask over my eyes and the cowboy hat on my head, I hurried to the front door to discover a tall, dark-haired Native American standing on my front porch. He whistled, flashing me a wicked smile, and pointed at his white Lexus SUV. "Ke-mo sah-bee, your horse awaits."

Laughing, I locked the door and took Preston's hand. "Then let's saddle up, Tonto, and hurry along before we miss all the fun."

"Didn't you tell me that this party is being given by that famous author who writes those erotic vampire books?" Preston asked me once we settled into his car.

I adjusted the toy gun and holster strapped to my hips before fastening the seat belt. "Yeah, Vanessa van Allen and Mama are close buddies. She mentored Mama through the process of writing her cookbook. Since it was just released, Vanessa had the idea of combining a Halloween party with a book launch. The caterer used only recipes taken from Mama Tucker's Ole Fashioned Southern Good Eats."

"Hey, catchy name," he said. "How do I get my hands on one? No, make that two. I'd like to give one to my mother for Christmas. She collects cookbooks, you know. She's got all of Trisha Yearwood's. Maybe your momma will become a famous Southern chef, too."

I considered my newest beau and a warm, fuzzy feeling washed over me at his enthusiastic prediction of Mama's future. Preston Neally was a nice guy. Not handsome, but presentable. Younger than me by several years, and a successful doctor to boot. We'd met through an online dating service. He'd been a welcome surprise after I'd endured several disastrous first dates with my other daily matches. At least he still had his natural teeth! You wouldn't believe how many toothless guys I've met these past eleven months. I'm tempted to swear off dating completely. I can't face another blind date no matter how "cute" he promises to be.

Bradford's rugged face resurfaced in my memory before I could stifle it. The previous warm, fuzzy feeling vanished under the onslaught of piercing blue eyes that seemed to mock me and cause my insides to clench with despair. Whiskey Creek Police Detective, Samuel Bradford, my former boyfriend. He dumped me over a ghost, and I'm still fantasying that he'll see the error of his way and beg me to take him back. At the moment, my fantasy's failed to materialize. He's moved on with another woman more to his liking.

A heavy sigh escaped my lips. Preston reached out, lacing his fingers with mine. "Worried about tonight? I wouldn't fret overmuch. I'm sure your mother's cookbook will be well received."

My stiff face relaxed into what I hoped was an engaging smile. "You're right, Preston. Everything will go off without a hitch. What could possibly go wrong on a night such as this? Although anything can happen with that weird group of writers Mama's hanging around with. Wait till you meet them and you'll see what I mean."

He brought my hand to his lips, gently dropping a kiss on my gloved knuckles. "Everything will be perfect, you'll see. Most authors are normal people. I'll bet they'll be on their best behavior tonight."

"You would think that, but writers and alcohol don't mix, and from what I've heard of their parties, I'm not sure someone won't end up face-first in the punch bowl."

"Relax, sweetie. It'll be an enchanting evening."

Whether or not it would be an enchanting evening I couldn't predict. Bradford would be there, and the grapevine had it that he and Vanessa van Allen had hooked up, and this would be the first time we would come face to face since our breakup last year.

Oh well, one could hope. But for good luck I crossed my fingers and sent up a silent prayer. Oh,

Sweet Jesus, Chief of the Supreme Mystery, please don't let me be the first one in the punch bowl!

A word about the author...

Penny Burwell Ewing was born and raised in Fort Pierce, Florida. Growing up in a southern coastal town gave her the best of small town living where the residents look out for one another. Her interest in writing began in the 1970s when she consumed every bodice-ripper published and decided to try her hand at entertaining herself. It worked and she is now working on her fourth novel. Once a professional cosmetologist, Penny draws on her humorous experiences behind the chair to add spice to her Haunted Salon series. She now resides in Tifton, Georgia with her mini-dachshund, Gator.

~*~

Another Penny Burwell Ewing title
available from The Wild Rose Press, Inc.:
DIXIELAND DEAD
Book One in the Haunted Salon Series